Sandra lives in Melbourne with her son and pets. Family is important and she has a close relationship with her loved ones. Counting her best friends on one hand and having support and laughter when needed. She always had a dream to publish and share her romantic stories. Always believing if you can dream it, you can achieve it, anything is possible, just believe.

This is for everyone who believes in destiny and true love. To my son Michael, my number one little man, always believe in yourself.

Sandra Vogt

Main Attraction

AUSTIN MACAULEY PUBLISHERS™

LONDON · CAMBRIDGE · NEW YORK · SHARJAH

A CIP catalogue record for this title is available from the British Library.

ISBN 9781398466364 (Paperback)
ISBN 9781398470002 (ePub e-book)

www.austinmacauley.com

First Published 2022
Austin Macauley Publishers Ltd®
1 Canada Square
Canary Wharf
London
E14 5AA

To my sister, mum and son for being there, for Connie for putting up with my stories and dreams. To my publishers Austin Macauley, thank you for having faith in my story. To my favourite musicians for being my inspiration towards my journey and for giving us all joy with your songs and to everyone who reads the story - I hope you enjoy it!

Looking back on my life, I have lived in a fantasy land. True love! Does it exist? In some yes, in mine no. I have never been in love, never known how it felt to truly love someone. I didn't believe I deserved it, so I just married the first guy that asked me. As I was always told fat girls like myself did not deserve anything, only skinny, good looking blondes did. And I would have to just accept what I was offered. If I didn't lose my fat, I would be forever single and that was from my dad and grandmother! So I know that my only true love is my son and that doesn't really count, he is my Number one and will be till I take my last breath and then till.

Movies, although they are great for escapism, they aren't really real. Yes, they make ordinary people who are born the same way that we all are with extraordinary talents to mega stars, does this make them any more special than the average Joe? Yes they have money, adulation but do they true friendships, trust, love? From where I stand, if you're a celebrity all people want is to take, take, take, they don't want to give, they don't want to know the real person. If you're lucky enough to meet a celebrity, are gorgeous, skinny, you don't have to have a brain, you can bag an celebrity or wealthy person and then rip his private life through the ringer, try to destroy his soul and put it down to it's for the best.

To me, an average person, that is absolute bs. I call it as it is. When people break up it's not to destroy who you once loved, not to bring them down, not to use children as weapons between the parents. A child is a gift, love is a gift, life is a gift.

This Now Starts My Adventure.

It was a beautiful June day and I was travelling to the USA with my son to visit all the touristy places. Finally after Covid and saving for what felt like centuries we were boarding the plane. I hadn't been to the states since 1995. I knew it would be a different world post-divorce, post Covid, post giving up but I was at least going to give my angel the best trip of the lifetime so, at least he has some good memories of his grumpy Mum.

Boarding on the plane, he asks why we don't go on first. 'Well mate, the thing is we are in cattle class; first class and business class go first. Then cattle class goes on last, we will still get there but it takes longer to load us all on,' I say quietly.

He responds, 'what makes them more important than us?'

'Well Michael, the thing is they either have more money, are famous celebrities so they need more security and need to be kept safe.

'But that is not fair,' he responds.

'It is what it is mate,' I respond.

'Mum if you could meet anyone in the world who would you meet?'

'Alive or Dead Michael.'

'Mum that's silly you can't meet someone dead!' *Smartass,* I think, but say, 'Good point Michael.'

I think deeply and go through my list of would be metres, If I could. Chris Hemsworth, Aussie legend; John Edward medium; Jon bon Jovi, rock legend; Bryce Johnston...words can't describe him. And the list goes on and on. I finally say, 'Well baby if I could meet ANYONE I would say Bryce Johnston.

He comes back. 'Why him?'

God give your mum a break, I'm thinking, quick witted smarty pants...

'Well honey, he looks like a kind man, a loving father, a funny monkey, he is a singer, musician, actor and he is a decent guy, a loving son, brother and he is absolutely adorable and completely unattainable to someone like me PLUS he has had a lot of crap thrown at him trying to break him. I would like to sit down with him and tell him he has support that he isn't alone and all I would love from him is to get to know the real Bryce.'

'Well, that would be nice Mum,' he says, 'maybe you might meet him when we are in America.' *Baby I could only hope but I am not a model, actress or anyone special. But it would be nice...* I think to myself, it would be nice I keep thinking if only. If only dreams and movies were real. He would meet me, fall head over heels in love with this short, fat smurf and be forever my number two man. But dreams don't come true. Movies aren't real. Life is as it is. Good for the rich and famous, crap for the norms.

'Good Morning, this is Captain Smith, Welcome aboard QF236 to Sydney and our final destination of LA. If you are travelling with us all the way to LA we will be travelling together for the next 15hrs, say hi to the person next to you as they will be your travel buddy, if you are travelling with children, please try to rest as I am sure you will hear, "Are we there yet?" For your convenience we have installed a button on your chair saying, NO.' Captain Smith laughs. 'Only joking everyone, please sit back and enjoy your trip with the flying kangaroo.'

'Mum,' Michael asks.

'Yes mate.'

'How long till we get there?'

'GOD! It's only been ten minutes, it will be at least 15hrs, go to sleep.'

'I'm not tired Mum.'

'Then go play your games, I don't know how to set them up.'

'Well, read a book,' I say

'I don't have one.' 15hrs of this I love him dearly but god help me...

I press the hostess button. 'Yes ma'am, can I help you?' she asks.

'Firstly please don't call me ma'am, I'm not 80.' I laugh. 'I am Sandy and this is my son Michael, I am a bit of a dumb cookie, would you mind showing me how to set up his game console so he can play and I can read.'

'Of course,' she says. God these air hostesses are amazing. How nice, so much better then when I travelled in the 90s. After what seemed like only five seconds, he was set up. Oh the peace. Bring on my intercept to my diary to what we are doing. Where we are staying and how much fun and embarrassment, I can be at Disneyland. I snigger to myself and put on my music, which is of course Bryce, George Michael, Kelly Clarkson, Jersey Boys' soundtrack and the list goes on. I put my headset on and listen, relax and dream.

I go back to my conversation with Michael that maybe I could meet Bryce, how, when, where, can I be that lucky. I know he lives in LA but where, how could I meet him, it's not like I can Google his address and go knock on his door and say hi Honey I'm home!! But that would be funny. I go back and start to wonder what he is really like? He is absolutely adorable, sexy, a great dad; would he even give me a look in the day or even in the night? No doubt he would never give me a thought, I am a no one, a normal person. At times I feel a waste of space, but I am me and love my son so I will just try to be happy. I think again about Bryce. He was married to a model. LOL. Dream on chook, you have no chance, you have a better chance to meet and greet an ompa loompa.

The flight is chaotic, it is noisy. There are 6 babies crying in cattle class, so I go for a walk to the toilet, peer into business class and think, *Wow! that looks so nice and quiet, wonder what first class is like?*

'Excuse me,' I ask the air hostess, her name shows Charlotte, 'where is first class? I have never been on an A380 this is my first trip on it.'

'First class is above us,'

'Really?' I say. 'Wow, how cool would that be to travel in. Do they have much up there?

'Yes,' she says, 'there are showers, beds, bars. They have everything you would need.'

'Gosh, how good would it be to be wealthy to travel like that?

Would you like to go up and see quickly,' she asks. I nearly fall over my feet to respond.

'Only if that won't get you into trouble, I promise, I won't make any noise.'

'OK,' she says, 'follow me.' We walk up the stairs and as we come around the corner, my eyes fall out of my head. OMG, it is like a first class hotel, not that I have ever stayed in one. There are pods where the people sit, I can see up ahead the bar and doors. I ask, 'Are those doors to the showers,'

'Yes,' she says.

'Wow, Wow, Wow,' I say in complete awe. 'Are there any out of ordinary people on the plane now?'

Charlotte says, 'We have a few American celebrities, Hugh Jackman is on the plane and there is a prince.'

'Oh Okay,' I say. 'Charlotte, thank you so much for letting me see how the other half or other quarter lives I better go back, thank you so much. I really appreciate it.'

'No problem,' she says and off I trot to cattle class.

I get back and Michael is still on the game, he had no idea I was gone, so I go back to my music, my book and rest up.

'Ladies and Gentleman, we are about to make our descent to LA. When you arrive, please ensure you have your declarations. If this is your final stop to your holiday, please enjoy and we hope to see you on your return trip, if this is your return to home welcome back and if you are travelling further with us, we will enjoy your company.'

'Well this is it Mate, we are about to arrive at the airport, look at the window Michael, that is Los Angeles, where dreams are made and broken. We have two weeks here and then we are going to New York and Niagara Falls.'

'Mum,' Michael asks.

'Yes mate,'

'When are we going to Disneyland.'

'Tomorrow baby, today we will walk around, settle in our hotel and go shopping.'

'Mum, do you think we can go to the game shops? So I can buy more games, and can we go and get Legos, and can we go and get Nikes, and all the cool things?

'Baby I would like to say yes, but we are on a limited budget, I have all our tours and entries paid for, we do have some spare but I don't know how far it will go.'

'Oh Ok Mum,' he says with a downcast face. Shit great start Sandy; you are already ruining the holiday. What can I not buy so I can give him everything he wants. I will use my credit card, not pay the mortgage, transfer what I can and work it out when I get home, hopefully that will work out, fingers crossed.

'Ladies and gentleman welcome to Los Angeles. Please move forward at a slow and steady stream, you will all get out and enjoy your time, local time is 10am and it is a lovely 92 Celsius.' I feel like I am melting, why did I come to LA in their summer?

'Come on mate, we need to go through customs, declare what we need to, get our luggage and find our car.'

'You are not driving Mum, are you?'

'No Michael, I booked a car to take us but you never know your luck in the big city I just may.' I laugh. That will scare him. Ha ha.

We finally make it out of customs, start to walk to the exit and low and behold there are cameras everywhere, thank god we are no one special, I feel sorry for any celebrity they have no peace, imagine not even being able to leave the airport in peace, imagine not being able to go anywhere without a camera in their face. *Poor bastards,* I think.

We find our car, go to get in and nearly get pushed over by an absolute rude person. 'Hey, you mate who the fuck do you think you are you can at least say excuse me.' He looks frazzled. I instantly feel for him and apologise, I ask, 'Do you need a lift to town?'

He looks at me, looks around and says, 'if you don't mind it would be easier than looking for a cab.' He hops in and we all go on our merry way. I think to myself he looks like a nice guy, nice smile, sounds American obviously but a bit unsure. I say, 'I am Sandy and this is my son Michael.' and he looks at me, nothing. So I say, 'Generally when people introduce themselves the other person does too! I don't mean to intrude.' and he looks at me queasily. 'Oh sorry, I thought you knew who I was, my name is Bry….Bryson.'

'Wow, it's nice to meet you Bryson. Are you from LA?' He says, 'No I am from Modesta.'

'Oh that's nice, is that near here.'

He laughs.

'Sorry, if I am sounding stupid but typical Aussie, I don't know much about America.' I then go on and say, 'I am sorry for being so rude, I got a fright and didn't know what was happening, I hope you can forgive me.'

'No problem,' he replies.

I ask the driver whose name is David. 'How long till we get to the hotel?'

'About 30mins ma'am.'

'Oh ok.'

'Bryson, do you need to be dropped off anywhere,' David asks him.

'After we drop off Sandy and Michael that would be good, thank you.'

'So, Bryson what do you do for a living?' I ask.

'Oh this and that, nothing too special,' he responds.

'Do you live in LA now or still from where you are?'

'No, LA now.'

'Oh, that would be nice,' I reply.

'It's a very busy city. So what are you both doing today,' he asks.

'Well, we will go to the hotel, check in and then walk around, Michael wants to get some games, clothes, Legos and things, so I am going to budget so he can get it all.'

'And what does Mum want,' he asks.

'I sit there, stare at him and say I have absolutely no idea.' We both laugh. 'If you want to know what I want in life, it is the same for everyone our age, sorry I am assuming you are similar to my age.'

He laughs. 'I am nearly 50.'

'Well welcome to the 50 club. It's all downhill from there. As soon as I turned 50, the eyes went, glasses became my friend, the grey hairs became dominant, so colour is my best friend and I swear the wrinkles just appeared overnight. At this point we are both in stitches.' I actually start snorting which then makes him cry with laughter. Talk about making a good impression. 'Okay, so back to your question, what do I want? Now to get to the hotel, get changed and enjoy the sun and maybe go to Venice beach, I believe that is close to where we are staying. For my life, it would be nice to find a nice guy, who doesn't hate the look of me, happy to spend time with me and Michael. Happy to have fun, laugh with both of us and enjoy a peaceful life. To support each other in good times and bad and always have each other's back. Too deep?' I ask.

'No, perfect.' he says.

What seems like only a few minutes, David says, 'Sandy we are here at your hotel.'

'Oh, what a shame I was enjoying chatting to Bryson. Oh well I guess this is us. It was lovely to meet you, do you ever get called anything else instead of Bryson, that seems so formal.'

'What would you like to call me,' he asks,

I reply, 'Bryson. Bray or what is your surname?' 'Johns,' he says.

'Cool, I could call you BJ?

'I like that how about BJ,' he replies.

'BJ it is,' I say.

'But you know what else is called a BJ?' I say.

We look at each other and laugh.

'Yes, well maybe not BJ,' I say.

'Nah all good, only the cheeky ones will know,' he says. 'What will they know,' Michael asks.

We look at each other and say together, 'Nothing Michael.' I look at Bryson and think I like us speaking together.

Oh well, I think.

'Anyway, it was an absolute pleasure to meet you again, thanks for the chat and maybe we will see each other again. How long are you here for,' he asks.

'We have 2wks here, then we are going to New York, Niagara Falls and New Hampshire to see our relos. We have a total of four weeks over here.'

'Okay,' he says, 'lovely to meet you both.' He gives Michael a high five, gives me a hug and a kiss on the cheek. Wow, I get butterflies when he touched me and his lips felt so soft. I pull away, act casual.

'Thanks again Bryson,' he looks at me with a raised eyebrow. 'Sorry BJ. Take care sweet and remember to always have a laugh. David thank you so much for the lift, you are a wonderful person and thank you for taking Bryson home, just put it in on my card.'

'No need Sandy it is all good. Well, bye then and again thank you.'

Michael and I turn around, grab our bags and enter the hotel, I then turn around again and I see Bryson looking as the car is driving away, I wave, smile and think wow what a gorgeous man inside and out.

'Welcome to hotel LA, how can I help you, I am Stefan.'

'Hi Stefan, Sandra and Michael we have a reservation.'
'OMG, I love your accent,' he says, 'Australian?'

'Yes, but we don't have an accent you do.' We both laugh.

'Can you say that thing you Aussies say,' he asks.

I reply, 'Put a shrimp on the Barbie? G'day?'

'No,' he says.

'Well you tell me when you remember and it will be my absolute pleasure.' I say.

'Okay, you are on the top floor with Disneyland in your view; we have room service, 3 pools, 2 bars and a courtesy bus to the shops.'

'Oh that is great, thank you Stefan, do you have a timetable as we want to go up the shops and look around, is Venice beach far? Can we walk it?' He gives us all the information and we walk to our room. Home sweet home for the next two weeks.

'Come on Michael, let's get changed into something cooler and go out.

'Okay Mum.'

'Michael we are leaving in 20mins. Move it baby.'

In the meantime, David is driving Bryce back to his house. 'Mr Johnston, it is a pleasure to meet you, I am quite surprised that you were not recognised by Sandy.'

'Yes it was a surprise, normally people jump at me or want something, she is quite refreshing. Do you think she actually had no idea?'

'Well, I can tell you this, she was listening to your Ep on her phone as I picked them up she was humming *Main Attraction* and I asked her what she was listening to? and she said, "Bryce Johnston' s Ep from last year." "His music has helped me stay alive," she said, she went on and said, "there were times when she just wanted to end it all but every time she listened to your voice and lyrics, it made her want to be a better parent." She went on "how she loves *Best Part of Me*, *Love is a war* and *Sign*," she said. She also said that when she hears *December days* she starts to cry as she said she can feel your pain and then just as she was about to hop into the car you banged against her.'

'Yeah that was funny the way she let it rip to me, no one has ever spoken to me like that and then apologise for speaking to me like that.'

'Well, Mr Johnston, most people when they meet you know who you are, I am sure no doubt that even if Sandy knows or works out who you are eventually, she will already know who you are really.'

'You know what David, I think you may just be right. Can you do me a favour?' he asks.

'Yes of course.'

'Can you take me back to the hotel? I want to spend the day with them both. I just have to go in and get changed first.'

19

'Of course Mr Johnston,' says David. David asks Bryce, 'Do you have a mobile number for Sandy?'

'Yes I do, but we sign an agreement not to pass the numbers on,' he says.

'I get that but on this one occasion can you give it to me. Let me check with Sandy while you are getting changed,' David says.

'Oh, Okay cool', and he goes into his home.

Phone rings. 'Hello, Sandy speaking.'

'Hi Sandy, it's David your driver from earlier.'

'Oh, hi David, long time no see!' Silence. 'I'm joking David.' I laugh.

'Oh Okay, I was just wondering if it would be Okay to pass your mobile number onto Bryson? He was asking if he could have it,' David says.

'Oh, of course David,' I reply, 'I have nothing to hide, no secrets. Go for it.'

'Thanks Sandy.'

'No problem David and David,' I say, 'when we are leaving in two-weeks' time can we request to have you be our driver?'

'I will put it down for you.'

'Thanks David and I forget to tell you, in the back of the seat I left a tip for you too, I got flustered and forget to tell you. Very good, thank you.'

'Anyway, Sandy, are you guys still at the hotel?'

'No, we have just left, we are walking down to the shops I hear there is a Nike and Ray ban factory, so shopping we are going.'

'OK, Have fun,' he says. And hangs up.

'Who was that Mum?' Michael asks.

'Just David, he wanted to know if he could give my number to Bryson. It would be nice to have a friend in LA.'

'Yeah maybe he knows someone, who knows someone who can help you meet Bryce Johnston.'

'Yeah maybe mate but if it's meant to happen it will. Let's go shopping.'

'Mr Johnston it was Okay, here is her number.'

'Thanks David. Are they at the hotel still?'

'No, they were walking down the shops.'

'I will call her now.'

'Hello, Sandy speaking.'

'Hey Sandy, B J here.' I get all flushed, he is calling. *This has to be good?* I start to shake, *seriously girl,* I think.

'I was just wondering if you and Michael would like to have company?'

'That would be good if you have time, it is always good to have a local help.'

'Good we are about 20mins away from the hotel, where are you both.'

'We are at the end of the street, there is a strip of shops and we have just gone into the Ray ban shop.'

'OK, I will call you when we get there and you can hop in and we will go shopping together,' he says.

'See you soon Bryson, sorry BJ,' I say.

'Come on, Michael, we have a local helping us with the directions, Bryson is on his way. I can't wait to see him again. Do I look okay? Shit my hair, makeup, is it Okay?' 'Mum, you look fine. Don't stress Mum, anyway he saw what you looked like when you came off the plane.'

'Thanks Michael smart ass.' Still thinking, *I hope I look Okay and also why is he wanting to catch up? Have I done something? Did he forget something? Chill stupid. Maybe he is bored or maybe he is being nice. He is a really nice guy so maybe, just maybe he is bored or maybe for some unknown reason he actually likes me. Now that would be wonderful but completely not going to happen.*

What seemed like only 5mins my phone binges with a message. *Hey Sandy, I'm outside the shops which one are you in?*

I message, *give me a second just paying for something.* We come out and standing there against the car is this amazing person, looking completely different, jeans, t-shirt, runners, hat and of course his sunnies. Absolutely, the sexiest man I have ever seen. 'Cool down Sandy,' I say to myself. 'Hey gorgeous,' I say, 'long time no see.'

He grins. 'Yeah it's been a while. Hey, you were saying, you wanted to go to Venice beach hop in, we will go and I will take you guys on a tour of LA if you want.'

'Thanks Bryson you are an absolute angel.'

'Thought you were going to call me BJ,' he says.

'Yeah about that, nah I think Bryson is better,' I say and try not to go red.

You can call me "Johno" if you want, that is what my mum calls me as a nickname,' he says.

'I am so confused,' I say, 'so many names for such a dummy like me, I should just call you honey.' I laugh.

He looks at me smiles and says, 'I like that.' We just stare at each other. We are sitting in the car looking at all the sights. I feel like a dog, I have my head out of the top of the window gawking at everything.

'Oh my god this is amazing,' I say. 'It's so sunny here, everyone is so happy. I love it. Michael and I are in absolute awe.' Every time I ask, Bryson responds with the history of the place, what happens where and when! What it is like at night in these spots, how LA livens up after dark but also how quiet it is. I sit in fascination just listening to him all awhile thinking god he is gorgeous. This is the most gorgeous man I have ever seen and he is spending time with me and Michael. My god how lucky are we. I must have done something good in my life to have bumped into him.

'So Bryson,' I ask.

'Yes Sandy,' he replies.

'Can I ask something and not get you upset, like I don't want to upset you and we have only known each other for such a short time, but being I am a female and we females like to know everything, I was wondering if I could ask you something.' He looks at me and I am staring back, my god his eyes, his lips, his smile, I could die and never wake up he has the bluest eyes I have ever seen, they are like the crystal blue waters in Isle of Pines.

'Sandy,' he says, 'are you going to ask or just stare.'

'Was I staring?' I ask, knowing full well I was.

'Yes.' He laughs.

'Oh, Okay sorry, anyway what I was going to ask was…I appreciate you spending time with us but does your girlfriend mind that you are not with her? Why are you spending time with us, not that I don't mind, I am so happy but just surprised!'

'Firstly, I don't have a girlfriend.'

Thank god, I think, Tick.

'Number 2, I like spending time with you and Michael you are both fun and I like spending time with people who make me feel happy and comfortable.' TICK 2.

23

'I know the feeling,' I say. It is hard to find people who make you feel comfortable. Don't take this the wrong way but I feel like we have known each other for years,' I say.

'I feel the same way,' he says.

We sit there looking at each other, I think wow I wonder what it would be like to kiss those lips. When he smiles he brings out the cuteness with his eyes and the smokiness of them. What would it be like to have his arms around me, hmmmm. I start to get a bit hot.

'It's a bit hot in the car isn't it?' I ask.

'No, all good here,' he says.

'Shit, how I do explain my red face. Ignore it and just keep talking.' SO, I SAY. So he says. Ummmm.

'Mum.'

'Yes Michael.' Thank god a distraction.

'Where are we going?'

'Not sure mate. Bryson, where did you say we were going?'

'To Venice beach,' He says. 'Everyone has to see Venice beach.'

'Okay cool.' Then we go back to staring out of the window.

'Sandy.'

'Yes Bryson?'

'What are you guys doing tonight?'

'I have no plans. Why?'

'Nothing just wondering.' Okay. This is getting ridiculous I think I am constantly smiling, get a grip girl he is just being nice. We are here. Come on you two come and see what all the fuss is about.

We exit the car and all I see are beautiful, skinny women, tanned and in skimpy bathers, now I know why we are here for the boys to perve. All good.

'Hey, why don't you boys go off and check out the girls and I will just look at the shops.' Bryson looks at me.

'You don't want company,' he asks.

'Yes, but I know that guys like beautiful women and I ain't that.'

'As I said I am a short smurf and that is why I am single.'

'I don't want to cramp your style, you might want to find a date,' I say.

He looks at me and then says, 'Well that won't do. I didn't come to spend time with you to leave you alone, we need to talk,' he says. *Shit Ms un confidence you have done it again.*

'Okay, go for it, what do you want to say?' I ask exasperated.

'Firstly, why do you question why I want to spend time with you,' I go to answer and he cuts me off, 'number 2,' he says, 'do you not enjoy my company?' Again I go to speak, 'Number 3, if I wanted to check out the females on this beach I wouldn't have come with you.' And then looks at me.

'Ummmm, Okay. Firstly, I am not used to people wanting to spend time with me and I am absolutely loving your company but look at you, you are the most gorgeous man I have ever seen, you have eyes like a blue clear ocean, your lips are so kissable I can't stop thinking about what it would be like to be kissed by you, your arms, fuck me, if I was wrapped in them I would never want to leave. So, yes I am enjoying your company and am so grateful I could just die now and be happy.

He is staring at me, and asks, 'You think I am gorgeous and am picturing all that? I stare at him.

'What did I just say, did I say too much, no I wouldn't do that, would I. I was thinking it surely? I didn't say it out load did I? Sorry what was the question?' I asked.

'You said that I am gorgeous, kissable lips, blue eyes etc. I go bright red and am completely rooted to the spot.'

'Ummmm yes,' I say.

He laughs at me, grabs my hand and says, 'Come on smurf lets go shopping.' I cannot feel my hand, it is getting sweaty but I don't want to let go, it feels so right to have his hand in my hand. I can't breathe properly.

OMG, what is happening to me, I think to myself. Put it down to lack of sleep, I didn't sleep on the plane much and I think I have been up for a day. So I just hang on to his hand and look at the shops. In the meantime Michael and David have gone up ahead and are looking at all the shops.

'Is there anything you want to buy,' Bryson asks.

'Yes,' I say, 'but I am on a tight budget and everything is for Michael. I might buy something small but I want to make this the best trip for Michael. He is my number one and always will be.' This makes him smile.

He says, 'I have a daughter and she is my number one.'
'Do you get on well with your ex,' I ask, 'sorry if it is a bit personal.'

He replies, 'No, I never should have gotten married but I wanted my daughter to have both parents as mine divorced when I was younger.

'Mine too,' I reply, 'I was 6 when they separated, I always blamed myself why they split maybe if I hadn't of been born, they may have stayed together. When I got married to my ex, the day before the wedding, I remember fighting with him at the rehearsal and went to walk out, the minister said, "it was nerves." On the day, I remember saying to my dad that I didn't want to get married and he said, "Walk away," but I felt bad. Everyone was there, we had purchased a house. Well, I did and I didn't want to let him down. On the honeymoon, I remember hating my ex. It lasted 7yrs, so yes I know regrets.

'Is Michael his son,' he asks.

'God no,' I say, I had a one night stand and oopsies, I feel pregnant so it is just me and Michael.' He looks at me.

'Well kids aren't mistakes,'

I reply, 'No they are gifts. He smiles.

'Looks like we have a lot in common, he says.

I ask, 'How?'

He stares ahead, looks back at me and says, 'Looks like we both have regrets but won't allow it to decide our futures.'

'Yes,' I agree.

'Mum,' BJ move it, 'come look at this.' So, we go ahead.

'What do you want Michael?' I ask.

'Mum, 'can I get this? It is a surf board that has the picture of Venice beach on it.

'Michael, you don't surf,' I say.

'Yeah, I know but it is pretty picture and I can put it on my wall at home.'

'Michael we are not buying a surf board to take back to Australia and put on the wall. Take a picture mate,' I say.

'Kids,' I say.

We continue to walk along the boardwalk and look at the shops, everyone is happy around us and all I can think is, I don't want this day to end. We have been walking for a while when David comes back and says, 'Hey guys, do you want to go and get dinner?' I look up and notice that the sun is going down.

'How long have we been walking along here,' I ask.

'A while,' Bryson says.

'It is beautiful here,' I say.

'I could stay here all day, it's so peaceful.'

'Come on,' he says, 'let's go and get some dinner.

We get back to the car. David asks, 'if I want to go back to the hotel to get changed.'

'Do I need to? I ask, 'where are we going for dinner?' 'Well,' Bryson says, 'we can stay local, we can go into downtown LA or we can go to my place.'

'Nah, I don't want to put you out. How about we just get takeaway and go somewhere quiet to eat it.'

'Good idea,' he says. 'David lets go to the local shops and get takeaway.'

'Do you or Michael have any preferences,' he asks.

'No, just no salmon for me, otherwise all good.'

'Okay, let's go.'

We end up in mid-town, grab dinner and drive back to the beach, we sit on the benches watching the sun go down and enjoying the company.

'Mum.'

'Yes Michael?'

'Can we go back to the hotel? I'm tired.'

'Of course,' I say, look at my watch and it is 9 pm. 'Shit I've been up since 6 am yesterday Melbourne time,' I start to get tired.

'Bryson, I hope you don't mind but we better go, I'm getting a bit tired. God knows how long we've been up. This time difference is getting to me.'

'No problem,' he says and we go back to the car and David drives us back to the hotel. I am about to get out and say goodnight when Bryson says, 'Let me walk you to your room to make sure you are Okay.

How sweet, I think, *gorgeous, sexy and kind*.

'Okay, thanks.' As we go in, he puts his hat on and we go into the lobby go to the lift and press 15. Standing in the lift, I start to waiver and I get caught. 'Oh sorry honey, just a bit tired now, all good Sandy, glad I came up with you.' He grabs my hand, puts his arm around me and holds tight, *a girl could get used to this,* I think.

'Come on Mum we are on our floor.' We walk to the room open up and I am about to say good night when Bryson walks in.

'This is your room,' he asks.

'Yes why?' I reply.

'Well, it's a bit small.' I laugh.

'We only sleep here, yes it's not the best but it is what we can afford, it's clean and look at the view.' We go to the balcony and I can see the lights of LA and on the side Disneyland. 'The view is the best,' I say turning to look at him.

'Yes, the view is worth it.' Is he agreeing with me or is he saying something else, no, he is agreeing with me.

'Do you want a cuppa before you go or a drink or do you need to go.'

'I will stay a bit if Okay,' he says, 'I don't have my daughter till tomorrow.'

'Okay, but please chat with Michael, this smurf needs to have a shower, hope you don't mind.'

'Nah, go for it.' I hear.

This is the best shower, I feel so dirty from the travelling, shit, what am I going to wear it's not like I can go out in my nightie. I try to think but my clothes are out in the wardrobe. 'Hey Michael?'

'Yeah Mum?'

'Can you grab my bag? I forgot my clothes.' He passes my bag and I put on shorts and a t-shirt. Well this is it, I have to go out, wonder if Bryson has gone, I hope not but I really don't want him to see me in shorts and a t-shirt as no doubt he is used to the skinny girls. *Deep breath and walk out, Sandy,* I think. I take one step at a time. I go out and yep, he is on the couch watching TV, Michael is in bed snoring. That's my boy. Snoring away. I laugh.

'Hey Bryson,' I said, 'I thought you may have gone.'

'He replies, 'I thought it was BJ or Honey you were going to call me?' He says.

'Oh, I don't know what to call you,' I say. I look at him and laugh and say, 'I will work it out.'

'He then says, 'Not a problem but to your question before, I wouldn't leave and not said good night.' God, he is so sweet. Some girl is going to be lucky to end up with him. 'And why are you not taken? You are absolutely adorable and so kind,' I say and then turn and put the kettle on, 'coffee or tea or chocolate,' I ask.

'Coffee, thanks,' he replies. I make myself a tea. We are sitting on the couch and Titanic comes on; 'I love this movie,' we both say, lol.

'I say, 'This is my favourite movie.'

He says, 'It would be a lot of peoples, but yes I love it too.' So, we sit on the couch and start to watch it. I snuggle into him and start to watch it, I can feel my eyes starting to close but I don't want to miss any minute with him. I know that this will be the last time I will see him so I want to savour all the time I can. Man, he feels so good, he smells so good, I really could get used to this, leaning into him watching TV. Next thing I wake up and we are both on the couch, we both fell asleep. I stare at him and look at his eyelashes against his cheek; he looks so comfortable, so calm, so gorgeous. Do I wake him or let him sleep, I look at the clock it is 1 am. I better wake him. 'Bryson, honey, wake up.' He stirs but doesn't move. *Oh Okay, well I will just snuggle back into his arms and go back to sleep what a way to sleep. Sweet dreams,* I think and go back to sleep.

'Mum, Mum wake up!' What is that god almighty racket. Mum wake up and so does Bryson. We both look at each other and laugh. 'Morning.' I look at Michael.

'Morning baby, what time is it,' I ask.

'It's 7 am Mum, we are going to Disneyland today, aren't we?'

'Yes mate, 10 am. We still have a few hours, Okay, go get dressed and we will eat breakfast.' I turn and Bryson still has his arm around me. Man this would be the perfect way to take my last breath in his arms. I look at him and he is looking into my eyes.

'Morning sunshine,' he says.

'I am so sorry I fell asleep, are you Okay? I didn't hurt you,' I ask.

'No all good, I haven't slept like that before and yet it was very comfortable.'

'David, Oh shit I hope he didn't stay all night.'

'No, I let him go when you were in the shower, I could have caught a cab home, all good.'

31

'Now what are you two up to today,' he asks.

'Well Disneyland today, we have entry at 10 am. Do you want to come,' I ask.

He looks at me and then says, 'You know what maybe not today as I am getting my daughter today but how about tonight we do something together?'

'Will you have your daughter tonight?' I ask.

'Yes, I will have her for the rest of the week.'

'Good, that will be nice. Maybe we shouldn't intrude,' I respond.

He looks at me, raises his eyebrow and says, 'Are we going to do this again?'

'No we aren't, sorry honey, I mean Bryson', and smile. We leave together, he goes down stairs to the car and offers to drive us to the entry. 'All good,' I say, 'I am sure we can walk it.' but then decide to hop in the car as we get to spend a little bit more time with each other. I think to myself, *can you fall in love with someone you hardly know. I never believed in love at first sight, but if this is how it feels, not wanting to not spend time with someone, happy to always have them around, well count me in cookie. Sign me up to whatever I need to, I am a goner.* We are here, I hear, bugger, but say, 'Fantastic, come on Michael lets go. I turn to Bryson and say, 'Thank you for yesterday and last night, thank you for the lift, I hope you have a good day with your daughter and just in case you change your mind about tonight, thank you so much for spending time with us.' I lean in and give him a hug and then we look at each other and give each other a kiss on the lips. Okay, I don't think I can walk, wow he does have soft lips. Hello god help me, I am drowning. 'Um thanks again.' I hop out of the car, *put one foot at a time*, I think, *don't trip over*

32

and try to be graceful. I turn around to wave and he is staring. God, he is so gorgeous and I slept in his arms last night, hehe… heaven is real. I smile wave and we go into Disneyland. This place is huge! There are 4 lands to view.

'Okay, Michael, which one first,' I ask.

'Let's do the rides Mum.'

'Okay mate.'

'Hey Mum.'

'Yes Michael, Why didn't Bryson join us?' he asks. 'Well Michael, he has to go and get his daughter, plus we can't monopolize his time, although I would be happy to be forever with him but we can't.'

'Oh Okay Mum, it's just when you were in the shower last night, he was asking all these questions, I think he likes you.' I go red.

'Well Michael, I will tell you a secret, I don't know what love at first sight feels like, but if it is anything like how I am feeling, I am in love with him. But it will never work as I don't really know him and he lives in LA and we don't. Come on, let's go see Disneyland.'

It is a magical day, we ride all the rides we can, we get sunburnt and have heaps of water and take heaps of photos. My phone battery is getting low so I go plug my phone with my portable charger and there is message. It is from him. *Hey sunshine, just wondering how you are going and what time do you want me to pick you guys up?* It says.

I call straight away. On the second ring he picks up. 'Hi you,' I say, 'sorry my phone battery was low and I just plugged it in, we are about to finish and walk back to the hotel, we need to freshen up, we can meet you wherever you want to save you come and get us if you prefer,' I say.

'Nah, all good,' he says, 'we are just leaving now to meet you. We are about 30mins away. When we get there we will come up to get you, see you soon.' Before I can respond he hangs up. Shit.

'Michael, we have 30mins to get back, showered and changed, Bryson is on his way.' I have never moved so fast. We bolt out the gates, cross the road and get back to our hotel. We have been back for 20mins, when there is a knock at the door, we have both showered and I am trying to dry my hair. 'Michael can you get the door please,' and continue to dry my hair.

As I come out there he is in jeans and a t-shirt, but this time he has a gorgeous little blonde girl with him, a mini version of him, so cute. 'Hiya, how's it going?'

'Good, you guys ready,' he asks.

'Can you give me 5mins? I just have to get my bag and shoes. Where are we going? Do I need to dress up a bit better or is this ok?' I ask.

'No Sandy, jeans and t-shirt is good, we are going to go to my place and have dinner and the kids can hang out, Michael bring your bathers and you too Sandy if you want, we have a pool.'

'Oh ok.' Shit, well once he sees me in my togs, it's over red rover. 'My bathers?' I ask.

'Yes, your bathers,' he says.

'I don't know if I can find them.'

'Mum, here they are,' says Michael.

I turn and look at him and if looks could have killed him he would be dead but instead I say, 'Thanks honey.' Maybe if I get him drunk he won't remember! Maybe just maybe he will forget, but a swim would be nice at least I won't get laughed at by all the girls. I put them in my bag with our towels.

'Sandy, you don't need to bring towels, I have towels.'

'I know, but I don't want to cause extra work for you.'

'Are you really worrying about two extra towels,' he says.

I look at him. 'Oh, Okay,' and take the towels out of the bag. We all go out the door and head to the lift, as the lift opens up I notice that Bryson steps behind me to let the other people out, geez he is so nice and polite, I notice that the other guests look at us quizzically but I ignore them and we hop in and take the lift down to the car park. Wow, what a car. There standing near the doorway is a black Jeep, and as we walk towards it, there is a driver and he opens the door for us. Wow, I feel rich. 'Thank you,' I say, 'but no need to open the door for me, I'm good. But thank you.'

'It's all good ma'am,' he says. 'Sir, are you ready,' he asks Bryson.

'Yes, let's go.'

'Bryson I can't call you this, it is too formal for me. Can I call you Brycie?'

'OK,' he says.

'Now Brycie, why is he being so formal?' I ask.

'It's just the service that I have when I need to get around, particularly when I have my daughter and guests, it's easier than worrying about the traffic.'

'Oh Okay.'

As we are driving, I am in awe of all the houses and the view out of the window. Wow, palm trees are everywhere, the streets are so busy and as we are driving further away the houses are getting bigger, the streets are getting wider and the views are stunning. We have been driving for a while when we turn into a street and then turn into a large winding driveway. My mouth falls open as we turn towards the house, Holy moley, my home would fit 50 times in the driveway alone.

'Um is this, um I, I am so flustered.'

'Spit it out, Sandy,' he says.

'Am I dressed Okay for here? This house is huge! I don't want to make a mess.'

He laughs.

'All good I am just renting it, it's a home, it doesn't matter what is around a home, how big or small it is, you make a home with love and company.' I am instantly in love with this guy. I look up and he is staring at me, 'Come on slow mow, we are here.' He gives me his hand and I climb out, the kids are both running around.

'Michael be careful, don't get dirt on the floor, be careful, don't make a mess,' I yell.

'Sandy it is all good, it is fine. He is safe as is Amy. They can't get into much mischief plus we are both here. So come on and let me show you around our home.' I like the sound of Our Home. *Jeez woman, get a grip,* I think. As we walk in all I see is space, a beautiful entry, ahead there is space, high ceilings, glass everywhere, the kitchen looks like it belongs in a showroom.

'Come on this is the lounge,' he says, if we go ahead, there is a sitting room where Amy plays her games, the bedrooms are upstairs on the left, outside on the right is the back yard, come on the kids are out there near the pool.'

I am in awe. This is an absolutely beautiful home. It looks like it is in Perfect and Pristine condition. It reminds me of the do not touch signs in a museum. Bryson looks at me. I am standing in the one spot. I look at him and say, 'I think we have to go.'

He walks towards me. 'Sandy, it is all good.'

'I don't want to break anything, I don't want to make a mess. This house, it's absolutely beautiful, what happens if I break something or Michael does, what happens if I dirty something, I don't want you to hate me.'

'I would never hate you,' he says, 'Plus if it gets dirty you can clean it, if it breaks we fix it, OK,' he says, and then smiles at me. I am a goner. Hook, line and sinker I am in love with him. *Now I know what love at first sight is, but it's one way so keep cool girl,* I think. He grabs my hand and we go outside. He has the BBQ on and the kids are in the pool. Michael looks so happy and I start to relax and laugh, this is Okay. *Wow I could so live like this for the rest of my life, just breathe,* I think, and of course stare at the gorgeous man at the BBQ, He is still holding my hand. "Earth to Sandy,' he says.

'Oh shit, sorry,' I say. *I'm fine just admiring everything, not to mention you,* I think to myself. 'Just enjoying the company and Michael is having a ball so all good. Can I help with the BBQ or do something?'

'Nah all good,' he says.

'Can I do a salad or set up the table?

'No all good, I did it earlier.' What a guy. I keep staring at him and decide to just stay and stand next to him and talk. It feels so comfortable talking and being with him. It's like we have known each other for years, it feels like we are old friends or even better a happy married couple. *If only, if only,* I think.

'Hey Sandy, wakey.'

'I'm sorry, just thinking. Thank you for today it has been awesome.'

'It hasn't even started, after dinner, we are going to relax and watch a movie or we can do whatever you want. Amy is here all week with me so your wish is my command,' he says. Boy Oh boy, so glad he can't read mind I just stare at him and smile. This is such a perfect day. I wish it would never end but I know it will.

'Kids, dinner.' we yell together and we all sit down on the deck, eat away and chat. The sun is starting to go down, 'Hey Sandy, come here,' Bryson calls out. So, I follow his voice, he is upstairs as I turn the corner he grabs me and covers my eyes. 'No peaking,' he says, 'do you trust me,' he asks.

'Yes,' I say.

'Good now, Step, step, I will guide you, keep your eyes closed,' he says. I keep walking with him then he says, 'Open your eyes.' I am on a balcony, I can see the kids below but the view ahead of me is stunning, I can see the ocean and the sun is going down. I look at him next to me and just smile. 'Oh God this is Gorgeous, what a view, imagine living here and seeing this view every day. Gosh, if it was me I would have the curtains open so I could see the stars and in the morning watch the sunrise. How do you even get out of bed?' I ask. 'Thank you for letting me see this with you.'

He says, 'It's my pleasure but I wanted to share this with you and we have peace and quiet here, the kids are safe and we can watch the sun set.' And that is exactly what we do, we stand next to each other watching the sun go down, it must be getting a bit cold as I shiver and then he stands behind me and hugs me and we just stand there. Here he says, 'I will keep you warm.' *Damn straight you will, I will be so hot soon, I will be sweating*, I think. I calm my nerves and lean into him and watch the sunset.

After the sun has set, we are still standing there till we hear, 'Dad, Sandy come down we want to watch TV.' We look at each other and laugh and go down. I have been in LA for two days and I am in love not just with the place but with the man next to me, how am I ever going to leave him, but I know I will have to but I don't want to. *Enjoy the time together,* I think, *it won't last.*

We sit on the couch, the kids are on the floor and we have settled in watching a movie. The kids are laughing at it and the oompa loompas. 'Man this is such a good show. Do you prefer this version of Charlie and the chocolate factory or do you prefer the newer one with Johnny Depp?' I ask. 'They are both good, the new version is different and has funny parts but Gene Wilder was a legendary actor,' Bryson says. I lean into him again and we watch the movie. This is getting to be a habit, leaning into him. A girl could definitely get used to it. I keep thinking this. He starts to rub my neck and shoulders, how am I ever going to leave but then I know I will only have good memories of LA and Bryson and Amy.

The movie finishes and I look at my watch and realise it has gone quiet, both kids are asleep on the floor and we are just leaning into each other. I get up and say, 'Thank you for tonight you have definitely made our trip so wonderful and to think it all started with me yelling at you, I am so sorry about that honey. But I think it's best if Michael and I get back to our hotel as we have a full day at Disneyland again tomorrow with a 7am entry. Do you have a phone number for a cab?' I ask. 'And please say bye to Amy for me she is absolutely adorable, just like her daddy.'

39

He looks at me and says, 'Why don't you guys stay the night, there's heaps of rooms and in the morning we get up and all go to Disneyland.'

'Can you do that? Don't you have book for early entry? I ask.'

He replies, 'it's sorted I got my manager to sort it out.'
'Manager?' I ask.

'Yeah, my business manager.'

'Oh ok,' I reply.

'But if I stay, I have nothing to wear or change into tomorrow, can we get up early so I can go past and get changed?'

'Of course, Sweetheart. Come on let's get the kids to bed and then we can go to bed.'

'Michael, wake up baby. Come on go to bed.' He gets up and we follow Bryson upstairs he has Amy in his arms and I am holding onto Michael, both kids get put to bed and then I go back downstairs to tidy up the dishes on the table.

'Oh, what are you doing? I hear.

'Just tidying up.'

'It's OK, I have a cleaner that can do that.

'Yes,' I say, 'but that doesn't mean I can't pick up and tidy plus it helps me relax.'

'Okay, I will help and we tidy up in harmony.' After a few minutes he grabs my hand and we go upstairs to go to bed. He says, 'You can sleep in here with me or if you want you can go sleep in the spare room, your choice, but…,' he says, 'you will be safe and I promise not to attack you.'

'Oh only if you promise,' I laugh. 'But then maybe I want to be attacked', and wink at him.

'Come on trouble,' he says, I will give you a shirt you can sleep in.' After a shower we both go to bed, I lean into him, hope I don't snore and try to go to sleep. Gosh LA is turning into a wonderful holiday. My mind is going at a 100miles per hour, I can hear his breathing and can't sleep as I can smell him and don't want to miss a minute of seeing him. I look at the clock and it shows 3 am, I can't sleep. I don't want to disturb him so I turn and stare at him. God he is beautiful. He looks so relaxed. His arm is still around me and I am looking up from his chest and just staring.

'If you keep staring at me you are going to be in trouble,' I hear. I go bright red, thank god he can't see it.

'I'm sorry, I just woke up and didn't want to disturb you. But…,' I ask, 'what trouble will I be in?' And next thing he has grabbed me, rolled me on top of him and says 'This.' OMG, we start kissing, his lips are so soft. I can't believe I am lying on top of this man and kissing him, Why is he kissing me, I am not a model, I am not skinny but yet he is kissing me, he is grabbing me and pulling me closer. I want to climb into his skin and never let go. We are rolling around, kissing, grabbing at each other and our clothes, when I say, 'I don't ever do this, pull away and sit up, I don't sleep with someone I don't know very well. I don't want you to think of me in the wrong way and I don't want to use you, I don't want you to hate me and I am enjoying our time together.' He looks at me, puts his hands on my face and says, 'I won't hate you, I have never felt this comfortable with anyone, not even my ex and if I didn't want to be here with you I wouldn't. Now come back here or I will have to come and get you.'

'Oh really and who's army,' I say. He grabs me, rolls on top of me and we start kissing, arms go everywhere, clothes get thrown around and we are in heaven, well I am. My god, his body is gorgeous, hair is in the right places and I start to trace his hair all the way down. Every bit of him is gorgeous. Boy oh boy, this is definitely going to be a night to remember. We end up falling asleep in each other's arms and then we hear, 'Dad, Sandy it's morning where are you guys.' I jump up and grab my shirt and bolt into the bathroom, in the meantime I hear him laughing at me as I have almost gone head first into the wall.

'Stop laughing at me,' I say with a look of thunder and amusement.

He just stares and laughs and says, 'Go gorgeous have a shower, I will be there in a minute, I will get the kids sorted out with the housekeeper.' His bathroom is enormous, my bedroom, spare room and lounge would fit into his bathroom alone. How did I get so lucky? There is a god and I start to sing while in the shower. *You're just too good to be true, can't take my eyes off of you. You are like heaven to touch, I wanna hold you so much at long last love has arrived and I thank god I'm alive, your just too good to be true can't take my eyes off of you* and then I have company singing with me. We are both in the shower, washing each other's backs, hair and singing. I normally get shy but I know this is the last time I will see him so let it all go and we start kissing again.

'Dad, are you in there?' We hear Amy says. 'When are we going,' she asks.

We look at each other. Laugh and he says, 'Give us 15mins baby and then we will go, Sandy is just drying her hair.' I am standing there naked in the shower and I am drying my hair, I giggle and get out of the shower.

42

At exactly 6 am we are all in the car, driving back to our hotel. Michael and Amy are in the back seat, Bryson and I are in the front, I have my hand in his and if I was to die now it would be worth it.

I have only known him for two days, but it just feels right, I feels like he is my soul mate. I am in awe, he is the most amazing person. I keep looking at him and wonder to myself what happened with his ex, why didn't they stay together? And why or why would anyone leave him. If I was his partner I would move the moon and sun to protect him and to always be there for him. I sit there thinking how good it would be if this was my life. Michael would have a dad and a step -sister, I would have a man I could be with, someone who would always be there next to me. I am imagining what it would be like to wake up next to him every day, snuggling into him every day and every night. My god, how good would it be to be with him.

'Sandy, we're here at your hotel, we drive down to the underground car park', and just before we get out he grabs my hand. 'Sandy,' he says, why don't you guys stay with us, you go pack your bags and stay with us for the rest of your holiday. That way we can spend as much time together as we want, if I have to work, I can work around it and we can all spend time together like a family and see how it goes.'

I look at him, I would love to say yes. I say, 'But I don't want to intrude and I feel we have already put you out a lot all ready.'

'Sandy,' he says, if I thought you were intruding I wouldn't of invited you, if I didn't want to spend time with you I wouldn't find any excuse to see you. I want to spend as much time with you as I can, I want Amy to get to know you and Michael and show her that adults can live happily ever after. So I am going to ask again and I hope I get a different answer,' he says. *Shit I have upset him,* I think. 'Now I want you and Michael to come and stay with us till you leave, would you like that?' I look at him, at the kids and back at him, 'Well you didn't have to ask twice,' I say. He laughs. 'God, woman what am I going to do with you.' I shrug and say, 'Maybe never let me go.' We look at each other and we all get out of the car. *SHIT*, I think, *I shouldn't have said that, stupid, stupid girl,* I think.

'Amy, you go up with Sandy and Michael and help them pack they are going to come and stay with us for the rest of their holidays.' Both kids yell, 'YEAH.'

I say, 'That makes 3 of us,' and Bryce says, 'No, it makes 4. I will go and sort out the refund and the bill for the hotel and meet you in your room.' We go our separate ways, the kids and I in the lift, Bryce goes to reception. We are nearly packed when he walks in.

Okay Honey,' he says, 'all sorted the refund is back on your card and they said they hope you enjoy the rest of your holiday, so let's get your stuff in the car and go to Disneyland together.'

'Are you sure I don't need to pay for both your entries?' 'It's all good,' he says, it was organised yesterday.' We drive up a back entrance and a security guard waves us in, wow that is service.

'Bryson, isn't this is the wrong entry?' I ask.

'No, it is for early entries for big groups.'

'Oh Okay.'

'Mr Johnst.' the guard stops. 'Mr Johns, welcome to Disneyland, we have a golf cart to help you all get round as quickly or slowly as you want.' Bryson smiles and we all get out of the car, grab our bags and hop on the cart. The kids are in the back, we are in the middle and the driver is in the front. This is so much fun, we go through a few of the lands, we all go on the rides, we laugh at not just ourselves but all the people walking around having fun.

'Bryson, do you want to join us on Splash Mountain?' I ask.

He looks at me. 'Um maybe,' he says.

'Come on, scaredy cat, I say, I will beat you to the queue.' The last one there has to kiss the nearest person and we all run. 'I won,' I yell and the kids come too. *'Where is Bryson,* I think and he grabs me, pulls me close and gives me a passionate kiss in front of both the kids and the operator. I go bright red and he pulls me back up, 'Payment made,' he says and winks, grabs my hand and we all hop in the ride. I am in an absolute tiz, I am so confused, why did he kiss me like that and in front of the staff member and both our kids, why would he do that? I question. He still has his hand in mine and yet I am not sweating anymore, it feels so comfortable, so right. *Does he feel the same way as me? Or is this just a thing he does*, I think. *Yeah that has to be it, a guy like him would never be with someone like me, just enjoy the time together,* I think, *when it is over and believe me it will end soon, then I will have beautiful memories but I don't think I will ever love again, he has ruined it for me now.*

We go on all the rides, laughing constantly, take selfies of each other and end the day like we started together, smiling, laughing and all of us are exhausted, we get back to the car and as I open the doors for the kids I notice that the back is full of souvenirs, teddy's and assorted items.

'Bryson,' I ask. 'I do hope that all the stuff in the back is for Amy and yourself.' He smiles. 'No, not just Amy, but you and Michael too.'

'Seriously,' I say. 'And how do you advise we get this all home, it will cost a fortune for me to send it,' I say.

'I got this,' he says. *Man he annoys me when he says things like that, I tell you one thing*, I think. *You got me and you will never get rid of me until you want.* I just wish I had the guts to say that out load. But the chicken in me smiles and I start to drift off. He grabs me and says to lean in we won't be long to get home. The kids are asleep in the back and I am lying back on the seat and looking at him.

'Bryson,' I say.

'Yes honey,' he replies.

'I just want to say something, I don't want to upset you but I need to say this.'

He looks at me. 'Okay,' he says.

'I just want to say that.' I pause, I start to get teary and go on, 'I just want to say that these past days have been the best days of my life, the only thing that beats it was Michael's birth. But spending these days with you and now Amy has been so memorable and I don't know how I am going to go home and not have you both in our lives. I do hope we stay as friends and I do hope that we never lose contact. I will always cherish our time together and although we really don't know each other very well, I just want to say that you are the most adorable, gorgeous, caring, wonderful person in the world and I wish it would never end, that we could stay here forever but I know that that is just a dream.' I look at him for some comment or movement but his head is looking ahead as he drives.

Shit I have done it now, again. Me and my big mouth. I have always been too honest for my own good. I wonder if he will drop me off to the nearest hotel. At least, I didn't tell him I loved him. That would really ruin it completely. Maybe he will just think I am an idiot. Oh well, at least I told him the truth well most of the truth.

I sit there in silence, he hasn't said a word since I spoke. 'Hey guys,' he says, 'we are home, come on kids, dinner will be soon, I have organised takeaway. Come on we all take something out of the car it will be quicker.' We empty the car in record time and yet he still hasn't spoken to me. I must have upset him.

'Michael,' I yell, 'Hey Michael, come here please.' 'Coming Mum.'

'Mate we are going to have to leave and go stay at a hotel.'

'Why Mum,' he asks.

I told Bryson what I was thinking and he hasn't spoken to me since, so grab your bags, I am going to try and find a hotel and get a cab. While he is out getting takeaway I should be able to find something and we can go.'

'But Mum why can't we stay.'

'Because I ruined it baby, thank god I didn't tell him that I loved him, that would have been worse.'

I find the house keeper. 'Excuse me, do you have a phone book I need to find a hotel and a cab.'

'It is in Mr Johnst, Bryson's office, that is upstairs on the right.'

'Thank you,' I say. I go upstairs find the phone book and start calling hotels. I am on the phone when I hear steps behind me.

'What do you think you are doing in here, Missy?' I hear. I turn around and he is standing there with his hands on his hips. God he is gorgeous.

'Just trying to organise Michael and myself a hotel.'

He frowns like a grumpy cat, walks toward me, puts the phone on the hook and pulls me to him. 'And why would you be doing that?' he asks.

I look at him, Okay here goes. 'Well in the car when I was talking to you, you know about how much this has meant to me, you went quiet, you didn't say anything, then when we got back you still didn't say anything, you just emptied the car with us and then you went out, so I assumed I had upset you and you wouldn't want me around so I thought I would be gone before you came back.'

He looks at me. 'Just because I didn't say anything doesn't mean I don't want you here. I had to do something and get something.'

Oh, I say. Nothing more, nothing less. Now he says, 'Let's go and eat with the kids and we will talk later, Okay?' he says.

Okay, so he doesn't hate me but why does he want to talk to me, what will he say? We go downstairs there is music, the table outside is set up near the pool, there are candles lit all around, how romantic I think.

'Wow what a spread, how many people are you expecting to come for dinner,' I ask. He smiles. 'Just wanted to make sure there was something for everyone plus tomorrow we can have leftovers. I smile well at least there is a tomorrow. We eat in silence but not silence, if you know what I mean, we talk about the day we had, what plans for tomorrow and the rest of our weeks.

'So honey,' I say, do you have any work plans, I think we have taken a lot of your time so far.' He grabs my hand. 'It has been a pleasure to be spending this time with you plus I have a surprise tomorrow night for you,' he says. 'Tomorrow night?'

'Yes, tomorrow night, and all will be revealed tomorrow.' Man he is driving me crazy, but a good crazy.

What has he got planned for tomorrow, I think.

'Any hint?' I ask. He looks at me and says, 'Nope, no hint, you will have to just wait and be patient.'

I look at him and say, 'I am not one of the most patient person, just one little hint, please!!!' I beg.

'Nope, and if you ask again I will have to punish you tonight.' I smirk as he does.

'Well maybe I might want to be punished', and we both laugh. The kids are oblivious, which is good.

After dinner, the kids get ready for bed. 'Bryson and I clean up and make a cuppa and sit in front of the fire. I love it here,' I say, 'it is so peaceful. I can't believe we are in LA and yet I can't hear any traffic.'

'That's why I live here, laurel canyon is close enough to be in LA for work wise but far away that we don't get much traffic plus the views are beautiful,' he says.

'Yes, they are,' I say while I am looking into his face.

'It is getting late, we have been chatting for hours and look at the clock and it is 1am. Come on sleepy head,' he says, 'let's go to bed.' We go upstairs, get changed and go straight to bed, I lean into him, he puts his arm around me and we fall asleep till morning.

I wake up first and look at him he always looks so restful. I am going to miss this. This is my fourth day here and I only have ten days left. *Oh well, enjoy it while you can,* I think.

'Morning sweetheart,' he says.

'Morning gorgeous,' I reply.

'I could get used to this,' he says. Wow, I wasn't expecting that. 'Now for your day sweetheart, I have made you an appointment at the hairdressers at 1pm, I have some surprises coming here at 4 pm and we have to leave by 6 pm for our special night out. Now don't say anything it has all be arranged, this is something I booked on the first night we met and I can't change it, it is going to be tricky logistically but it will be fine. Now for the kids, we are all going to stay here and relax till you have to leave. Do you want to join me in my studio while I work out some songs,' he asks.

'Of course,' I say.

The kids are playing in the pool, I am watching from the studio upstairs while he works and think he is absolutely perfect. 'Do we have to go out tonight?' I ask. 'I am quite content to just stay here with you and the kids.'

He looks at me. 'Yes we do', and then says, 'come on gorgeous it's time to go to your appointment.'

'Do I really have to? Can't we just stay here,' I query. 'Go,' he says, 'for me please, I will see you soon.'

So, I go downstairs and say bye to the kids, jump in the car and off I go. I arrive at the hairdressers but it looks too swanky for me.

I ask, 'David, if this is the correct place.'

'Yes, 'it is,' he says. So I go in. The door opens and a model answers it, 'Hi Sandra, I am Sharon, I am going to do your hair so please come in and relax, Do you want a glass of champagne?' She asks.

'No thanks, I don't really drink that much. But please call me Sandy.'

Well I think you will be doing a lot of different things soon so I think you better get used to it,' she says. I stare at her and am about to say something when she says, 'Now please sit here, face away from the mirror and we will get started. I put my headset in my ears, listen to my music and just in case Bryson calls and wants to cancel but it never happen, in the meantime I am chatting away to Sharon, she is masterful, so clever, after she finishes she turns me around to face the mirror. 'All done Sandy, you can look now,' she says. I look up and I can't believe this, I look so different, my hair is up in a knot and framed around my face and I don't look like myself.

'Thank you so much Sharon,' I say, 'you have done a miracle.'

'It's my pleasure Sandy,' she says, I don't do miracles, it's what you really look like.' I am in awe. *I hope he likes it*, I think. I say thank you again, hop in the car and we go back to Bryson's. I hope he doesn't mind what this looks like, I feel so different. We arrive back and there is a strange car in the driveway.

'There you go, Sandy,' says the driver.

'Thank you so much,' I reply and go in. Bryson is standing there as I walk in.

'Hi honey,' I say.

'Hope this is Okay, the hairdresser just did it, you look gorgeous, but it is not over yet. Go upstairs to our room go get changed and I will see you soon.' I walk up bewildered, why is he doing this. But I go up and when I walk in the door there are 5 people.

'Hi,' I say.

'Hi Sandy, now take a seat, we have to get you ready.' I sit down and watch them go to work. My makeup is being done. I have shoes and dresses flying around.

'Do you like heels?' I hear, 'or flats?'

'Heels,' I say.

'High heels or reasonable heels?'

'As Long as I can walk I don't care.'

'Right.' I hear. 'Close your eyes,' I hear and I do as asked. I am trying to ask questions about how much this is, where do they know Bryson from and how did he organise this so quickly but I am told to enjoy this as it rarely done and to just relax, so I dose off a bit. I feel a tap on my shoulder. 'Open your eyes, Sandy.' And I am looking in the mirror.

'Who is that,' I ask.

'It's you,' I hear them say.

'No.' I say suddenly, 'that's not me, it's a trick mirror.' 'No, they say that is you. You are absolutely stunning. Now let's get Cinderella dressed and her prince can take her out.' I walk in silence and awe. This is what dreams are made of. I get dressed in a bright blue dress, look in the mirror and my mouth flies open. The dress is absolutely stunning, it clings to parts that I didn't even know I had. It sits perfectly on my breasts and falls beautifully past my enormous hips, it is one shouldered dress. I just stare in the mirror.

'Are you sure this looks OK?' I ask. 'I am not asking to be told I am beautiful as I know I am not, but I just want to make sure I don't embarrass Bryson.'

'Sandy this is the real you, when people get their hair, makeup and dressing done it is the real person. We can't make something that isn't already there, we just improve on what is already there,' they say.

'I still can't believe this is me. I am the short fat smurf, yet I don't look like that, I look like a different person.' I turn around and ask, 'Do you think Bryson will think I look OK, I don't want to disappoint him and do you guys know where he is taking me?' I ask.

Cheryl says to me, 'All we know is you had to be ready by 6 pm which you are, he planned this the day you guys met and he is said it is a very special night.'

I look at Cheryl and then the others and nod my head and say, 'Wish me luck.'

I walk out the bedroom door, hope I won't fall over my feet and start to descent the stairs, I have my bag in my hand and as I start to walk down the stairs I see Bryson standing there looking at me. 'WOW,' he says, 'Sandy you look absolutely gorgeous.'

I turn a bright red and say, You don't look so bad yourself Mr J. You are a very sexy man and I am so lucky to be here with you and thank you for today and this, I have never felt so special.

'Well, the night is only starting,' he says and grabs my hand. Amy and Michael come and say good night, we give them both a hug and kiss and I say, 'Michael behave please, listen to Christy and do what she says, I have my mobile if you need but please only ring if it's urgent.' Bryson puts my jacket on my shoulders, grabs my hand and we walk out to the car. David is there, opens the doors and we hop in the back.

'Hi David, how are you tonight.'

'Very good Sandy you look stunning.'

Again I go bright red and Bryson snuggles against me and says, 'No David she doesn't just look stunning Sandy you look perfect.'

'Well, it always helps when you get pampered by professionals, I say.

'True,' says Bryson, 'but they can only improve on what there is, they can't make a mutton look like a lamb.'

'Honey, where are we going? I ask.

'Well, I have somewhere very special for tonight, it is very exclusive and it will be perfect.'

'As long as I am with you,' I say, 'it will be.'

We arrive at the most beautiful building, there are lights everywhere, cameras are everywhere and I am frozen to the seat. 'Bryson what are we doing here?' I ask.

'This is the surprise, but we are going in the back Okay,' he says.

'We are going to see a premier of my new movie tonight.'

'Really which movie?' I ask.

'It is new one and there are heaps of celebrities there so that's why we got dressed up.'

'Oh Okay,' I say,

'I guess that's Okay.'

'Are you sure it's Okay I come with you? I can wait but I don't want to get in the way.'

'No, all good but we are going to have dinner first,' he says.

'Okay honey.' We go in and are directed to a private room, no one else is around, there are only us and a waiter. We sit down and the meal arrives. It is a perfect delicious meal, beautiful wines and a perfect companion. Bryson starts to speak and pauses.

'What's wrong Bryson?' I ask.

'Sandy, I have a confession to make but I don't know how to say it.' I gulp what is going on, have I done something wrong, does he not want me here anymore, has he got me dressed up to tell him he wants me to leave, we have been together for four days and I can't believe how much time we have spent together, I don't believe anything except that I love him and I never want this to end but I know that it can't be. He is still looking at me.

'Sandy, before I tell you what I want to say and confess I want to say something else.'

I know we have only known each other for four days, I know we don't really know each other that well but these past days have been perfect, both our kids love spending time together, we love spending time together so I think this is the night that I tell you everything.' But, he is sweating, he seems unsure.

I say, 'It's Okay you can tell me anything, I promise I won't be upset.' He is looking at me, takes a drink of wine, puts it down and is fiddling with his napkin. 'Honey, it's Okay if you want Michael and I to go we can, if we are in your way, I understand, you didn't have to go out of your way, I understand, it's been less than a week but I get it.' 'No, no that's not it Sandy,' he says. He grabs my hand, gets up and drags his chair next to me. 'The thing is,' he says, 'the thing is, these last days has been amazing, I have never felt so close and so comfortable with anyone who is not my family before. Even my ex, I never felt this way.' He is holding my hand and rubbing my hand, I can't concentrate, but I look at him, he looks so nervous. 'The thing is honey,' he says, 'the reason why I did tonight is I wanted to tell you how I feel and what I want. I never thought I would ever feel this way, when I first got with my ex and married her, I did it so Amy could have both parents together and the minute we got married I regretted it. But spending this week with you has changed me, it has changed the way I feel about love, it has shown me that you can find the right person for you, that you can find your soul mate, that there is love for everyone out there. Sandy I love you,' he says. He is looking me in the eyes and says, 'I love you so much and I don't want you to go back to Australia, I want you and Michael to stay here with Amy and myself forever, logistically I know it will be hard, I know your home, family, work, Michael has his school over there but I hope that we can build on our relationship, I hope that you both can come over here and live. I want you to be here with me. I don't want to lose you. He has tears in his eyes...' I wipe at his face and put my hand on his face.

'I love you too, crazy that it is, but I do. I loved you from the moment I yelled at you for bumping into me. But how would it work? I am no one, I am nothing like the women here, I am not a model, why me? I think to myself the last bit.'

'Sandy, the only thing matters is that we love each other and we can build on this relationship but there is one more thing I have to tell you.' I look at him. Okay here goes. 'The day you met me I was running away from the paparazzi.'

I look at him. 'I don't understand,' I say. 'Why would you?'

'The thing is I haven't been so truthful to you completely. My home isn't a rental I own it and I own a place in Reno too. Reno is my farm.

'So you have money who cares,' I say, I don't love your money, I love you and Amy.'

'I know that but the thing is I haven't been truthful of who I am. Now I am getting worried.'

I sit up and look at him. Then I say, 'We can get through anything unless you're really a girl or gay then that breaks it.' He laughs. 'I am not a girl and gay, not that being gay is bad but it's you that I love,' he says.

'Good,' I say. 'So what did you have to say?'

'Sandy, the thing is, the truth is, my name is not Bryson Johns.

'It's not,' I ask.

'No, my name is Bryce Johnston.' He looks at me, I start to laugh.

'Good one, as if I have to admit you look a lot like him but if you were Bryce Johnston then why would you be with me?' I ask. 'So, yes Bryce Johnston is a sexy and gorgeous man but you are not him, you're Bryson.'

'No honey, it's true I am Bryce and the reason I am with you is because you know the real me, the crazy me, the one that likes to spend time at home, the one that loves his daughter and the one that loves you and Michael.'

I look at him. 'Yeah right,' I say. 'You're Bryce Johnston?' I ask.

He shakes his head, 'Yes.'

'You're Bryce Johnston,' I ask again. 'Yeah sure,' I say. He grabs his wallet and shows me his license. Yep on there is a picture of Bryce and his name shows Bryce Lou Johnston. Holy fuck I am with Bryce Johnston, I swallow hard, start to shake and look at him. He is staring at me. I can feel myself start to faint but realise I am not going anywhere as I am sitting down. 'Okay, so you are Bryce Johnston,' I say. 'Tell me everything. Why me? Why now? Why didn't you let me go on thinking you were who you were?'

He starts to speak. 'Firstly, I am with you because you are you, you didn't give a shit what I looked like, you were kind to me even after you cracked it, I like spending time with you. The reason I wanted to tell you now is I don't want any more secrets being kept from you. I have to work on my album and the premier for my movie and I wanted to share it with you. I didn't want you to find out from anyone else. Plus I really didn't like having to keep who I was from you.' I look at him and I can tell he means it.

'I don't know what to say. Um Bryson, Bryce I say. I umm, I, I want to say that I am so confused but the bottom of it is, I don't really care, I love you but are you sure you want me to come to the premier, wont there be photographers there? Won't they ask who I am? How are you going to explain that? From what I know you are a very private person and if I go with you how are you going to explain me? I ask. Plus people wouldn't expect you to take someone like me, they would expect you to be with a model. Surely, you won't want me there with you? I can go back to your place?'

'No, I want you there, he says. I want to experience this with you and I will tell them you are my girlfriend.'

I stare at him. 'But you are a private person, you don't discuss your private life, you never have, why now?' 'Because I don't give a shit what anyone thinks of, and I want to show everyone who I have on my arm proudly.' *Good answer,* I think. We are sitting there when there is a knock at the door.

'Come in,' says Bryce.

'Mr Johnston, are you and your party ready, everyone is starting to arrive.'

'Come on gorgeous,' says Bryce, 'let's go.'

I get up with him, nearly trip on my feet but save myself, we go out to the car, sit in the back and it drives around the corner.

'Ready honey?' he says. I shake my head, check my makeup, all looks good, check my dress that there is no food left on it, powder my face as it is shiny.

I turn to Bryce and ask, 'Are you sure? I can go home and wait.' The door opens up, he hops out, grabs my hand and pulls me out of the car, puts his arm around me and we walk to the carpet.

'Come on honey let's do this,' he says.

'Bryce, Bryce over here.' Cameras are flashing left right and centre, geez it is bright, I can't see for the love of god.

'Bryce, how are you? Who is your date? What's her name? Are you a couple?'

'Sandy, smile, relax I have you,' he says. He is not letting go of me, I am on auto pilot smiling, he is pulling me along, I try to pull away so he can have photos on his own, but he pulls me against him and leans me into him. Flashes are going off like you wouldn't believe. 'Bryce, Bryce, Bryce over here. Who's your date?' I hear.

The rest of the cast and partners are arriving and I just keep walking and holding Bryce's arm. I have no idea how long we are on the carpet, I have no idea where we are, all I see are stars in my eyes from all the flashes. We walk up the carpet.

'Hi Bryce, Michelle from E News, Congratulations on another blockbuster, how are you today?' she says. 'Will there be a sequel and I know everyone is wondering who is your date today?'

He grabs me. 'Firstly, it is such an awesome time every time we get together for a premier, it is great to catch up with the cast again and this beautiful lady is my girlfriend Sandy,' he says. 'Normally, I keep quiet about who I am dating, but this woman is the most wonderful special person who has fitted so well into my life and I want the world to know that I love her completely.' The camera goes onto me and then onto us both.

'Well Bryce, I think you have broken many women's hearts tonight but I can see that this lovely lady makes you very happy, over the years that I have seen you I have never seen you so happy.'

'Yes,' he says, 'when you meet the right person and you know that they are the right person, you don't care who knows.'

'Well, congratulations on the movie, can't wait to see what happens in the movie and what happens with you both.'

We walk away, I have no idea what he said or what was asked. All I know is I am on auto pilot and I just keep walking, I am thinking, step left, step right, keep walking I think. There are more cameras going off, I can't see in front of my nose. Bryce leans into me every time we stop. Pulls me close to him and whispers into my ear, 'Smile baby, just relax,' he says.

'Are you sure you are happy for me to be here,' I whisper back. He grabs me in front of everyone, leans me back and gives me a massive kiss. Cameras are flashing, everyone is yelling out, 'Bryce over here, Bryce look over here.' I am completely frozen, I have no idea what is happening, I just keep walking up the carpet, smiling and looking like a deer in the headlights. All along, Bryce is holding onto me and reassuring it is all Okay. We finally get to the doorway and he says, 'Now let's go sit down and you can meet everyone.' Everyone, he means the cast. As we walk into the theatre, there are 300 eyes turning towards us. 'Bryce, they are all looking at us and wondering why you are with me and what bet you lost,' I say. He stops in the walkway, looks at me and says, 'No they're not, they are looking at me and wondering how happy I look and where have you been all my life.' I go bright red and as we walk to the front, I feel everyone staring at me. I have to just remember I am not part of this world, this is just a two week stopover on our holiday. He won't remember me after I leave, no one will care who I am tomorrow morning. All they will think about is how good this night was and that the entire cast are here.

We go to our seats and I am sitting next to Tom who has his partner next to him. 'Tom this is Sandy, Sandy this is Tom and Maria, there's Chris, Melissa, Matthew, Susan, Marta, Sam, Josh, Jasmine and Curtis. Everyone this is Sandy.'

'Hi Sandy,' they all say. Wow this is real. This is not a dream I think. I am sitting with all the cast at the world premier and I am next to the most gorgeous man in the room, my Bryce. I think this is going to be one of the best nights of my life. I am feeling really comfortable and happy sitting here.

Bryce says, 'We are going to watch the movie and then we do a Q & A. It should finish approx. 11 and then we go home Okay honey.'

'Not a problem,' I say.

'Thank you for letting me come with you.'

He grabs my hand, kisses it, looks into my eyes with his clear and crystal blue eyes. 'I wouldn't want to spend this night with anyone else,' he says. I am in heaven. We lean into each other as the movie is on and he makes comments to me about what happened, I am sitting there just staring, this is amazing, to see a movie at the premier is one thing but to be with Bryce and knowing he is with me. Wow this is, it's just so wonderful, overwhelming but wonderful. The movie finishes and the cast get up to go on stage and start the Q & A. All us partners move together and sit with each other and just watch…

Maria sits next to me and asks, 'How did you guys meet?' Then says, 'I have never seen Bryce so happy and comfortable, even when he was married he always looked like he was on the edge and ready to spring up, but he is so calm and happy with you,' she says. I look at her and before I can speak, all the other girls come up and ask the same thing, I pause, look at them. 'I would love to tell you but I don't want to be rude and tell as Bryce may not want me to tell you. But I can tell you this I met him at the airport when I arrived and yelled at him.' They laughed. And I say, 'I have never, ever, ever loved anyone as much as I love him. I loved him before I knew who he was, I love him for the man he is, I love him for the father he is, I love him for the man he is with myself and my son and I love him for the man I know he always will be.' They are all staring at me and have tears in their eyes.

'Wow,' they say.

'I think that he has found his soulmate,' Jasmine says.

I look at them all and say, 'All I know is I am enjoying this time with him, I have one more week and then my son

and I are leaving, at that time I am sure he will forget out me.'
They look at me, shake their heads together.

Maria says, 'Sandy I have known Bryce for over 12yrs, I have never seen him so open with a female, he is normally very, very private and yet with you he is open. I don't think he will forget you, I think deep down that he will always have you in his heart.' I look at her, look at him up on the stage and my heart is soaring, could this really be it, could he really love me, could they be telling the truth or are they just pulling my leg?

'Maria, I would love to believe that,' I say, 'but we have only known each other for just under a week, can you really fall in love in less than a week, true forever lasting love?' I ask.

'Sandy, I fell in love with Tom in a moment.' We all sit back in our own thoughts and listen to our partners talking, every time I look at Bryce he is looking at me and smiling. *God I love this man*, I think. I am a goner, hook, line and sinker.

'Thank you very much on behalf of everyone tonight for sharing the premier with us all and our loved ones,' Tom says. 'We can't wait to hear the feedback, thank you for all your questions and behalf of us all. Thank you and Good night.' They all get up and start to walk to the side. An usher comes up and advises us to get up and we walk towards the back of the room and out the side door, as we enter the side our partners are there. Bryce walks towards me, grabs me for a hug and a kiss, pulls away but still holding onto me and asks, 'So did you enjoy it and are you ready to go home Cinderella?'

I look at him. 'I would go anywhere with you honey.'
'Good let's go home baby.'

We say goodnight, go to the side entrance and hop into our car.

This has been so surreal, on the way home, we are leaning against each other in the back, I turn towards him and ask, 'Bryce, are you happy?'

'Did YOU have a good night?' He pulls me towards him.

'Yes, it was a great night and the company was even better.'

'I love you Sandy and I never want to be away from you or Michael again.' I am looking at him trying to read his eyes, but it is a dark in the car, I think to myself he is just drunk, he won't remember this, I lean into him and say, 'I love you too. I am going to find it hard to leave.' Then silence, it is a comfortable silence, I know we are both either thinking or he has fallen asleep.

We get home and hop out, we walk in hand in hand. I take my shoes off and go inside. We both check on the kids and then go and sit down on the couch and have a cuppa. I don't know what to say, my mind is going at a hundred miles per hour. Did he mean what he said in the car?

'Bryce,' I ask.

'Yeah baby,' he says.

'When you said that in the car did you mean it?' I whisper.

'Sorry honey,' he says. I look at him.

'Umm, are you ready to go to bed,' I ask instead. 'Plus can you do me a favour and unzip my dress, I had the guys help me get in to it but I just can't undo it.' He laughs and undoes it, I go upstairs with him and we both go in the shower and get ready for bed.

I can't sleep. Every time I close my eyes the night re runs in my mind, did he really say what he said? Did he really say he was going to miss us? I rerun his looks at me over the night, the way he held onto me whenever he was next to me, when he was on the stage doing the Q & A, he was looking at me the whole time, did I imagine that? Every time I look at the clock it is still night time, 1am, 2am, I close my eyes, 3am, 4am, this is ridiculous, the kids are going to be up soon. I decide when I look at the clock at 5am that I am going to get up. I know Bryce will sleep for a bit longer, so I decide to go in to the kitchen to cook a feast for breakfast for the kids and us. It's Friday and Michael and I have one more week here, I don't know how I am going to say goodbye to Bryce and Amy, this is going to be so hard I think. I go back to our room, grab my phone and headset and listen to my music while breakfast is cooking. I check the muffins, the bread all going well, bacon won't take long, I have the pancake mixture ready to go, the fruit is ready and on the tray in the fridge. I am just standing here waiting, it's 6 am and all is ready to finish, Okay I think, what to do now. I will clean the kitchen and make sure it is all clean, I set the table, get some flowers from the garden, that has killed 20mins, now what..... I will call Louise my sister and see what she thinks. She answers on the 3rd ring.

'Hey Louise, it's me, how is Mum, Ziggy, honey, Sparkie, Pastel and Nugget going? Is everything Okay,' I ask.

'Yes,' she replies, 'They are all good and so am I.'

'Shit sorry sis, I meant to ask how you are going, if you need any more money for the bills or food etc, my card is in the drawer with the itinerary.'

'Hey Louise, I need to ask you something,' I ask.

'Go for it,' she says. So I tell her everything that has happened. It goes quiet.

'Are you there?' I ask.

'Are you sure he said that?' she asks.

'I think so, he has said I love you quite a few times, but can you fall in love so quickly I ask.' I go on and tell her how I feel. I say to her, 'I think I was in love with him before I met him, he is so adorable, so loving, so much fun, I knew he would be I go on, I even think if I hadn't of met him I still would have loved him, you know what I am like, I fall to quickly but this is so different Louise, I have never felt this way, I just can't imagine not having him around, how am I going to leave in seven days. It feels like we have known each other for years,' I say.

Louise listens and then says, 'It is just an infatuation on your end Sandy. He is only being nice for the sex and once you go he will forget you.' I am sitting outside on the side of the pool thinking. 'You know what sis,' I say. 'I get what you are saying but last night he introduced me to his friends, he introduced me to the press, if he was going to forget me why would he do that. I love him, I do, I just don't know if I can go home, I know I have these plans to see Roger and Verdi but I don't want to, I know we have New York booked and Niagara Falls but I don't want to go, but on the other hand I can't afford to lose the money and deposits,' I say. 'Well where I see it you have two options. Number 1, stay there for the entire holiday and let the family down, don't go and see what you want and then in three weeks come home and forget about Bryce and his life.'

'OR,' I say.

'Number 2, stay the week and then go on your holiday as planned and then come home and forget about him.'

'Is there a 3rd option sis that doesn't have me with a broken heart and forgetting about the best man I have ever met and don't get me wrong,' I go on, 'I loved him the minute he got in the car when I first met him and It's not because he is Bryce Johnston but of who he is the person.' 'NO,' she yells, 'it is just a dream, it will have to end, he won't want you to stay there, he won't want you to be a part of his life forever, it is a fantasy. I don't mean to say this but I have to keep you grounded. Bryce Johnston will NOT', and she yells this part, 'he will NOT want you to be with him forever. Get over yourself stupid and go on the rest of your holiday as planned and come home.' I go quiet, I start to cry and she says, 'Pull yourself out of this shit and stopping being so dramatic,' she says, 'that is what sisters are for, to make sure you don't make stupid mistakes.' I sit there with my feet now hanging in the pool, I have no idea how long we have been talking for but the sun has come up and I am sure everyone will be up. 'I better go Louise, I will get Michael to speak to you when he gets up, thanks for the chat, I have a lot to think about.'

'Don't make a mistake, go on your holiday and come home,' she says and then hangs up. I am staring at the water in the pool, as I move my feet there are ripples in the water, that is how my heart is feeling, rippled, it is broken, I don't want to leave him, but would he want me here. The phone call hasn't helped at all, it has made it worse, *what am I going to do*, I think.

I hear a noise behind me and wipe my eyes, it is Michael thank god.

'Hey baby, morning,' I say.

'Mum, are you Okay,' he asks.

'Baby we only have a week here and then we have to leave.' I start to cry. 'I don't want to leave, I want to stay here with Bryce, Would you like to stay here and go to school here if we could or do you want to go back home?' I ask. 'Do you want to go see Roger, Verdi and our planned trip or do you want to stay here a bit longer,' I ask.

Michael looks at me. 'I am Okay with whatever you want to do Mum, but can I ask you a question?' he asks.

'Go for it,' I say.

'Do you love Bryce?' Because if you do, does he love you and if he does then I want you to be happy Mum,' he goes on, 'I have never seen you so happy Mum but it's up to you Mum,' he says.

What a mature little man, I think.

'Baby, this is our trip of a lifetime. I don't think we will ever get back here, this is our chance to meet Roger and his family and meet Verdi, to see NY, Niagara Falls, this is my last chance to see them, It took me years to save the money for this trip, I don't know if we can ever come back baby, if we do stay here for the rest of the trip are you going to be happy not to see what we planned?' I ask. 'I don't want you to miss out Michael, Plus I say, what happens if Bryce decides he doesn't want us here anymore, what would we do? I look at him with tears in my eyes and a solon look. 'Mum,' he says, 'Just ask him, if he doesn't want us to stay we will go but I beat you a thousand v bucks, he will want you to stay, he loves you Mum.' I just stare ahead and look at the water how it is moving when we splash our feet.

I look at Michael. 'Baby how did I raise such a wise young man?' I ask.

'Just lucky I guess Mum,' he says, and then gets up and go. My phone then rings and it is Louise. 'Hey sis what's up,' I ask. She said, 'I thought of a 3rd option.'

'And,' I say.

'Talk to him, ask him what he wants or go speak to his family. Has he introduced you to his family? His mum? If he is serious about you he would've introduced you. I have met his daughter, I met his brother yesterday, and the cast from the movie.'

'But sis, it has only been a week.'

'Exactly,' she says, 'it has only been a week.' Finally, she says, 'You are not thinking like your age but thinking like your shoe size. Grow the fuck up Sandy, it is fantasy, it is not real. I haven't met the guy and I don't ever want to meet him,' she says.

This gets me angry. 'Look Louise, I do not like your tone, I love him, regardless how he feels and If you EVER say that again I will never speak to you again, I don't give a flying fuck what you think, I am going to sort this out myself, I only called because I wanted clarification, I didn't want you to knock him, or destroy my feelings, you are meant to be my sister, you are meant to care about me, I know I am being selfish and I have spoken to Michael and he is happy with whatever I chose, but it isn't just about me, there is Michael, Bryce and his daughter's feelings too. I tell you this one more time and then it's not to be discussed again, I love him, there I said it, I love him for the man he is, I love him for the father he is, I love how he smiles at my stupid jokes, I love how he looks at me, how he spends time with Michael and myself. I love how when he wakes up in the morning he looks so relaxed, I love waking up next to him every morning, I love going to sleep next to him, knowing he is next to me and I love being with him. If this is one sided then it is one sided and I will just deal with it BUT I just don't know how he feels, he says, he loves me, that he is enjoying our time to get her but I just am so confused. You know how I felt about him even before I came here, I never thought I would meet him and now that I have I am going to be forever spoilt and will always compare every other man I meet to him. I know this isn't real, I know this is fantasy but I can't help how I feel.'

'Do whatever you want,' she says and hangs up. My music plays again and I am lost in my thoughts. Far out that didn't go well. I have so many thoughts going through my head. I know I have to speak to him, but if I do, will he get angry at me, will he deny it, will he tell me he does love me. Just as I am about to get up and see if he is awake. *Dreaming of you* starts playing in my ears and I start to sing with it, the more I sing, the more I start to cry. It is just a dream, this whole trip, I don't need to ask him, I know the answer… He is being nice, if he really loved me he would introduce me to his family surely, I am so confused. I am so in my thoughts singing the song that I don't hear the noise behind me. *I can't stop dreaming of you*, I sing, *late at night when the world is sleeping, I stay up and think of you and I still can't believe you came up to me and said I love you, I love you too,* I sing. *Oh man, life sucks,* I think. How the hell am I going to leave in a week. I have made my decision, Michael and I will go soon, Louise is right, it is a dream the poor guy is probably sick of me. The next minute I feel arms encircling me and I look up and its Bryce.

'Morning gorgeous,' he says, 'I woke up and you weren't there, I was worried,' he says.

'Sorry honey,' I say, 'I couldn't sleep so I got up to prepare breaky.'

He looks at me. Are you Okay?' he asks. 'You look sad.'

I just, I just, god what do I say, My sister is a bitch and doesn't like you, do you love me I think, do you want me to stay, am I being a pain. I am just looking at him and say, 'Yeah, I am Okay was just listening to my music and one of my favourite songs came on it always makes me sad.'

He looks at me and then grabs me and says, 'Okay, let's get breakfast. He helps me up, gives me a hug and passionate but quick kiss and says, 'What I said last night at the premier and in the car is true. He looks at me deeply. 'I do love you Sandy and I don't want to be apart from you. Before I can say anything we hear, 'Dad, Sandy we are awake is it breakfast time yet,' asks Amy.

So we eat breakfast and while we are eating, we start to chat with what is happening over the day, so anyway Bryce says, 'I was thinking as it was a late night last night and it's Friday, I thought we would go to Mums so you can meet the family,' he says. I look at him, in my head I hear Louise's comment he hasn't introduced you to his family has he. I look at him and he says, 'I hope that is Okay, we are expected there for lunch.'

'Um honey, question when was this organised,' I ask.

'I spoke to Mum on Wednesday when you guys stayed here, we couldn't do it earlier as this is the only day my whole family and partners can make it and I thought it would be good that everyone meets you both together.'

I smile and say, 'that will be lovely. What should I wear?' I ask. 'Can I buy them a present each? Can I make something to take?'

71

'No, all good honey, Mum has it all organised.'

'Okay, but I want to take something, maybe a nice wine and flowers, can we stop and get that at least.'

He looks at me. 'You're not going to accept 'no' are you,' he asks.

'Nope, no way charlie brown,' I reply. He grabs my hand kisses it, I didn't think so.

So I am going to meet his family, he loves me, shit, now I am in deep trouble.

'You ready Sandy? we have to go,' he yells.

'Yep, coming now.' I walk down the stairs and I decided to wear my favourite outfit. I have my bright blue off shoulder top, my light black skirt and my wedges. As I walk down the stairs he turns towards me and say, 'Wow you look gorgeous,'

'I bet you say that to all the girls,' I reply.

'No, just to you.'

'Well Mr J, you look absolutely gorgeous too and I have to admit I love the glasses and give him a kiss.' We all pile in the car and drive to his mums place, I have the wine, flowers and chocolates in the back in a basket, I went out earlier with Michael and bought flowers for his sisters and beers for his brothers, but for his mother I went all out, flowers, wine and handmade chocolates.

'Hey Bryce, can I ask you a question and get an honest response.'

He looks at me quickly as he is driving and says, 'I have always told you the truth.'

'Good,' I say, 'me too. Do you think your family and Mum will like me, I ask. Not that I want a big welcome, but they are used to you being with gorgeous skinny women and that isn't me.'

He gets a frown on his face, yep grumpy cat look I think.

'Honey,' he says, 'not all that glitters are gold.' And then he looks ahead and keeps driving.

'I'm sorry honey, I just don't want them to hate me.'

He grabs my hand and says, 'They will love you because I do and so does Amy. I am in heaven I am a pig in shit. Here goes,' he says, 'we are here.'

I recognise the place from the magazines and the internet. It looks so cute, so full of life. There are heaps of cars outside the front and he pulls up behind and parks in the driveway. We all get out and I go to the back to get the baskets of goodies. I press down my skirt and top take a deep breath and next to me he is standing.

'Relax, it will be all good.' He grabs the biggest basket, grabs my hand and we walk to the door. In the meantime Amy has run up to the door and ran inside, as we walk to the door I see both front windows with eyes looking out. I look at Bryce and he kisses me and says, 'Let's go.' Gosh I am so nervous but I believe him and make a silent pray, Please god I know I am not really religious and I am asking for a lot, I know you have a lot of things on your mind to fix but please let his family like me I love him so much.

We walk towards the door, he grabs my hand.

'Deep breath sweetheart,' he says. As he is about to knock the door flies open, I see it is his mum.

'Hey Mum,' he says, walks in, puts the basket down and gives her a massive bear hug. 'This is Sandy and her son Michael, Honey this is my mum Wilma.'

'Hi Mrs...'

'No, call me Wilma,' she says.

'Hi Wilma, it's lovely to meet you and thank you for letting myself and Michael join you all,' I say.

'All good,' she says, 'come in to the cool, it's a hot day.' I walk in with the basket and then I see all these eyes on me. 'Hey everyone,' Bryce says, this is Sandy and Michael, this is my family' and he goes and introduces me to them all. I am so lost, I know faces but I am terrible with names.

'Hi everyone,' I say, 'just letting you know upfront, I am hopeless with names but good with faces, so I will apologise now in case I get them all wrong.' They all laugh and I think I will be Okay. I give the gifts out and then I go the Wilma and give her basket. 'I just wanted to say thank you again Wilma, this is for you, I didn't know what to bring, please don't think it is a bribe but I always bring something with me as I think it is rude not to bring something.'

She looks at me, gives me a hug and says, 'I know what you are saying I do the same thing', and then she says, 'I knew I'd like you.'

I stare. 'Um thanks,' I say. I look to see where Bryce is and he is outside with his brothers and I assume brother in-laws at the BBQ, I smile and next thing I am surrounded by all the sisters and his mum. 'So, Sandy do you love my brother,' I get asked. 'How long are you here for?' another sister asks. 'Are you after something from him,' the third sister asks. 'Give her a break girls,' says Wilma. 'I can tell how much she loves Bryce, he told me about her on Monday after he got home and was driving back to her hotel.' I turn and look at her. 'Is that true?' I ask her. 'Yes,' she says. He said, 'He has never been spoken like that before by anyone and he loved it as you were so refreshing and that was when he fell in love with you.' His sisters all look at me. 'Okay do

74

tell what happened on Monday.' So, I tell them exactly what happened how I yelled at him then felt bad for yelling at him, not knowing who he was and yet thinking he was the nicest person and the sexiest person I had ever seen. I went on and told them about our week and then about last night at the premier. They are all staring at me with tears in their eyes, Wilma comes around gives me a hug and says, 'He has been waiting for you all his life, he should never of married his ex, she was a gold digging green card mole.' We all look at her. 'Mum,' the girls say in unison in shock. I laugh. 'Sorry, but that is what I was thinking.' we all laugh together. They ask me my plans, what is happening, when are we going back home and I tell them everything including the conversation with my sister early this morning. I also tell them how I am confused, how much I love him, that I know it is crazy and how if I had never met him I would still love him and miss him. I then go to speak and start to cry, they look at me and I say, 'I don't know how I am going to go back home.' They all come to me and give me a hug. Next thing I hear, 'what are you girls doing to my woman?' We all turn around and start laughing, we hear bloody women and then we laugh again. This is turning into a good night. I love his family. He comes around me, puts me in his arms and kisses my neck, I go bright red and then he walks outside again.

'How many girls has he brought here to meet you all?' I ask.

His mum says, 'You are the first one he has brought home to any of my homes to meet us all, so don't break his heart.'

I stare. 'Wow, I would never hurt him Wilma, not intentionally but I do have to go home, do you think he will be Okay with that? My sister says he won't mind but I am not sure. I am so confused.'

Wilma grabs my hand. 'We need to talk,' she says. 'Great we need to talk chat. Bye Bryce I think. We go into the lounge and we sit down. She looks at me and then says, 'Sandy, I know what you mean to my son, he has never brought any female here to meet the whole family, when he was with his ex, it was rarely a group event, he would always make it a few of us, we never liked her, we knew she was no good for him but she fell pregnant and he wanted both parents there for Amy.'

'I understand that,' I say. 'When I fell pregnant it wasn't planned but I vowed I would never force anyone to be with me for any reason, It was a one night stand after I separated, you see I was a good girl all my life, I never slept around so I thought I am in my 40s so why not have fun, the first time I went out and did the deed I fell pregnant and you know what it was the best thing that happened to me. I would never not of had Michael and I would never take it back. I am lucky I don't have to worry about an ex but at times I feel bad he doesn't have a dad but I think he has 3 women around him that love him so I hope that is Okay.' I say.

She looks at me and says, 'You are just what he needs. Welcome to the family.'

We are talking about how cute he was as a child, what mischief he got unto and how adorable he is now when he walks in and says, 'Foods up.' He puts his arms around my neck, looks at his mum and says, 'I hope you have been behaving Mum.' We all laugh and then I turn around and say, 'Yes Munchkin, all good.' He gets the grumpy look and then laughs. 'No secrets,' he says. I am so happy. I love his family, love his mum and I love him. I think to myself what could possibly go wrong.

The night is going well, we are all laughing, one minute it is 2 pm and then the next it has gone quiet, all the kids are in the lounge watching TV, or sleeping and it's getting dark. I look at my watch and realise it is 10pm. Wow this has gone well. I feel so comfortable, everyone realises it is getting late and all get up to go. After everyone has left, I go into the kitchen and help finish the clean-up. Bryce is sitting in the lounge with the kids and his mum and I are chatting. He comes in and says, 'Come on honey we have to go, the kids are stuffed and I have to do some work tomorrow and then I have plans for us.'

I get up, say thank you to his mum and give her a hug goodbye. Bryce hugs his mum and we all walk out. 'Mum it's all good stay in it's late. I turn around give her a hug again and say, 'Thank you for tonight Wilma, thank you for making me feel welcome and thank you for such a wonderful man in Bryce.' She hugs me and says, 'My pleasure and remember I am always here for you if you need a chat and then hands me her number.' We hop in the car, wave goodbye and drive back home.

'Thank you baby,' I say, 'it was a lovely night. Did I get the approval?' I ask, 'really hoping that I did.'

He smiles, looks at me and says, 'maybe.'

Oh maybe that's not good, I think, *he must see I am a bit worried* and I have gone quiet.

He laughs I look at him. 'Yes, they loved you all of them even Clare and she doesn't love many outsiders.'

I feel a relief off my shoulders. 'That's good news,' I say.

'Yes,' he says, 'that's very good news. I am glad that I organised this it makes my next decision so much easier.' I must have drifted off because I didn't hear that last comment and I should have as it would have definitely changed my mind about what I had to do. Trust me if I had of heard that there would have not been a doubt in my mind.

'Sandy, wake up we're home.' I look at him and see that he is smiling. 'Come on sleepy head the kids are in, let's get you to bed.' I get out of the car and we go inside. I am so tired. This last week has been so full of emotions, now what do I do about the rest of my time here, I will think about it tomorrow I think. We go to bed and all I can think of is how fantastic he is, how wonderful my time with him has been and what the heck am I going to do.

I wake and I hear singing, laughing and I smell something delicious. I roll over look at the clock and realise it is 9am. Shit I slept in, what did he say he had to do today, work, I hope I didn't stuff up his plans. I roll over and there is a note on his pillow, It reads, *Morning sleeping beauty, I am in the studio recording a couple of songs, the kids are outside playing with Christy, have a shower and come down to the studio, I love you.* Oh he loves me, stick that up your ass Louise. I go shower, put on shorts and top and go downstairs and find him. God he has a fantastic voice, I love the tune, it is happy and beautiful, I look through the glass and he directs me to come in. I open the door and sit down while he is singing, I love this song, it is beautiful. The next thing he starts singing, *My Eyes Adored You.* I know this song and fall in love with him even more. He is singing then stops, looks at me winks and then sings more. I am watching in awe. I have never been in a studio before, Amy and Michael have both

78

come in and we are all sitting on the couch watching him, once he finishes singing he is on the guitar and then the piano. He is so talented and I maybe a bit bias but a very sexy, gorgeous man and I can't believe where we are after just six days. *Stop thinking,* I say to myself, *once it gets to 14 days you have a flight to catch.* I look at him and start to get teary.

'Drink,' I ask.

He shakes his head. 'Yes', and then says, 'give me 5mins.'

The kids and I go out and start to organise drinks and food for him and the guys. I am about to turn around when he comes behind me. 'So gorgeous, plans for today, how does coming to Lake Tennyson with us?' he asks.

Lake Tennyson,' I say, where is that, can we drive there?'

'No, we fly and it's all booked, I thought we could spend a few days away from LA and you could see the farm.'

'I would love to, when are we leaving?' I ask.

'In an hour, but I have already packed you and the kids have packed their bags.'

I look at him. 'You packed my bag?' I ask.

'Yep, just chucked what I thought you would need, I did it while you were asleep plus I didn't want you to worry about what to take.'

'Okay,' I said, 'worst case scenario I will just buy if I need anything.'

Next minute there is a knock at the door, our bags are loaded and we are being driven to the airport.

'Lake Tennyson here we come,' says Amy and Bryce.

Michael and I look at each other smile and laugh. They both look so happy. I am sure everything will be fine.

'Welcome Mr Johnston, the flight is on time and we are scheduled to leave in 15mins, the bags are loaded.'

I get out of the car and in front of us is a private plane. 'Bryce, please tell me we are not flying in that?' I ask.

He looks at me. 'Of course we are.'

'Um I am scared of small planes,' I say, 'last time I got on a small plane I had a panic attack.'

He looks at me and then says, 'How about this, we try it, if it is too much for you we will take a later flight and I will get us on a commercial flight but I will let you know I would never let anything cause you grief or hurt you. I am with you and will protect you.'

I look at him. 'Okay, I will try.'

My legs feel like jelly as we are walking up the steps, I don't know if I can do this. Michael and Amy are both sitting in the plane already and they are both talking and playing games. I feel my head beading with sweat. I am shaking and I am now in the plane, it is so small there are only 10 seats. Bryce directs me to sit next to him on the couch seats and buckles me in and then holds my hand. 'Are you Okay?' he asks.

I shake my head. 'I, I, don't know but I can't let the kids down.' So, he grabs my hand. I hear the door being shut, I start to shake and I feel like I am going to be sick, I can see the pilots ahead and feel the engines get louder and the plane starts to move. I am shaking like a leaf and Bryce looks at me. 'It's Okay honey', and then starts to kiss me. I am all good. I am in the kiss, I feel his arms around me, I hear the kids laughing and then he pulls away, we are in the air honey. I look out the window, look at him and say, 'You did that to distract me didn't you,' I ask.

'Yep,' he says with his adorable smirk.

'Good play,' I say. And then unbuckle my seat belt and sit on him. 'You are a naughty boy and will have to pay the toll later.'

He laughs. 'My pleasure ma'am. Happy to pay the toll and what shall that be?' He asks.

I wink and say, 'Well you will have to wait and see.'

We have been in the air for what seems like an hour and the pilot says we are going to make our descent down to land.

'Do you always fly private planes,' I ask.

'Only when there are a lot of press around so we make it as easy as possible so we don't have to worry about the paps,' he says.

'Are there issues with them now,' I quiz.

'Yes, there are as they are trying to get pictures of us together and the kids, I am just trying to protect my number one girls,' he says.

'You mean Amy,' I say.

'No, not just Amy but you too and of course your young man too. I just don't want you to stress about anything, just to enjoy our time together.' He smiles, makes sure we are all having our seat belts done and then starts to tell me about Lake Tennyson.

'Is your place far from the airport,' I ask.

'No, it's only about 15mins, we are very secluded so no one will annoy us plus I am known quite well here so we don't get the usual questions, here we are just locals. So we will get our peace and quiet. I can't wait to show you my place,' he says, 'we have a pool, heaps of land, our own forest and creek and in winter, it's so gorgeous with the snow and all the sites. But the good thing is this weekend there is a local show on and a parade so we can go to that if you want,' he says.

'I will do anything you want me to do as long as it's legal.' I laugh.

The plane lands and we are directed out to the tarmac where there is a car waiting for us, the bags have been loaded and we all hop in. Gosh I am just in awe of this place, surrounding the airport there are all these mountains, the air is so clear and the sky is so blue, I just look out the window, look back at Bryce and back out the window, I am like a kid in the candy shop, this place is perfect. I can see why he loves it here. I turn to him. 'This is beautiful honey. I'm surprised you don't live here full time,' I say.

I would but it would mean a lot of travelling to get Amy back to her mum's and then to work. It is easier to just stay in LA and when we can we travel here as often as we can.'

'I can see why,' I say and snuggle into him.

We start to turn and all I can see are these beautiful maple trees lining the road.

'Wow, they are beautiful are we far? I ask.

'This is the start of my property,' he says.

We drive for what seems like 5mins and then turn and all I can see is this massive timber structure, it is architecturally beautiful. I am in complete awe. 'Bryce this is not a farm this is a mansion, this is absolutely stunning. Oh my god I say, this is perfect. How can you call it a farm, I was expecting a farm this is like a hotel.'

He laughs. 'To us, it's just our holiday home/farm. But I can see what you mean.'

I hop out of the car and turn to him. 'Did you renovate this?' I ask. 'This has your touch,' I say.

'Yes, I did with Christy.'

'You are not just a sexy man but a very talented man. You definitely could use this as a fall back career.' I say. 'We do,' he says.

We walk towards the door, go inside and if I thought the outside was stunning the inside is like a museum, everything is perfect, there are windows all-round the place, I look up and there seems to be forever space.

'Bryce, this is gorgeous. OMG this is beautiful.'

In the meantime, Amy is running around. 'Come on Sandy, come see my room', and grabs my hand. I laugh as I am being dragged by his princess. *I think I am going to need a map to get around here,* I think.

'This is my room,' she says.

Her room is bigger than my lounge and kitchen at home. I am so happy for Amy that she has Bryce as her dad and that he can provide for her like this. I just wish Michael had as good as life as Amy but we are two different people from two different worlds. I know this can't last. We are just too different. I am smiling at Amy as she is running around so happy, so free and then Bryce is behind me.

'Come on sunshine let me give you a tour of the house,' he says.

'Amy I am going to show Sandy around do you want to come or stay here and play?'

'I will come daddy,' she says.

So, we walk around together, every corner I turn I am in awe, I must look like a deer in the headlights as he says, It is nothing Sandy, just be yourself, here it is just us, no one else, we can and are always ourselves here, we could walk around naked and be safe.'

I raise my eyebrows and look at him. 'Now that would be a nice sight to see in the morning but I don't think it would be wise with the kids', and we both laugh. God I love his laugh. He looks so relaxed here. I can see why he loves it here. The kitchen is fully stocked, the air conditioner is running and the house is spectacular.

'And this is where we sleep,' he says.

We are upstairs and I walk towards the window, all I see are mountains and a clear blue sky and on the right there is his pool, back yard and land everywhere.

'This is gorgeous,' I say. I turn and look at him. 'Thank you for this Bryce, thank you for allowing Michael and I into your life and thank you for being you. I don't know what I did to deserve this but all I can say is thank you and I am so glad I yelled at you at the airport.' We laugh. 'Yeah,' he says, I' can just see the story at the wedding and how did you guys meet,' he says. I just stare, laugh and we start to walk downstairs.

'So, from here, where are the kids' rooms?'

He points towards the stairs again and says, 'Our room is on one side of the stairs and the kids are on the other side, it is like our retreat and they have their own,' he says.

'Come on let's go outside and you can come and meet the animals and the staff.'

Of course he has staff if he isn't here all the time someone has to look after the place. We walk down to the back and there are horses everywhere. I can see lambs, cows, alpacas and of course the horses.

'Come on sweetheart I want to introduce you to my favourite horse.'

We walk towards the stables and I see this beautiful gentle horse, she is rolling on the ground and I am laughing. 'She does that all the time,' Amy says, 'she must have an itch.'

'She is beautiful,' I say. I haven't been this close to a horse since I was 12, Michael has never been this close to a horse,' I say.

Michael and I are just leaning on the railing watching Bryce and Amy, they look so happy, they are laughing and I say to Michael, 'Baby, I am so sorry you never had this, that you never had a father and that I am not a very good mother, but I love you so much.'

'Mum it is all good, some have a lot and some don't, we have what we need' and I hug him and cry. I have raised a wonderful, caring young man. I just hope that he gets all he wants in life.

Bryce comes towards us and asks, 'What's wrong baby, why you crying?'

'I am just happy honey, plus I feel bad for Michael as I have never been able to give him any of this. I feel like I am not a good Mum but I am so happy that you trust us to be here.'

He grabs my hand, pulls both me and Michael and says, 'Come on and see my girl up close.'

She is so big, I go to reach out and pat her and she brings her nose down towards me and nudges me, I am smiling from ear to ear, I start to pat her and then hug her neck, I look at Bryce and he is smiling. What I ask. He stares at me then says, 'I have never seen her do that to a stranger, she is normally reserved with strangers.' I then start to pat her long lean neck and body and say, 'Us girls stick together, hey beautiful', and I get a nudge again and then laugh. I walk towards Bryce and watch Michael as he is patting her and Amy is with him too. So it is just Bryce and I on the side. Michael has the biggest grin on his face and Amy is going through everything with him. I feel Bryce's arms around me and I lean into him. 'Honey,' I say, 'I don't know what else to say but thank you again, this is wonderful.'

'Come on let's go in, it's dinner time, come Amy, Michael,' he says, 'let's go in. we will come out tomorrow and spend heaps of time outside.' He grabs my hand and we all walk inside again.

As we go inside I can smell this delicious smell. 'What's that,' I ask.

'Oh, it's the cook, she lives on the property in her own place and caretakers the property and when we are here she helps with the cooking and cleaning.'

'Well that's not right,' I say, 'why don't we get all the staff tomorrow to come and have dinner with us and I will cook a feast for them as a thank you. Would that be Okay I ask.'

'Yeah baby, let's do it in a couple of days so we can all do it.'

'Okay,' I say.

'Marissa, this is Sandy and her son Michael, they are staying with us for the week.'

I introduce myself and ask, 'If I can help with anything.'

'No, it's all done,' she says.

'Well let me help set up the table and help with something at least.'

She looks at me and then to Bryce, I look at him too. 'Please,' I say quietly.

Okay,' he says.

So, I am in the kitchen helping Marissa.

'I hope I haven't done anything wrong,' I say, 'it's just I don't like being waited on and think it is good if everyone helps.'

She looks at me. 'Well, most people that come here demand to be served, when all the young girls came here they would bark orders to me and my husband.'

I stop. 'Well that isn't me Marissa, please call me Sandy and I would like to do something for you and your husband. Are there many other staff here?' I ask.

'Only my husband Miguel, he does all the maintenance here, the gardener Thomas comes once a week and then there is Stuart who looks after the animals.'

'Does Thomas and Stuart have partners?

'Yes ma'am.' I look at her.

'Sandy, they are partners.'

'Oh that is good,' I say, 'it is good not to be away from your partners too long. Do you think I can meet them tomorrow?' I ask.

'I am sure it can be arranged,' she says.

Next thing I feel Bryce behind me the tables all done and we are ready for you. Marissa and I carry the plates out and she goes back into the kitchen.

'Baby, I maybe putting my foot in my mouth but I am happy to clean up I am sure Marissa wants to go spend time with her husband Miguel.'

He laughs. 'It didn't take you long to work out their names,' he says.

'Well, that's me I don't like not to know everyone,' then I say, 'did you know that Thomas and Stuart are partners.' He

87

looks at me. 'The gardener and the animal guy.' I shake my head.

'I had an idea,' he says, 'but never really knew.'

'Well you know now,' I say.

He comes to me kisses me and then hugs me. 'My angel who is so kind.' I go bright red. 'I'm just me.'

He sits down and we all eat. After we have eaten the kids go to have a wash and get ready for bed and I am in the kitchen tidying up. I am making a coffee for Bryce and a tea for myself when he walks in.

'Honey, are you going to come and join me in the lounge?'

I turn around. 'Sorry sweet, I was just finishing up the cleaning and while you were busy with the kids I made a cake.'

He smirks. 'Is that the smell, I smell?'

'Yep, very easy hot caramel sponge cake, it only took 15mins to make and it will be ready in 10mins, does Amy want a hot chocolate?' I ask. 'I know Michael will just have water,' I say.

'I will check and off he goes.

The buzzer goes off, the sponge comes out of the oven, I have whipped cream just in case plus I have taken out some ice cream. I put on the tray plates, Bryce's coffee, my tea, and a cup of hot chocolate just in case for Amy and Michael's water. I am walking into the lounge when Bryce grabs the tray off me. 'I got this,' he says. 'Come sit down and relax,' he says. We sit next to each other on the couch and the kids are on beanbags on the floor and they are watching TV. I start to shiver and then realise although it has been a warm day it gets a little bit chilly at night or is it just me as he is sitting so close to me. He puts his arm around me and I lean into him as we watch the movie. Every night we tend to cuddle each other. *Boy Oh boy this is going to be so hard to leave him,* I think. I start to cry. He pulls my face up so he can see. 'What's wrong?' he asks. I don't want to lie but don't want to tell him the truth so I just say, 'This movie makes me happy so it's happy tears. I cry at toilet roll commercials,' I say. 'Put it to old age.' He looks at me and then seems to accept this, I lean back into him. I can smell his aftershave and his own aroma and it makes me want to cry again, far out I am going to miss him so much.

'Come on baby, let's put the kids to bed and get ready ourselves, we can sleep in tomorrow.'

I grab the cups and plates and the tray and take them to the kitchen, I load the dishwasher and then start to walk out to the lounge when he grabs me, lifts me up and starts to carry me upstairs. I am laughing and saying, 'Bryce stop you will break your back, put me down.'

'Nope,' he says.

'Bryce, please don't.'

He is still carrying me upstairs, next thing he kicks a door open and I look around, we are in the main bathroom, there are candles everywhere he puts me down and says, 'Now undress, we are going to have a nice relaxing bath.' 'But the kids?' I ask.

'Asleep plus I can hear them if they wake up.'

I hop in the bath and he comes in and he is as naked as a baby, Oh boy, he is an Adonis, no matter how many times I see him naked it never surprises me. He jumps in the bath and sits behind me and starts to wash my hair and body, I just lean in and am in absolute heaven, I have no idea how long we are in the bath but I can feel the water cooling so we hop out, get dry, dressed and go to bed. We start to kiss and get intimate. Every time we do this it gets better and better. I run my finger nails down his back and he is running his hands along my back and body. It is getting hot and heavy, I am in sex heaven, we are tossing and turning, rolling onto each other and then we climax and fall against each other. I start to laugh and say, 'Now we need another wash.'

He laughs, kisses me and says, 'let's sleep angel.' He pulls me down next to him and we fall asleep in each other's arms.

I wake up and look at the windows, all I see are the mountains, I get up to put my clothes on and hear. 'Where do you think you are going young lady?

I turn and he is looking at me. 'I was getting dressed so I could go down and make breakfast for everyone.'

He raises his eyebrow and says, 'Get your sweet ass back into bed, the kids will be Okay as I asked Marissa last night to watch them for us. So unless you want me grumpy I think you better get back in here.'

I smile, jump back in bed and round two starts. I love him so much. I can't believe that after being a fan for so many years, coming to US and actually meeting him seven days ago that I am in his arms in his bed. Shit, I only have seven days left and then I am leaving him.

I say, 'Honey I am going into the shower, you're welcome if you want.'

He says, 'He will be there in a second.'

I go in the bathroom, run the shower go under the rose and start to cry, fuck I am leaving soon for NY and to see my relos, would he come with me, would he want me to stay. Luckily, when he comes in he doesn't notice I have been crying. Good thing about crying under the shower, you can hide it. We are both clean, get dressed and go downstairs. It is a beautiful day, so peaceful.

'Plans for today,' he says, 'is there are no plans.' 'We do what we want to do.'

'How about a walk?' I say.

'Good idea,' he says. 'Come on kids lets go for a walk around the property', and off we go. The kids are in front of us and we are behind them holding our hands. We have been walking for a while and come upon a creek.

'Oh Bryce this is beautiful and so peaceful. This is the creek I saw on Instagram a couple of years ago, isn't it?' I ask.

'Yep', and when we came in the trees where the start of the path from the video.

'I can see why you like it so much here, everything you need is here. Honey I need to say something and ask something.'

He looks at me and says, 'That sounds interesting.'

I can see the kids ahead playing. 'As you are aware we are in LA for 14 days and then we have a booking in NY and Canada. I have booked the accommodation and tours. What I wanted to ask was do you and Amy wants to join us or are you happy for us to just go?' I ask.

He looks at me and then says, 'There is another option.' I look at him. Not sure which way this is going to go but can only hope it is what I was hoping. He goes on. 'You can both stay with us for the whole trip and not go, and while I am making suggestions, you could always just stay here forever.'

I can't breathe. I look at him. 'Are you asking us to stay for another two weeks or for always?

'Both,' he says.

'Oh god, I was feeling the same way.' I look at him. 'I want to say yes but I saved for so long and I don't know if we will ever get another chance to go see New York and Niagara Falls, plus we are going to meet my cousin Roger and his family. I just don't know,' I say. He looks at me and seems to be sad, I go on. 'How about we do this, we see how it goes and if you can come you come with us to NY and Niagara falls, I can cancel the accommodation for the time and just make it for a couple of days so we can all fly in together and then you can meet Roger and the family over here.'

He looks at me, smiles, comes to me and kisses me. 'That will be perfect,' he says.

'Good but I need to organise it ASAP. As soon as we get back to the house I will help you,' he says.

I am happy and know that this is the right decision. 'But,' I say, 'we have to go to town tomorrow so I can get all we need to cook for you and your staff.'

'Of course honey,' he says. 'Anything you want.' *Anything I want,* I think. *All I want is to be with you forever,* I think. I don't want to leave your side. But I know that, that is just a dream, that eventually something will burst this bubble and I will be left heartbroken, regardless of what happens over the next 21 days Michael and I are booked to go back home to Australia as I have to go back to work and Michael has school. But this is not something I am going to think about till I have to.

We slowly walk back to the house and we all go in, the kids both go off to play, Bryce and I go into his study to organise the trip and all the changes. 'Are you sure you want to join us?' I ask.

'Of course I am enjoying our time together and it would be good to meet your cousin and his family plus I haven't been to NY for years for a holiday it would be good to see the sights with you, Amy and Michael. Will your ex be Okay with you taking Amy?' I ask.

'I will sort it out,' he says, and we organise all the flights, changes to the accommodation and the tours. We have been at it for a couple of hours when we finally stop and stretch, I get up and walk to the window and realise it has gotten dark, Shit I forgot about the kids and their dinner. 'It's all done,' he says. 'I got it organised it while you were investigating the tours etc. and now sweetheart let's go and see the kids, game night after dinner?' He asks.

'You're on,' I say, 'how about girls against the boys?' I say.

'You Okay with that kids?' I ask.

'So it's on, Okay and when one of us wins, what's the prize?'

'Anything you guys want,' he says. I smile and look at him, he laughs. 'Okay, I think that will have to be regardless who wins.'

I look at him innocently and say, 'Oh I have no idea what you are thinking Mr J.'

He grabs me in a bear hug, kisses me and we all go and sit in the lounge and play. It is getting a bit loud and we are all laughing, but eventually both kids go against us adults and they win. We may have let them win but we won't tell them that.

'Okay,' Bryce says, 'what do you guys want as a prize? I shake my head. 'No.'

He goes. 'Nah all good, a bet is a bet.

They say, 'Junk food for breakfast lunch and dinner.'
'That is definitely my son,' I say.

'How about this,' I say. 'A good breakfast and if it's Okay with Bryce junk food for lunch.'

I look at him and he says, 'Well I think that maybe Okay', and laughs.

The kids are happy and then Amy says, 'Is it Okay if we stay home tomorrow and swim, while you guys go shopping?'

I look at Bryce and he looks at me. 'I can go by myself tomorrow, how about it daddy stays home with you both and when I come back you can help me in the kitchen and cook, Amy how does that sound?

'Cool,' she says.

Bryce then says, 'I am happy to come with you if you want, Marissa can watch both of them, I want to show you something and it is best not to have the kids with us.'

I look at him. I have no idea what he wants to show me but say, 'If it's Okay with Marissa.' He comes back in 5mins. 'All sorted, now kids it's late, let's all get ready for bed,' he says.

'Sandy,' Amy asks.

'Yes sweetheart?'

'Can you come and tuck me into bed?'

I look at her and Bryce. 'If it's Okay with Daddy.'

'Yeah of course,' he says. He gives her a big hug and kiss and says, 'I will come in later and say goodnight.'

Amy grabs my hand and pulls me towards her room. I tuck her in, give her a hug and then say, 'I will go get daddy to say goodnight.'

'Sandy,' she says.

'Yes sweetheart.'

'Can I ask you a question?'

'Of course.'

'Why is it mummy and daddy no longer love each other?' I look at her and want to cry, keep it together I think. 'Do they not love me anymore because all they ever do is argue in front of the suit men'

I realise she is saying the lawyers. 'Baby girl, they do love you very much but sometimes parents are the wrong pots and lids, daddy is a blue pot and mummy is a red lid. Sometimes they are good together, yet they just don't fit each other well. But that doesn't mean they don't love you, they both want the best for you and that's why everything is happening. I know for a fact Amy that your daddy loves you so much and that you mean the world to him and I am sure mummy feels the same way?

'Oh Okay that makes sense, can I ask something else? 'Of course,' I say.

'Do you love daddy?'

'Oh that is easy to answer, Amy I have never loved a man as much as I love your daddy, I know it has only be a short time but I would move the moon if I could if it made daddy happy and you.

'OK,' she says.

'Sandy.'

'Yes sweetheart?'

'Are you and Michael going to stay with us forever?' 'Wow, that is a surprise, Honey, I just don't think it is possible, my home, work, bills and family are in Australia and Michael has his school and friends.'

'But if you both stay here I can have you as my step mum and Michael can have daddy as his stepdad.

Oh my heart is breaking, I look at her. 'Amy I will tell you this and you have to promise not to tell anyone for me. She looks at me with her gorgeous blue eyes, so much like Bryce's. I pause, trying to stop the tears from falling, which I am losing. 'If I could I would. It is something that would be absolutely wonderful but it isn't up to us sweetheart, it is also up to daddy. Now I think it is time to go to sleep, I will go check on Michael and I will get daddy for you.' I give her a massive hug and kiss and wish her good night. I walk out her room and Bryce is coming towards her room.

'She wants to say good night, I am going to check on Michael,' I say.

'Do you want a drink or go to bed.'

'Bed,' he says, 'I am stuffed,'

'Okay,' I say, 'I will see you up there. I go check on Michael give him a kiss.'

Little do I know that when Bryce goes in to Amy he gives her a kiss and says, 'Thank you angel for asking Sandy about staying, good girl. Love you sweetheart.' he gives her a kiss and she turns around and goes to sleep.

I am standing at the window in the lounge room and looking out to the mountains. I think to myself that I have major problems, I love him so much but know deep down it can't happen, this has been a dream I know if I pinched myself I would wake up but don't want to wake up. He comes behind me hugs me and says, 'Let's go to bed', and we do. We walk up hand in hand up the stairs and go to bed.

We have been lying in bed for a while, when I realise I can't sleep, I know that when we part after NY and the west coast it is going to be harder than now. Maybe I should just tell him not to worry about it. But then he has paid for his side and I am a typical tight ass I don't like money being wasted so I turn and look at him, he is fast asleep and looks so peaceful. I lean into him and he lifts his arm up for me to curl into and I fall into a deep sleep. I am home as far as I am concerned wherever he is, it's my home.

We get up in the morning, get dressed and go get the kids who happen to be still in bed.

'Come on sleepy head,' I say to Michael, 'do you want to come to town with me baby and look around or do you want to stay here with Marissa and Amy.'

'If Okay Mum, can I stay here?'

I feel a bit flat as he doesn't want to come but I get it. 'Okay baby. Now get up and get dressed I will make you your breakfast before I go.'

I am in the kitchen mixing and making breakfast. I have on the bench pancakes, egg and bacon muffins, there is strawberries sliced on crepes, omelettes and toast when Bryce and Amy walk in, they both run to the bench and can't believe what is done already. I call out to Michael and he comes in too.

'Come all of you, breakfast is up.' They all help put everything on the table and we all sit and chat away.

'Thank you baby,' says Bryce, 'this is a feast.'

'Well it's the least I could do for you,' I say.

'So what are you guys going to do today while I go into town,' I ask the kids.

'Nothing much,' they say together. They have something up I think to myself, but surely they are just being kids. They wouldn't be up to anything would they? Nah don't be silly. 'OK,' then I say.

'Bryce, are you going to stay as well and look after the kids?' I ask. Just in case he changes his mind. I don't want him to take time away from Amy.

'No as I said, I am coming with you, I have a couple of things to do and Marissa and her hubby will be here, we won't be long in town will we? he asks.

'No, I just need to go to the shops and I have to pick up something I have ordered.'

He looks at me. 'Ordered?'

'Yep, I ordered it on Thursday, it's something special,' I say. He looks at me and I can see he is trying to work it out but I hold my stance.

'Okay kids you go and play, I will clean.' So they run off and Bryce is with me.

'Sandy what are up to?' He asks.

'Nothing I just had to get something in and as we are here I got it redirected that's all.' I just hope he doesn't find out about it, for Last week I found a photo of him and Amy and got it enlarged, decorated and framed. I hope they like it. But with him coming it is going to be tricky.

'Hey Baby, give me a second before we go I have to go to the toilet. I go in and call the post office. Hi I have a parcel to collect however, it is for the person that is coming with me, is there a way of disguising it or can it be delivered?'

'We don't do deliveries as it's not a weekday.'

'Oh OK.' Shit, how am I going to get it here without him seeing it, will he know what it is.

Shit, I will have to fib to him and tell him it is for Marissa. I hope that works.

'Sandy you right?'

'Yep, on my way.' We say bye to the kids, Marissa and her hubby and hop in the car. Every time we drive around I am in awe.

'Bryce this is so beautiful, how do not live here full time. I would never want to leave?

'Well with the business and my ex in LA, I have to stay there a lot plus my family are close too so.'

'Yeah, it makes sense,' I say.

'But still this is so peaceful, doesn't anyone annoy you up here?' I ask.

He looks at me. 'Not really,' he says, 'I am considered a local, if the press come here no one tells them where I am unless I say it's Okay. Here we are norms.'

I laugh. 'Such a gorgeous norm too', and wink at him. He laughs, grabs my hand and says, 'Scoot over here and sit closer.' I do as asked, I don't need to be asked twice. We put the radio on and *Dreaming of you* is playing.

'I love this song,' I say, it is from the movie about Selena, such a talented person. So, sad she died so young.'

He looks at me and realises I am teary again. 'Sandy now you have to tell me what's wrong.'

I turn and look. 'Nothing I am just a sook, it is such a beautiful song, imagine feeling like that, knowing that the person you are with is the one for you, your soulmate, it's just beautiful.' I want to add that I am feeling everything in the song about him, that he is my soulmate, my one and only love and although he has said he loves me, I still can't believe it. So I put it aside and file it in my head under dreams.

We arrive in town and I say to him, 'I have to go and collect something from the post office and then go to the supermarket, shall we meet here in an hour.'

'You think you are going without me,' he asks.

'I just thought you had things to do.'

'I do but I want to do them with you.'

Shoot, I think.

'Okay no problem, post office first and then the supermarket.' We go get the parcel and he carries it to his car for me and we go to the supermarket. I feel like everyone's eyes are on us and we enter, he grabs my hand. 'Don't stress, let's go.' As we walk around, I am loading up the trolley with all the food and trimmings needed, as we near the end and walk to the registers I say, 'Hey honey, can you go get a couple of bottles of wine, I will wait here till you come back to pay.' He looks at me, raises his eyebrows and goes. 'Okay just wait.'

'Will do,' I say. As soon as he goes, I unload all the shopping and ask the cashier to try and rush through as I want to pay for it and then ask her to add some flowers and chocolates. She smiles and says, 'You are the first female he has brought here that actually had paid for anything, normally when he does bring people he always has to pay.' 'Well, I'm not like that, I am just me and this is my treat.'

I pay for the shopping put it in the trolley and wait for Bryce at the car. He comes up to me and says, 'You are a very naughty girl.'

I turn and giggle. 'Well may be you will have to punish me later', and we both laugh, he then grabs me pushes me towards the car and kisses me passionately. 'Honey, you shouldn't do that,' I say.

'Why not?' he asks.

'Because people will see.'

'So? I don't care.' Oh I love this guy, he is so open and happy here.

'Come on gorgeous,' he says, 'get your butt in the car, the quicker we get home the quicker you can get a spanking.'

'Oh yes please Mr J,' I say.

We get home and it is so quiet, we start to unload the car when Michael and Amy come out skipping.

'HI Dad, Hi Sandy.'

'Hi Bryce, Hi Mum.'

We look at each other and say together, 'What do you two up to in unison.'

'Nothing we missed you both.'

'Okay then,' I say, 'come help unload the shopping and I will start to get cooking.' After everything is in the kitchen, I send Bryce and the kids out. Then Amy comes back in. 'Sandy,' she says.

'Yes sweetheart.'

'Can I help you with the cooking? I like to help when Dad cooks, but mum doesn't let me that much.'

I look at her. 'Of course Amy, let's get an apron on you.' So here we are, the radio is playing, Amy and I are fiddling around with all the food. We have been in the kitchen for a couple of hours, when Bryce walks in and is just standing there watching.

'What I say?' I love this, it feels so right.'

I smile. 'Yeah it does.'

'Honey, can you get the roast out of the oven? While we get the cake out so it can cool.'

'Okay,' he says.

'Michael,' I yell, 'can you come here baby please', and he actually comes.

Can you help me take stuff out to the table please?

So, all four of us are working together, it does feel right, it feels like I always wanted, this is it, Perfection. Whenever something good happens something bad will happen. But I will only think good things. Law of Attraction, you think of only good things and be positive.

We are just finishing up setting the table when the front door opens, Marissa, Miguel, Thomas and Stuart walk in. 'Hey all. We're here.'

Bryce comes into the kitchen, hugs me from behind, kisses my neck and says, 'Everyone is here.'

I take out all the food, Roast Pork, Roast chicken, baked photos, Roast pumpkin, Veggies, Gravy, homemade rolls, 3 salads, plus more. The table is brimming with food, everyone is sitting down and I stand up and say, 'Now that everyone is here, I hope you don't mind Bryce but I want to say a few words.'

He shakes his head and says, 'Go for it.'

'Firstly, I want to thank you all for being so kind to myself and Michael while we have been here, thank you for all you do for Bryce and Amy for all the years he has had this place and thank you for coming today and joining us for dinner. I just want to say that this has been a great holiday and I know I have made good friends. Now on that note, I have pressies for you all. Firstly Marissa and Miguel, I know that you are always here but you do get time off, so I have paid for you both to go away for a week and stay at a resort not far from here, Bryce helped me with the place, hope you will like it. Thomas and Stuart I understand you go away often, so I have paid for you both to have a couple of experiences for when you go away, again Bryce helped me with the destination.

102

Now baby." I look at him. 'This is something that I found on the first day at your home and then when I met your mum she helped me with the other portion I needed.' I go into the back room, grab the parcel and say, 'This is for you and Amy. I hope you like it.'

He grabs it and opens it and starts to cry, 'Wow.' I hope he likes it. He turns it around and shows Amy and everyone comes to me and gives me a massive kiss and says, 'It is perfect, thank you so much. What it is?'

'It's a photo of him and Amy from the time she was born, to his first daddy and daughter trip and then the last portion is of them that was taken a few weeks ago when they were outside in the yard. It is a collage of them and it was absolutely worth every cent,' I say, 'Well that's it, but I do want to say one more thing to you.' I pause take a deep breath, 'baby... thank you for all you have done for Michael and I, thank you for being you, thank you for being the best person in the world that I have ever been with and I just want to say and it may be too soon, but I absolutely, irrevocably adore you and I am going to miss you so much when I go home. Now that is it, I will go get sweets.' And I bolt from the table. I didn't want to see any of their faces as I know I had said too much, but I don't care, when you love someone you want to tell them, you want to yell it out as loud as you can and make a fool of yourself, and this I had done.

I am in the kitchen and start to cry, I have done it now. I shouldn't have said anything but I had to tell him. How am I going to go back in there? I can't stop crying so I just get the sweets ready, trying to finish off decorating the cake which I had done as a surprise for everyone, it is in a heart with the words 'Thank You All' on it and an edible snowman just because I like snowmen. I am getting the dishes and cutlery on the tray when Bryce walks in, thank god I have my back to him.

'Sandy,' he says. 'Are you Okay? you have been in a while,' he asks. I wipe my face and bend down to the oven to try and put off my red face to the heat of the oven, I just hope he believes it.

'Yeah, all good sorry,' I say. I was just finishing off the cake.'

He looks at it on the bench and then pulls me up from the oven, turns me around and lifts my face up with his hands, he looks at me deeply, gives me a kiss and then says, 'Why have you been crying?'

Shit, I thought he wouldn't know. 'I wasn't crying,' I said.

'Don't lie to me sweetheart,' he says. 'I know when you're fibbing.' He looks at my face, puts his hands against my face and says, 'Tell me please.'

I am staring into his gorgeous eyes and say, 'I am sorry for what I said, I had no right to be so forthright but I had to say it and now I don't know how to go out there and be casual with you.' I start to cry.

He wipes my face and say, 'Sweetheart, you, Amy and Michael are my life, I love you and I feel the same way, we can do this, we can work this out, I know you live in Australia and I am over here in the States, but it will work out. We just have to give it time, now are you going to bring the cake in or do I have to carry you with it?

'Um you will have to carry me with it.' I say and he goes to lift me up.

'Bryce, you will break your back,' I say laughing.

He twirls me around and puts me down. 'Come on sunshine,' he says, 'I am starving for that delicious looking cake', and we take it in. I make everyone coffee, tea and the kids milkshakes. After we put the kids to bed, we are all sitting back on the couches talking, I am leaning in Bryce as I am getting tired and look at the clock and it shows 2 am. I am wondering when everyone will go home but realise that it has been a good night. All of sudden they get up and say, 'Shoot, we didn't realise what time it was.' We all say goodnight, and as we reach the front door Marissa gives me a hug and whispers to me, 'Remember dreams can come true, just don't listen to the negative and believe he loves you.'

I look at her and say, 'Thanks Marissa.' We hug each other and they all go. Next minute my love is next to me and says, 'Bedtime Cinderella', and we go up to bed.

In the morning, I wake and just stare at him and think I still can't believe that my time is nearly up. We have spent a week here and now this is my last day with him. Here in this beautiful man's life with just us.

'Bryce, what time are we leaving?' I ask him, 'for LA.' 'A few hours,' he says.

The car is loaded and we wave goodbye to Marissa and Miguel. Marissa hands me an envelope and says, 'My number and address is inside. Don't lose contact,' she says. Okay and I hug her. We all hop in the car and drive to the airport. I still can't believe that we are leaving this beautiful place. I just hope nothing gets in our way. We arrive at the airport and there are press everywhere, I am in shock, I look at Bryce and he looks pissed.

'Do you think they know about us?' I ask.

'I don't think so baby,' he says, 'but let's try to get on the plane quickly.' We get dropped off on the tarmac and all go into the plane, thankfully no one saw us. We take off and I am so stressed about the press and if I did something wrong that I don't even stress about the flight. Bryce is on the phone and then says, 'SHIT', and hangs up. Thankfully, the kids don't hear him as they are watching a movie and have headsets on.

'What's wrong honey,' I ask.

He looks at me. 'My ex has told the press where we are and all about us and they are crawling everywhere, NY may not be able to happen together.'

I try not to show I am upset. 'Oh well I guess that would be the best. Do you want me to stay on the plane when we land and then catch a cab back to your place and get our things and then leave?

He looks at me. 'God, no honey. We will leave together but if the press are there I just want to protect the kids.

I smile, God he is wonderful. 'OK, only if you are sure.'

When we arrive back at LA there are no press on the tarmac which is a good thing, he has organised for us to be collected off the tarmac as it is only a local flight. We load up in the car and start to go back to his place.

As we arrive, he looks a bit shitty.

'What's wrong honey?'

'It's my ex,' he says. I look at her as we pull up and she is absolutely gorgeous, I feel like the ugly duckling compared to her. Oh well, here goes nothing I think, Amy jumps out of the car and runs to her Mum.

'What are you doing here?' But still gives her a hug.

'I just wanted to see you honey, I need to talk to Daddy.'

'Okay.'

I take the kids inside with the bags and then say to Michael, 'Tomorrow we are leaving to go to NY. Are you ready for the big trip honey?' I ask.

'Mum,' he says, 'do we have to go?' he asks.

'You don't want to go honey?' I ask.

'Yes and no. I like it here with Bryce and Amy, it's like I have a Dad and it feels like a family.'

'Oh baby,' I say. I try not to cry but hold my chin up. 'Baby, he isn't your dad and not sure if he wants to be, he already has his family baby, although I do love him I just don't know if it will work out, this has been a whirlwind trip and he is dealing with his ex-wife now, so let's see if all is Okay when he comes back in but baby he did say they were going to come so let's just see Okay. Now let's make sure we have all our things, I am going to confirm our flight for tomorrow.'

I am about to go into the study when his ex-Simone comes up to me. 'You Sandy we have to talk,' she says scathingly to me.

'Excuse me, please don't speak to me like that I don't care who you are don't you dare speak to me like that. Now what can I do for you Simone.'

'Well the first thing is leave my family alone, you know he is only with you for the publicity, he doesn't love you, he just told me it is just for fun.'

I stare at her in complete disgust. 'I can't believe that,' I say to her, 'after everything that we have said and done, he is not like that,' I say to her.

'Well he is an actor and he just told me that.'

I stare at her, I know she is lying but it makes my blood boil, but I go ahead and give it to her. 'Well, I don't care what you say or think and while we are giving advice to each other, why don't you just back the fuck off from him and let him live his life and get on with his life. You only married him for a green card and he only wanted his daughter to have her family together. If it was me, I would never have hurt or lied to him, to have his love and then try to destroy him like you are not just personally, emotionally, financially but professionally you should be absolutely disgusted, you are not a nice person, you are venom, you are a waste of space on this earth and draw to much air from the universe. So how do you like the truth bitch!' I say venomously, I feel bad for saying it but someone has to stick up for him and if it is over, well I am going out with a fight. 'And another thing, your daughter is devastated she said to me a couple of times that mummy and daddy don't love her anymore as you are both constantly fighting. You need to grow the fuck up woman! You need to remember that this precious angel did not ask to be born, that she was created from love, yet all you seem to care about it is money. I have spent two weeks with both of them and all he cares about is his daughter, all you care about is money. How dare you put Amy in the middle of greed you are not worthy to be her mother. I would give anything to have her and Bryce in my life forever, I love him so much, so much so that I am going to walk away as I have just realised you still want him, don't you.' I just stare at her, the evil bitch. 'That's right isn't it, it isn't because you love him but you love his money, his fame and all the trimmings and you will never give up will you until he gives in and takes you back will you?' Then a light bulb went off in my head. 'That is what you want isn't it?' I question, 'You want him back! You will never give up will you? I just stare at her and know this is her plan all along.

'You have dragged him for years through the courts just so he gives in, just so you can get your fangs back into him. You pathetic peace of shit,' I yell. 'You know what you win, I love him so much but I cannot be here anymore seeing you do this to him. I would stay with him and fight, I would give up my life in Australia just to be with him not for his money but because I love him, because he is everything I have ever wanted and even if he had no money or fame, I would still want him because he is a beautiful human being, he is a wonderful father, brother, son, he is a caring man with the biggest heart, he is so fragile yet so strong, he makes me feel safe just by looking at me and he has made me believe in love at first sight but you, you are just pure evil.' I am shaking at this point and crying but I go on. 'I want you to make a promise at least, drop the case, drop the fight and if you want him love him, he deserves it, he only wants to be loved and put him and Amy first above your own selfishness.' With that I turn and walk away from her.

I am shaking like a leaf but I know that Michael and I have to leave and we have to leave now. I go get Michael, 'Hey mate, get your things we are leaving in 15mins I have to call a cab.'

'But Mum,' he says, 'I thought we were leaving tomorrow.'

'Yeah mate we were but I have fucked up. I let it rip with his ex and I can see they are talking in the patio out the back. Go get your things packed now.'

In the meantime, I call a cab and say to come ASAP as it is an emergency. Luckily, all my things have been packed and if I leave anything I will just buy it again. I go into the study and write a note to Bryce.

My darling Bryce...' Tears start to stream down my cheeks. 'I know what I am about to write but I have to as this will be the final thing he ever reads from me so I start to write and try not to wet the paper too much.

I first want to apologise for how I treated Simone but I could no longer stand by and see you being ripped apart from her evilness. She loves you and wants you back, although this will break my heart I want to say the following:

Thank you for all you have done for myself and Michael, thank you for all the good times and fun times. Thank you for sharing your life and Amy with us. You have made me believe that love can exist and that there is such a thing as a soulmate, and I feel that I will never ever be able to find the love that I feel for you in anyone else. You are the most amazing person I have ever met. I thank god that the day at the airport when you bumped into me. Little did I know that in two weeks' time my life would change unconditionally forever, little did I know I would find the man that I will love till I die and I have. I love you baby always will.

I will always be watching out for you in my heart and dreams, I will always look out online to see that you are Okay and I promise I will never, ever, EVER tell anyone about what we have shared. Our relationship and time shared will go to the grave with me.

I am walking away so that you and Simone can be a family for Amy. I know that this is what she wants and I know that if I walk away you will get your happy ever after. By the time you read this, we will be on our way home, I am so sorry for causing so many problems for you all and I wish you all the happiness in the world, you deserve it baby.

I WILL LOVE YOU TILL THE END OF TIME AND FOREVER

With all my love Sandy xxx

I leave it on the desk near his keyboard and I call Jenny, the travel agent that we spoke to yesterday.

'Hi Jenny, it's Sandy, can you do me a favour? And please I beg do not tell Bryce.' I beg.

'Hey Sandy, what's up?'

'I need you to change my flight to leave ASAP. I need all my accommodation changed so that he cannot find me, I have completely stuffed everything up and I am about to leave and go to the airport, please I beg do not tell him where we are. If you can't change NY, just get me close to my relos in New Hampshire, he doesn't know where they live and then you can get our flights changed to home. Please Jenny.'

'Oh Okay, Sandy give me a few minutes, just go to the hotel near the airport, I have booked you both in as a package at the Ramada Inn. That will give you some time. But are you sure I can't tell him?' she asks.

'He won't even know I have gone, he is with Simone.' I say. Silence on her end. 'I have to go Jenny, I think the cab is here I have just got a text, call me on the mobile OK', and I hang up. I messaged the driver, *I will come out on the side door, please give me 5mins*. I go find Michael and we take our bags to the door, I go find Amy and she is in her room playing.

'Hi baby girl,' I say to her. She looks so happy. 'Michael and I have to go but I wanted to tell you that I love you and Daddy so much, I want you to be happy and I know that you will be, Daddy is talking with Mummy out the back and I am sure that there will be good news soon. Look after yourself

111

baby girl and Daddy Okay,' I say. I am trying not to cry as I don't want her to know what is going on. 'Love you sweetheart.' I kiss her head and give her a hug.

'Love you too Sandy,' she says. I turn and walk out her room, go to the door, grab our bags and shut the door behind us, closing the best chapter of my life.

'Where to?' the driver says.

LAX airport please, to the Ramada inn hotel.'

'No problem ma'am,' he says.

I am crying in the back of the taxi and Michael is trying to soothe me.

'Mum, it will be Okay, don't worry. I know he loves you and me.' It is just a blimp in the ocean.

'Baby, you have no idea what I have done and said, he will never forgive me but the thing is we are going to see Roger, Canada and NY, we have two weeks left and then we are going home and this will be the last time we will ever be here in LA or Reno. It has been the best vacation; it has had romance, adventure, love and drama. The best holiday ever but it is now over.'

My phone then rings. I can see it is not Bryce so I answer, 'Hello,' I say.

'Hey Sandy, Jenny here, I have changed all your flights and accommodation, I have moved Niagara first and NY next, you fly into Canada tomorrow and you have the red eye flight leaving tonight. I just want to confirm are you sure about this?' she asks.

'Yes Jenny, thank you.'

'And if he calls?'

'He won't call,' I say, 'he is back with her. So, thank you I will speak to you later.'

'Excuse me,' I say to the driver, 'can you take us to the domestic terminal please, we are on the red eye and need to check in I assume, we are flying American Airlines.'

'NO problem ma'am,' he says.

'How long till we get there?' I ask the driver.

'5mins,' he says.

Good, it won't be long before we are on the plane. I just wonder how everything is going back at Bryce's but don't want to think about it.

In the meantime, Bryce and Simone are talking in the backyard.

'I can't believe she spoke to me like that she says. What an absolute bitch, how dare she say I am greedy and only care about money, how dare she speak to me like I am dirt, what are you going to do about it BJ,' she says.

He is staring at her. 'Well you are, aren't you? You never loved me did you? You only cared about my celebrity, my fame, my money, the notoriety, If I didn't know better I would say you got pregnant to trap me, to make me marry you so you could get a green card. With Sandy she met me and didn't know who I was, we feel in love without her knowing who I was. So, different to you. It's about time someone stood up to you.'

'But BJ I love you, I want us to be a family again. It has been so hard to be away from you.'

'Away from me? he questions, 'or away from my money! If you loved me you wouldn't try to ruin my life, you wouldn't try to hurt me professionally. When someone loves someone they will put themselves last, they will do the best for the one they love. You don't love me. It's over, you can take all my money but you will not take my spirit or my daughter. I will fight you till you give up. Bring it on bitch,' he says, now get the fuck off my property before I call the police on you.'

Simone just stares at him. 'I can't believe this I thought you wanted me, I am beautiful and skinny, unlike her, she is just plain ugh.'

'No to me, Sandy is my one and only, we love each other and I will not let you destroy what we have. So are we going to sort this shit out or do I call my lawyers?' Mexican standoff on the patio.

'Fine,' she says, 'let's sort this shit out so I can get on with my life and so can you. You know what else she said to me,' Simone says.

'What?' he snaps.

'She said that Amy said that we don't love her as we are always fighting. That I have to put her first and not my needs, she was right about that. Maybe I have been a bit selfish.'

'A bit,' he says scathingly.

'Definitely.'

So, they hash out all the agreement, co-parenting, money, holidays. It seems to take hours. When they finally finish they have both signed the agreement, it has been emailed and faxed to both sets of lawyers and it is dark. It is nearly midnight by the time Simone leaves and Bryce goes looking for everyone.

A note is on the table from the housekeeper, dinner is in the fridge. He puts the plate in the microwave and while it is warming goes checking on everyone. Amy is in bed asleep, he gives her a kiss, night my number one. He goes looking for Michael he isn't in his bed, maybe he fell asleep with Sandy in their bed. He goes into their room and it's dark, he goes to the bed and it is empty. He turns on the light and the room is empty, her side of the wardrobe is empty. Bryce grabs his phone and tries to call, it goes to voicemail, *Hi thanks for calling Sandy, I can't take the call at the moment but leave a message and I will call you back.*

Hey baby, it's me, where are you guys? You're not home and I am worried. Please call me,' he says.

While he is calling Michael and I are on the plane to Canada. I see my phone ring but put it to message bank. I can't speak to him, he will think maybe we have gone out but thankfully by the time he works out where we are it is too late. I really don't want to see Niagara Falls now or NY but I promised Michael. He is fast asleep next to me in the seat, all I want to do is call him but I know I can't he is probably calling to tell me that they are together again. I hope he is happy. All I want for him and Amy to be happy, to be loved. That is my wish for them both.

Meanwhile Bryce is frantic at home, he calls and wakes up Christy and asks if she has seen or heard from me, all she can say is Oh man it's after midnight, they probably went out.

'Not at midnight and not both of them, all their stuff is gone,' he yells.

'I don't know man. Ask the housekeeper or Amy. Can't you remember anything,' he asks.

'I didn't see her mate, can I go back to sleep now. All I know is Mary said she saw her and Michael leave and she said she left you a note. Now I am going back to bed, it will be Okay, give her time.' Bryce hangs up and runs around the house, he is looking everywhere, the lounge, kitchen, near the door, he checks his messages on his phone, checks his email nothing he goes into his office and sees the envelope leaning against the keyboard. He opens it and reads it and by the end of the note he is crying. Fuck she is on the way home, she isn't even going to the rest of her holiday.

I will call her and speak to her when she gets home, he thinks. Unless she is lying and is still going ahead with her holiday, yeah maybe she is doing that. He calls jenny. 'Hey Jenny it's Bryce can you call me urgently please it's about Sandy and Michael.' I can't sleep he thinks. Oh Sandy where are you?? And he eventually falls asleep on the desk.

'Good morning ladies and gentleman we are about to make our descent to the airport, please ensure all trays are put away and your seats are in the upright position.'

'Michael, wake up we are about to land into Canada, have a look out the window.'

'Wow Mum it's beautiful. Are you feeling better Mum did you get any sleep?'

'I'm Okay baby. I have our itinerary. We have a day of relaxation so that is good. Tomorrow we go to the falls and then the next day we are flying to NY.'

'Mum,' asks Michael.

'Yes baby.'

'Do you think Bryce and Amy will meet us in NY?

I stare at him and then I try not to cry unsuccessfully, 'Baby, I don't think he will ever talk to me again after what I said to his ex-wife. I just hope that they sort it all out for the sake of his sanity and for Amy, she is so sad baby, all she wants is for her mummy and daddy to be happy and all I want is for him and Amy to be happy and if that means I never see them again then that is OK. So to answer your question, no I do not think they will plus we were meant to be in NY now not Canada, I swapped our trip around and our accommodation so even if he wanted to see us he can't.'

Michael looks at me. 'Mum, maybe he wants to see us, maybe he is trying to let you know that.'

I stare at him after a few minutes I say, 'I can only hope baby but dreams don't come true for people like me, the last two weeks has been an amazing dream it almost doesn't feel like it happened but I know it did as I have photos to prove it but one day it will just be a fond memory.'

We look around the plane and it is emptying.

'Come baby, let's go and see Canada.'

We enter the walk way and go into the airport, I can't believe I am here finally, all I ever wanted was to see Canada, I wish he was here I think. As we walk towards baggage there is a movie poster of his movie, great I can feel the tears starting again, shit, I can't keep doing this, I can't keep crying, he said he loved me but she said it was for publicity, do I believe her no, not in anyway. Would I believe that conniving scant but I want his life to be easier. I put my sunglasses on and we walk out of the terminal and find a cab.

'Hey there welcome to Canada, where are you off to?' the concierge asks.

'We have to go to the Niagara hotel,' he tells the cab and we load up and sit in the back. Wow this place is beautiful, so white and clean. I could stay here forever, imagine being here with Bryce and Amy I am thinking, stop thinking about it woman I think, it is over, you will never hear from him again, he is happy now, he will put up with her just to make sure Amy is happy. I would do the same, we are very similar but god I miss him like crazy. I put my phone back on to get our reservation details and my phone is flashing, 10 messages and voicemail, I am not game to listen to them but I see two text messages are from Louise, two from Jenny and six from

Bryce. I will call my sister first, then Jenny I think, then look at the time and realise Louise is asleep so message her our itinerary and call Jenny. She answers on the first ring.

'Sandy OMG, are you Okay? she says.

'Yeah all good Jenny, why?'

'Well, you didn't have your phone on and I was worried something went wrong, where are you guys?' she asks.

'In the cab going to the hotel. I just want to say thanks for helping I hope I haven't caused any problems between you and Bryce.'

She goes quiet. 'He has called a few times, he is absolutely frantic with worry, he said if you called he begged me to get you to call him, he said he had left you messages but you haven't replied.'

'I can't,' I say. 'I just can't listen to them I am sure he is calling to have a go at me or worse,' I say. 'Jenny thanks for keeping my secret but I do have to ask one thing,' I ask.

'Of course,' she says.

'Have you seen him?'

'Yes,' she says.

'Is he happy? Is he Okay? I just want the best for him,' I say.

There is silence, then she says, 'No he isn't Okay, he called me in tears, sounded so frantic and he then turned up as soon as I opened and begged to tell me where you were, I wanted to tell him but I promised you, he was angry, threatened to boycott me and never use our services again but then we talked and he said he understood. Just do me a favour,' she says. 'Please call him.'

'I will tomorrow for sure, I didn't sleep and my battery is about to die. I will listen to the messages and send him a text Okay,' I say.

'Well, you should call him instead.'

'I can't Jenny. I will cry too much, that is all I have been doing the whole time, the air hostesses kept asking if I was Okay and all I could do was shake my head and then cry more... I need time to try, once I can pull myself together I will call him Okay.'

'Okay,' she says, 'but just message him please I have never seen him like he has been.'

I hang up and listen to the first message from him. *Hey baby it's me where are you. Call me baby, I am worried about you and Michael. I have news for you. Sandy, Honey, Sweetheart call me PLEASE.* I can't listen to anymore messages, I disconnect, I can't deal with it, I look out the window and the tears are rolling down my face. Get over yourself I think.

Ma'am we are at your hotel, I look up wow this is so beautiful.

'Thank you so much,' I say, I pay and tip and we collect our bags and go into the hotel.

'Welcome to Niagara hotel, how may I assist you?'

'Hi, my name is Sandra Wilson and we have a booking under our name for the next couple of days.'

'Of course Ms Wilson, I will get one of the ushers to help you with your bags and take you to your room,' she says, 'I am Kira and if I can help with anything else do not hesitate to call.' She goes on, 'I see you have the tour tomorrow to the falls, pick up will be at 8 am out the front and then you will be dropped off in the afternoon, all the meals and entries have been paid for,' she says.

'Thanks Kira, 'thank you for being so helpful and kind.' We follow the usher up to our room, our bags are put inside and I tip him.

'I'm not sure if this is enough or not,' I say to him but give him 20 US$.

He looks at me and says, 'Thank you but that is too much.'

'It's all good, I don't mind, you have been very kind so thank you.'

We put our bags on the bag trolley, open the curtains and wow, what a view, I can see the falls in the distance, 'Michael come look at this view baby,' I say.

We stand in awe, this is beautiful, god Bryce and Amy would love it here too, I think.

'Mum your phone is ringing.'

'Don't answer it baby,' I yell.

He stops. It has to charge. I know I can't turn it off as I need it but I have to keep ignoring the calls. I put it on silent and leave the cover closed. We go downstairs to look around, even the hotel and the surrounding area is beautiful. I can see why the romance movies are made here, it is so clean, snow is everywhere. This is so peaceful. We walk around and then go to the restaurant for dinner. By the time we finish and go back to our room I check my phone, there are quite a few more messages from Bryce. I know I have to answer them so I don't read them, just send a message, *Hey honey, we are all good, I hope you and Amy and your ex have it all sorted out, thanks for everything you did for us, thank you for all the time we shared, I will always remember our time together, I know that everything will work out for you. Regardless of what was said*

I am truly sorry and hope it didn't cause any problems. Love always Sandy xxx, then hit send and put it on silence as it needs to charge, I pop in the shower and leave Michael on his game.

I don't know how long I have been in the shower but it feels good plus I can cry and Michael won't hear or see me. I eventually hop out, dry off and hear Michael on the phone, SHIT, 'Michael,' I yell, 'get off the phone.'

He looks at me. 'Here Ya Ya, here is Mum.'

Oh thank god. I start to chat to Louise and tell her what happened. She listens and then said, 'I told you so, I told you he was using you, now maybe next time you will listen to your big sister.' I sit in silence and let her go on and on, I know in my heart he wasn't, I know what we had was something special but I also know it is over and I tell her that. I then finish off telling her what we are doing, then about going to NY and then to Rogers. But that we are going to cut short the trip by a few days to get home earlier. I hang up and then put on the news. Bryce Johnston and his Aussie girlfriend flew back from Reno on Sunday and rumour has it that there could be wedding bells happening soon, one source says that they are so close that as he has broken his privacy rule that she could be the one. There is a photo of us both smiling at each other at the premier, I can't believe that was a week ago, it seems so long ago. I turn off the TV and go to sleep.

It seems like I have been tossing and turning all night when there is a knock at the door, I go and answer it and it is Kira.

'Hi Sandra, just wanted to let you know that there are press all around, someone told the press that you were here and they are trying to get pictures of you and Bryce. I did

121

throw them out and security will watch all entries and when needed will help you, just want to confirm you still want to go to the falls.'

'But he isn't here, he is with his ex in LA,' I say and then add, 'Yes Of course we do, that's why we came here.' 'Good,' she says, 'we will take you out the back and you will be safe, are you still flying out Wednesday?'

'Yes we are. Also one more thing Mr Johnston called looking for you, I told him you were not here but I don't know if he believed me.'

'Shit,' I say, 'Oh sorry for swearing,' I say.

'Is everything OK,' she says.

'Yes of course, we just wanted a quiet vacation.'

'All good Sandy, I will organise breakfast to come up and will come and get you in an hour.'

We set our watches and get ready, we pack our bags, I call Jenny to confirm our flights and explain what has happened, I then ask if she has heard from him again? If so, is he better, has he forgiven her and if so, how does he look as I miss him horribly. Jenny advises, yes she has seen him, no he is not happy as I haven't spoken to him and he needs to speak to me urgent. She said that he had something urgent to do and has all his contacts trying to find out where you had gone, she goes on, he called the hotel in NY and was told that the booking had been cancelled.

'Sandy you have to speak to him, you can't keep ignoring him.'

'Jenny I get it and I will call him shortly but I did send him a text and told him we were Okay.'

'Okay then,' she says, 'if there are changes to your flight, so just confirming you are staying there for three days and fly out on Wednesday, I will let you know Okay, now I just want to confirm all your changes to NY and New Hampshire.

'Thanks Jenny, can you please email me all the changes? I really do appreciate all the work you have had to do and for not telling Bryce. I am so sorry for putting you in this situation.

'All good Sandy, speak soon', and she hangs up. I just sit there and try to find the courage to call him. It is still early in LA and I know he has Amy so I decide to leave it till we are back from the falls when there is a knock at the door. I go to the door as it must be breakfast and open it and it isn't Kira or breakfast but Bryce. I can't believe he is here. I am just staring at him, milking in everything about him, before I can just run to him and hold onto him I snap, 'How did you find us?' I go on and say, 'I changed all our itinerary around.' I look at him, I stare at his beautiful blue eyes, they have dark rings under them, he looks so tired, ashen, exhausted and yet he looks absolute adorable and beautiful. 'Bryce what are you doing here?' I ask and then say, 'I don't think your ex would be happy!!!' He is just staring at me, he looks like he has been crying, he is ashen in the face and my heart melts but I know inside he is back with his ex and probably just wants to have a go at me for what I said. I open the door and say, 'I guess you better come in.' he walks through the door, sits on the bed and drops his head. I forget what I am thinking and sit next to him, I want to put my arms around him but I know I can't because if I do, I will melt, so I keep my hands clenched together and in my lap. After what feels like an hour, he looks up at me, he doesn't look like the Bryce I know, he doesn't look like the man I love and adore, he looks completely deflated. To be honest he looks washed out.

'So, are you going to talk to me or do you want to stay here as we are leaving in 30mins to go on our tour and no one is going to make us miss it, this will be the last time we are ever here. So either talk or go, I don't really care anymore.' Inside I am shaking and crying but I have to be strong and pretend seeing him isn't ripping my heart out. He looks at me and goes to grab my hands and I pull away.

'Mr Johnston, why are you here?' I ask. 'If you want to have a go at me, go for it, you can't tell me off more than I have already.'

He breaths and then turns to me. 'I am not here to have a go at you, I am here because I wanted to see you, I asked Jenny, your sister and Christy no one knew where you were, it just happened that mum saw a report on the E News that you were spotted here, Amy and I were in NY at the hotel we booked so it didn't take long for me to fly up here.' I just stare at him, god I love him but I keep quiet. 'Okay here goes he says, I had a go at my ex and told her off for the BS she said to you, we argued and then called the lawyers and got it all sorted, we still have heaps to talk about but I just couldn't concentrate. I just want to ask you one thing and if the answer is Yes I am the happiest man on this earth but if the answer is no then I will go and you will never see me again...' He runs his hands through his hair. God I just want to grab him but I sit still. 'Sandy I love you, I know it will be hard I know my life is complicated and you will never have it easy, we will always have to be careful and always will be followed but I just need to know this one thing and then everything we can work out. Do you love me?' he asks He looks at me with his gorgeous tear rimmed eyes, I am screaming inside YES but then I remember what else his ex said, that he never loved me, that he is an actor and knows how to put on feelings as that is his job and above all, that Amy wants them together and not us and finally that if I did not go, he would lose his career and she will make sure that I am disgraced as a money hungry whore!…I look at him and say the only thing that I know will save him, that will make sure he doesn't lose Amy or his career, so I lie to him, one thing I said I would never do, I take a depth breath look away and say, 'I love you like a fan, all your fans love you,' I say. I am shaking and hope he doesn't see it.

He looks at me and sighs and then says, 'is that it, only as a fan, nothing more, after everything we went through, the time we spent together, all our plans.' he pauses and looks at me and quizzes you only love me like a fan to a star.

'Yes, Mr Johnston that is correct.'

'But after how we made love, how it felt to have you in my arms that was nothing to you?' He asks. 'Was it just a game to you, I introduced you to my number one, to my family and there is nothing there between us.' He just stares at me, I am shaking and hope he can't see it, I have tears welling up in my eyes but have to just go on and lie. 'Yes, only as a fan.' I say with my voice breaking.

He then gets up and says, 'I hope you and Michael have a good trip.' Goes to the door and walks out and walks away from my life. I stare at the door and I break down, I am shaking convulsively, I can't breathe, I feel like I am going to be sick, I can't stop crying. I have lied to him and my heart is broken into a million pieces, I just want to run after him and tell him everything about the threat, I don't care about me but him, he has worked so hard for everything, so I just sit there and cry.

'Mum, are you Okay? Michael asks.

I look at him and can't speak, I just shake my head and break down.

'Why didn't you tell him what was said to you?' He asks. 'Why did you lie to him. You do love him, you have been crying for days Mum, why didn't you tell him the truth?' Michael asks.

Sometimes mate you just have to lie to save someone, when you love someone you have to set them free, if they come back it is meant to be, if they don't it wasn't.'

'But he came to you, Mum.'

'I told him we were here, Mum I'm sorry I did.'

'I look at him. 'Baby it's Okay, as an adult you have to sometimes put your feelings aside to protect the ones you love and yes I do love him, I adore him but I had to lie to make sure he doesn't lose Amy, his home and career. I had to do it. He looks at me and then there is a knock at the door. it is Kira.

'Hi guys are you ready?'

I look at her and break down again. 'Oh Kira, what am I going to do?'

She closes the door and sits down next to me and I tell her everything. After I finish, she says, 'Call him, tell him.'

'I can't Kira, no matter what I just can't, he will lose everything.'

She looks at me and says, How do you know that she will destroy his career and all that?'

'I really don't know,' I say between sobs, 'but I just can't risk it, I love him so much and I just can't let him lose everything he has worked so hard for, I can't let him lose his daughter she is his life!'

She puts her arm around me and lets me sob. After what seems like hours, I slowly stop to sob and just whimper, I look at Michael who is on his game and realise I have ruined the trip to the falls.

'Oh baby, I am so sorry, we haven't gone to the falls.' 'It's Okay Mum, we can go tomorrow.'
My heart takes a flip, boy Oh boy I have raised such a beautiful little man.

'Kira, do you think we could go to the falls tomorrow? I ask, is it too hard to swap around or do we have to repay?' I ask.

'All sorted already, as soon as I saw Mr Johnston I changed them for tomorrow. So what I suggest is you guys stay in tonight, get a good night sleep and tomorrow at 6 am I will come and get you both and then if you want you can either stay here for a couple of more days as or I can drop you off to the airport in the morning.'

'Kira, we have our flight out now Wednesday night, I just don't think I can change it again, poor Jenny has done so much to accommodate everything, but I really appreciate it Kira you have gone above and beyond to help.'

'Sandy, the thing is I am a huge fan of Bryce and to think he has found love with a nice and normal person and not a using model or liar, it makes me happy to help.'

'But Kira I am not nice, I lied to him, I hurt him.'

'Sandy, you only did that to protect him, do you want me to call him and tell him to come back,' she asks.

I look at her and think it would be so much easier but then common sense comes in. '"No I will leave it as is, he is better off without me. As it is I am thinking of cancelling the rest of the trip but I just don't know.'

Kira gets up and closes the door behind her.

'Mate I am going to go to the pool to get some sun, do you want to come too?' I ask.

'Yes Mum.'

We get changed and go to the pool, there is no one around, just us two. I have my headset on and am listening to music and Michael is swimming in the pool. When I get a message on my phone. *You did the right thing sending him away now we can be a family and he will never lose what he wants*, it says. I know exactly who it is. I reply back, *Fuck off bitch, just warning if you EVER hurt him again I will make sure you will be punished and yes it is a promise not a threat. Now you got what you want leave me the fuck alone!!!*

I am shaking I should have kept my cool but she is such a manipulative cow, I have two options, tell him what she has said and have him hate her and lose everything, tell him what I said or just leave it. My instinct says to tell him, but I can't risk it so I keep my mouth shut. He hates me now. He could never love me. He would be disgusted with me and think that I was trying to use him like everyone, so I just give up and try to enjoy the sun and peace and quiet. It isn't working every time I close my eyes I see his face, fuck I have ruined it now. I start to cry again but I have to pull myself together. This is ridiculous. I call Jenny.

'Hey Jenny, its Sandy, can you do me a favour again, I know we have our flight out on Wednesday night but is it hard to change the rest of the trip?'

She says, 'Just email me what you want to do, I will do my best, the latest flight out of Canada is at 11 pm but I think it is a bit late, so how about we make it Thursday am and then you can arrive in NY early and enjoy the full day.' 'But if we do that what about accommodation for Wednesday night?' I ask.

'Sandy, I can add another night on where you are it is just another night or you can stay at the hotel near the airport, it is up to you.'

'Jenny it's all good, just let me know and email me Okay. I am so sorry for all these changes, I know I am the worst customer in the world but thank you for everything.'

'Sandy it is all good Okay, us girls have to stick together, so just confirming NY will be a day short and how much at New Hampshire?'

'Jenny, how about to leave NY at the four days and shorten New Hampshire, is that Okay?'

'Of course,' she says, Sandy can I just ask one more thing?

'Yeah go for it,' I say.

'Why are you believing his ex and not him?'

'Jenny I had to. She threatened his career and that he would lose Amy, I couldn't risk it, my heart is absolutely broken but I can't ruin the trip for Michael so I have to put my feelings aside and try to enjoy it. Have you spoken to him since he left here? Is he Okay?'

'Yes, I have and between you and me he thinks there is more to it then what you are saying, he is upset but not angry, the first thing he did was call me and changed his flight to go back to NY to get Amy. Sandra, I know he still loves you, you should call him.'

'I can't Jenny, I lied to him. I told him I would never lie to him and I did. Even if he works it out, even if he knows what is happening he will never forgive me because I broke his trust and lied.'

'Sandy, I think he would understand. Have you slept in the last two days at all?' she asks.

I think and say, 'Maybe an hour or two. My head is spinning and I feel sick all the time. I have never felt like this before, I feel like my heart has broken in half, that it can never heal. I love him so much but I, I… I just can't, I can't…' I repeat and then break down and cry again. 'Oh, Jenny I am so sorry. I just can't. I can't…'

'OK, not now but maybe later. Give me an hour or so I will fix everything and then I will message you the changes Okay.'

'Thanks Jenny.' I hang up.

'Bryce, are you still there? says Jenny.

'Yep.'

'Fucking ex, she is such a manipulative mole, I can't believe she would do that. Poor Sandy.'

'I knew something was up because Michael spoke to me but couldn't talk long but to think she would do that and put it all on Sandy's shoulders I just can't believe it. Do me a favour, change her flights and put her in the Waldorf, then I can get my sister to check on her as she is in NY for a business meeting. I am going to deal with Simone for once and all, she will regret the day she ever tried to destroy myself, Sandy or take my daughter away.'

'No problem, Bryce.'

'Hey Mark Its Bryce, I need you to do the following', and he tells him exactly what has happened. He goes through everything he knows and ends the call with the knowledge knowing Simone is going to get a visit from his lawyers, the police with an restraining order on behalf of himself, Sandy, Michael and Amy and that a warrant for her arrest for the threat against all of them. Well I wish I could be a fly on the wall to see that he thinks. Now to sort out what has happened with Sandy and Michael.

I wake up the next morning and look at the clock, it shows 4 am.

'God, did I actually fall asleep?' I ask? Michael, wake up baby we are going to the Falls today and then NY.'

He wakes up slowly but has a smile on his face, he then turns and looks at me. 'Mum, are you feeling better today?'

I look at him, although I am falling apart inside I say, 'Yes baby so much better. Can't wait to see the Falls and then we are going to NY tomorrow, we have tours and then we are going to see Roger and the family. So let's get ready sleepy head.'

We get up, get dressed, I pack our bags, make sure everything is ready and check my phone. I have 30 messages. Geez 30. I have never seen so many messages. I start to go through them. Jenny has sent me a few messages with tickets, accommodation details, booking details for the tours, flights to New Hampshire and then our flights home. There are messages from Bryce, I don't read these as I am not sure what was said and when they were sent, there are messages from his mum, a message from his ex and messages from unknown numbers. I delete the unknown ones, don't read the one's from Bryce but read the ones from his mum.

Sandy, it's Wilma here, can you please call me, I need to check some things from you, it's not urgent but need to know before Sunday. Oh this is interesting so I call.

Hi Wilma, it's Sandy sorry for calling so early, I am getting mucked up with the times between east and west. We are about to leave but if you give me a call tonight after 10 I should be back in the hotel. Speak soon, and hang up.

Knock, knock, knock, I go to the door and Kira is there, 'Morning, how are you both,' she says.

'Better,' I reply. 'I have our flight booked for tomorrow and I believe we are staying at the hotel near the airport so we can just walk over to the terminal early. Is that Okay to organise a lift to the airport?' I ask.

'All good, I can get it organised,' she says. 'So, come on lets go see the falls. We are only a 10min drive away from the entry', and I can smell the fresh air and hear the falls. I am getting so excited as is Michael. Kira parks the car and we all get out and walk to the walkway, as we turn the corner there are the falls.

'OMG, they are breath-taking. Kira this is stunning, absolutely beautiful. Imagine getting married with that view in the background, that would be amazing,' I say.

She looks at me and smiles. 'Yes we have had a couple of proposals but no one has ever been married close to the falls just on the top. But yes very stunning views. Every time I see them I am in awe,' she says.

We are walking towards the boat which will take us on a tour around the falls. Kira explains that we will be on the boat for a few hours, have lunch and then we are going on a helicopter flight over the falls. I look at her and try to keep my cool. Two things I like but am scared of. I get sea sick on boats if it is rough and I am scared absolutely petrified of small planes and a helicopter is a really, really small plane. I look at her and say, 'Fantastic.' I swallow and think be brave, what else can go wrong. It works out to be a good day, I put my fears aside and try to enjoy the day. My motto from now on is to enjoy the rest of the trip and try not to think about Bryce, I know this is the best but everywhere I turn I can see his face, it is like he is here. God I miss him but I no longer have any tears so I just go on the day in a haze and try to enjoy it all. I smile when asked to smile, but the smile doesn't reach my eyes, I answer questions when asked and I walk when I need to. I look at Michael and see his face is filled with so much joy so I know I have done the right thing. The falls are stunning, the mist from the falls gives a rainbow all around us, I see angels in the mist, I see my dad's face in the mist, I see Bryce's face in the mist. God I have it bad. TYPICAL fan I think. You had him, you stuffed it up, how will I be able to continue without him but know I will, I am a strong woman, I may never have loved before but now know what it feels like to have a broken heart, I have finally known what it is to wholeheartedly love someone and to lose them but it is better to have loved and lost than to never of loved.

The day is starting to wind down, we go back to the hotel to get a few hours rest before we have to leave to go to the airport hotel. I do some quick souvenir shopping and then go upstairs to the room. I check our flight and connections and then check with the front desk to get a taxi to take us to the airport.

'I am sorry Ma'am but your car isn't coming till the morning,' says the receptionist.

I don't understand,' I say, I spoke to Kira we are leaving tonight to go to the hotel near the airport.

'No ma'am you have one more night here, management have advised you are to stay here tonight in comfort and tomorrow morning the car will take you to the airport for your flight at 8 am.'

'Oh thank you.'

I advise I have some gifts is it Okay to bring them down, I go upstairs and then take them down to reception. I then leave a gift for Kira and the staff who I have interacted with over the three days and then go and get Michael. As I am going to the lift, I check my voicemail and hear Bryce's voice, I disconnect. I can't do this I think and then chuck my phone in my bag.

I open the door of our room and Michael is sitting on the bed playing his game. 'Michael we are not going till tomorrow morning now mate, so relax, have a shower and let's get ready for bed.'

I call Kira and she answers.

'Hey Sandy.'

'Kira, thank you so much for the extra night, I hope it has been charged? I ask. No, it hasn't my manager and I decided you both deserved an extra night of comfort.'

'But I can't accept this.'

'Yes, you can Sandy, just say thank you.'

'Thank you Kira, please keep in contact, I have left my details downstairs at the desk with something for you, I hope that is Okay.'

'You didn't have to but thank you,' she says and hangs up. We go to sleep for the last night in Canada. I am sitting outside on the balcony before I go to sleep and think of Bryce and Amy. I wish things had of been different, I am thinking how amazing it would have been to be here with them both but know that things are sent to challenge us and makes us better people. I will always love him and one day I know that I will be able to watch a movie or interview with him and have only fond memories, but for this moment in time, this one second, I am sad. I look at my phone, be brave I think and listen to his messages and then decide to sleep instead. I can hear a ringing in my ear, I look at the clock it is 4 am. I answer the phone.

'Good morning ma'am this is your wake up call, the car will be here at 6 am to collect you and take you to the airport.'

'Thank you,' and I hang up.

'Michael wake up baby, we have to get up and get dressed, we are leaving in two hrs.'

He gets up mumbling, 'This is bullshit.'

'I know mate but just think here we come NY.'

We walk around the room and check everything is packed and then I say, 'Have you got everything ready? I ask. 'Michael, are you listening?'

He is staring into his screen, Oh well, I will give him a break and go around the room to check everything has been packed, I then tap him on the shoulder. 'Come on mate, NY here we come', and we leave and go downstairs.

The taxi ride to the airport is non eventful, we arrive at the airport to go in and check in and go to the gate to wait for our flight, I call Louise and tell her what is happening and that we have four days in NY and then we are going to see Roger. I also advised we have changed hotels as I knew I couldn't afford the one that was booked so we are in the heart of times square but on the cheaper side and will be doing the tours. She asks how I am, have I heard from him and that there have been heaps of calls from newspapers, she has told them no comment and that they have the wrong details so hopefully that will sort them out. I just hope he is Okay and that all is good with him and Amy. My phone rings and I answer it, it is his mum.

'Hi Wilma how are you?' I ask.

'Good,' she says. 'I have to ask you something,' she says, 'and I don't care what the answer is as long as it is the truth, do you promise me?' she asks.

'Okay.' I say. I am a bit scared of what she is about to ask but I have made a promise and I have to keep it.

She goes on. 'Do you love my son?'

'Yes absolutely, more than I have ever loved anyone.' 'Good,' she says.

'Did Simone threaten you, Michael, Amy and Bryce?'

I breath in and out. 'Oh well here goes, I, I, would rather not say as I don't want to cause any problems.'

'Sandy,' she says, 'please tell me the truth.'

Here goes. 'Yes she did,' I say, 'BUT please don't tell him I don't want him to lose Amy or his livelihood.'

'Well that sounds right, it sounds just like her, we never liked her, yes she was a model and beautiful but we never liked her.'

I then said how she had threatened him, that he would lose Amy, that she would make me out as a gold digger and a user and would destroy him emotionally and professionally unless I did what I did, that I was warned to leave him alone or he would lose everything.

'And Yes that is all true... BUT Wilma, I lied to him, I told him I never loved him, he will never forgive me.'

'I am sure he will. Don't stress OK.'

' Wilma, we have to go. Our flight is boarding, can you do me a favour? Can you please look after him, make sure he is Okay.'

'Of course sweetheart,' she says.

'I will speak to you soon.'

136

'Sandy just one thing, I know that you and my son are perfect for each other, I saw it the moment he talked about you on the Tuesday. He was in love with you from the moment he met you.'

'Well Wilma, the feeling was and is mutual. I just wish I, I just wish I, nah all good. Take care Wilma and thank you.'

'Bye sweetheart speak soon.'

We board the plane and there are so many people on the plane, I don't get why so many people fly this early, Michael is next to me and he falls asleep, I stay awake as it is such a short flight and will sleep when we get to NY. I put my phone on airplane mode and decide to read all my messages. Most are good, Jenny has sent me all the details for the hotel and tours in NY and then the latest one is with the changes. I really have to give her a present as a thank you and a really big bonus, but it may have to wait till I get home. Home I thought it was going to be here but as usual I stuffed it up. Now the only messages are from Bryce here goes. *Sandy, call me. Sandy where are you guys? Sandy, call me I need to speak to you. Sandy why aren't you answering me? I am worried about you guys and it goes on,* then the last one is, *I am here in Canada we need to talk, I have so much to tell you, please speak to me.* That was three days ago, no more messages. Well that's it, it is over, he is with his ex and him and Amy have their happy ever after. Oh well, it was nice while it lasted. At least his mum knows the truth, I wonder how she worked it out. I decide to go on his Instagram and see what is happening, there isn't much on there, just the usual lyric videos, some pictures of him in the garden and nothing much. I wonder if he has blocked me, no that wouldn't happen otherwise I wouldn't see that at least. I so want to contact him but you have to accept what is done is done.

I decide to stop looking I will only upset myself, so I do the next worst thing, I start to go through my camera roll and videos. He is in nearly everyone, the first day at the beach, our time together at his place, the kids and I racing against him which we won, both of us playing in the pool, our time together at Reno, it is all there, I am crying but don't want to stop looking as I miss him so much.

'Excuse me ma'am,' says the air hostess, 'can I get you something?'

'Yes please, a new brain and the last few days back so I don't do what I did?'

She looks at me. 'I'm sorry I don't have that here in the trolley but how about a nice wine?'

'Yeah why not, but not too dry and thank you.'

'I hope you are Okay,' she says, 'I see that you are crying, just remember whatever happened love will conquer.'

'I wish,' I say, 'but some things just can't be fixed. If it could, it would be a miracle. But thank you for trying.'

She goes back to the back and I sit there and keep thinking. God I miss him. By the time we land, I have cried myself stupid, fixed my makeup, put on sunglasses and we exit the plane. As we come out of the terminal there are photographers everywhere, thank god he isn't with us. Michael and I come out and see a card with our name on it and we start to walk towards him. Suddenly, there are photographers around us and asking questions about Bryce and myself. 'Where is Bryce? When is the wedding? Sandy answer us. Did you know that he is back with his ex,' another says? Another says, 'Tell us it isn't true!' We are being followed to the car. 'Sandy how does it feel to be called a gold digger and that you never loved him but was using him for his fame?' One yells at me. I turn around look at the bitch and then turn around and continue to walk to the car. We are literally being chased to the car when security steps in and circles us and helps us get to the car, we climb in and then I just sigh a big relief. Holy hell how did they know we were there? Why would they ask these stupid questions? Poor Bryce, no wonder he gets annoyed with the press. I am just glad that I said nothing, but I knew I had to message him to let him know. So I do. I messaged everything that was said and then added, *I hope that you and Simone are happy baby, I know you won't want to speak to me but I just wanted to tell you about the press and what they said, I didn't answer them or react except when I turned around but then I just kept walking. I hope one day we can be friends baby please don't believe the press. I never used you, I will always look out for you, you and Amy will always be in my heart, l will love you forever Sandy,* and then hit send. Shit, I hope he doesn't read the last bit. Hopefully, he will ignore the message, I can't take it back now.

We pull outside the hotel and I say to the driver, 'Um this is the wrong hotel, we are meant to be staying at the budget one.'

'No Miss, this is the one that was sent to me.'

'I don't understand, I haven't booked this hotel or paid for it.'

'Miss, don't take this the wrong way but this is the one I have been told to drop you guys off to. So you need to get out of the car please as I have another job to go to.'

The door opens up, we hop out and the concierge greets us, 'Welcome Ms, we will take your bags up to your room, please follow myself to check in.'

I am shocked this is the most beautiful hotel I have ever seen, the ceiling has chandeliers that look like they should be in a museum, the furniture is stunning, there is so much space.

'Excuse me, I think there has been a mistake, can you please stop, I need to go back and get a cab.'

'Ms I am sorry but you are Sandra and Michael yes?'
'Yes, that is correct.'

'Then this is the correct hotel.'

We go to the check in and I call Jenny.

'Hey Jenny it's me again.'

'Hey chook,' she says.

'How are you both?'

'Not good Jenny they dropped us off to the wrong hotel.'
'You are meant to be at the Waldorf,' she says.

'Yes we are, that is the wrong hotel. We are meant to be at the Ramada,' I say.

'No you are at the Waldorf, I pulled some strings and due to the issue at the airport, my contact was happy to have you both there.'

'Oh, but I haven't paid for this yet,' I say.

'Sandy, it is all sorted don't worry about it, it has been sorted out, now go and enjoy, go to sleep and I will speak to you in the morning.'

'Thanks Jenny.'

I turn around and the lady has our key and welcome folder. We go to the lifts, the usher pushes 28th floor and we ride up.

'This is beautiful hotel; I saw it on the movie Serendipity. I love that movie,' I say.

'Yes ma'am it is a good one, my wife loves it too.'

He shows us to our room, opens the door and wow, the view, I can see the park. OMG this is beautiful. I can't believe it. I start to think about Bryce and wishing he was here. Why do I keep doing this, he isn't here, he will never talk to me again. You are such a loser I think to myself, you did the only thing you could do I think. Then my phone rings, I look at it and it's his mum.

'Hi Wilma.'

'Hey Sandy how are you guys? Did you arrive Okay? Where are you staying?'

'Yes we got here Okay, we are at the hotel, not the one I thought but it was a deal so all good. The view from our hotel room is overlooking the park, Oh Wilma it is so beautiful. I just wish I could turn back time and have Bryce here, I miss him so much', and I start to cry a bit.

'Call him,' she says.

'No I can't, I did text him but he hasn't come back to me which I expected plus he is happy with Simone so that is what is important.'

Silence. 'Sandy why do you think he is with Simone?' 'Because she told me that.'

'Who told you?' asked Wilma.

'Simone on Sunday, she said that he was just using me for publicity and that they were back together and if I didn't go he would lose everything so I went. But not after what I told her, I told her exactly what I thought about her and warned her to never hurt him again and that is why I left.' 'Do you really believe her? asked Wilma.

'I guess no, but I know that she is a bitch and very beautiful and if there was any chance he gets to have Amy with him and not have his career or livelihood threatened then I had to go. I saw him on Tuesday, he came to see us, I lied to him when he asked if I ever loved him. I lied, I told him no. But it wasn't true. I do, I do love him. I love him so much that I walked away. Oh Wilma what am I going to do?'

She says nothing for a while and then says, 'Tell him.' 'I can't, I just can't. Anyway we have to go and get ready. Can you please do me a favour,' I ask.

'Of course.'

'Please make sure he and Amy are Okay, make sure he looks after himself and make sure he doesn't read any articles from over here. I got hounded by the press at the airport, we are going to try and go on tours if not we will fly home early.'

'Okay sweetheart, keep me in contact,' she says. 'Thanks Wilma', and hang up.

Michael and I go to the lifts and decide to walk around New York. I can't believe I am finally here, this has been my dream. There is no one following us so that is good. We walk around and see all the shops that I have seen on shows. We walk past major shops, we stop for lunch, go shopping, walk to the Guggenheim museum, walk around blocks upon blocks, I see Tiffany's and have a photo outside, I will never afford to go in but I can't believe I am standing the same spot that Audrey Hepburn was standing. We keep walking past shops, there are so many people. I am such a tourist taking photos everywhere, this is such a lively city, it is such a dream. I look at my watch and realise we have to get back to the hotel as it is getting close to dinner time and tomorrow we have tours and we are going to see the statue of liberty and the sex and the city tour. So excited. I look at my phone and it is flat as a tack.

'Come on mate, let's get back to the hotel.'

As we walk back I see a newsstand and there is a magazine with Bryce's face on it. I pick it up, pay for it and put it in my bag. I will read it when I can face it. I am now just a fan, someone who was lucky to meet their favourite star and got to spend heaps of time with him. It is like a dream now, nothing more, just a dream. We walk past the library. I stand in awe, what a beautiful building. We even walk past stalls on the side of the road. I have to stop, I buy a fake bag and wallet. Michael sees t-shirts that he wants, we are both having a ball. This is the real New York, the one you see on the TV and movies. This is almost perfect. We finally make it back to the Waldorf and go back to our room. Tomorrow, we have our tours and then Saturday we leave and go to see Roger. This is something I changed myself just in case where we are gets leaked. We both go to sleep quickly and wake up refreshed. I turn my phone back on and there are five messages and three are from Bryce. Seriously dude I think, I don't need to hear about your happy life. I don't read them I move them straight to archive. We get dressed get up and go meet the tour at 8 am outside the hotel. This will be a full day and tomorrow we are catching the train down to New Hampshire. I can't wait to see Cousin Roger.

The day goes quickly and we both have an absolute ball. The statue of liberty is so beautiful, the tour around NY shows all the sights that you would ever want to see, I have souvenirs coming out of so many bags I think I will have to buy another suitcase just for the souvenirs. We have seen all the parts of NY I wanted to see including the zoo. We arrive back at the hotel to rest up and see press everywhere. I know it isn't for us as we haven't had any hassles all day and we just walk past quietly and go inside. Just as we go to the lift I hear my name being yelled out, I turn and see his sister Melinda.

'Oh hi Mel, what are you doing here?' I ask.

'I have been trying to call you to speak to you but your phone hasn't been answering.'

'No it's flat after all the pictures, plus we used Michael's phone which no one has the number for, what is up?' I ask.

She looks at me and then says, 'it is Bryce.'

I look at her in horror, I am sweating. Oh my god I am thinking. I start to speak quickly without a breath.

'Is he Okay? Is Amy Okay? What is wrong? What does he need? Is he ok? Talk to me,' I yell.

She says, 'If you would like me to answer you have to stop asking questions.'

We get in the lift to go upstairs and she says, 'Wait till we get to your room I don't want anyone to hear.'

We walk to our room and enter. Just as I step in I ask again. 'Is he Okay? Amy? His mum? Family? What is wrong?'

'He is very sad,' she says, 'he has gone quiet, he has refused to leave the house since he came back from seeing you. All he does is mope around all day and play with Amy.'

'Well, it has nothing to do with me,' I say, 'he has Simone, let her sort it out!'

'Sandy, he isn't with Simone.' I stare at her. 'But she told me they were getting back together, she told me he never loved me, she said he was using me for publicity, she said that if I didn't go he would lose everything, his home, Amy, his career, so I went, well after I told her what I really think about

144

her. Why isn't she sorting him out?' I have tears rolling down my cheeks. 'Oh god I am so sick of crying,' I say, 'I seriously have to get a life,' I continue.

'Sandy you need to speak to him, you are the only one he will listen to, he loves you.'

'No he doesn't, he walked out when I saw him, if he loved me he would've stayed.'

'Did you tell him you never loved him?' she asks.

'Well yes but I had to, I had to lie to him. I love him Mel, I adore him but I was warned to back off. I don't know what to say anymore. He won't forgive me for lying I always said I would never lie but I did. Mel you guys have to help him, I just can't anymore, I can't speak to him, I can't see him, if I do I will melt and he will lose everything.' Mel looks at me, she is aghast with what I have said, she then says, 'I will speak to him but please will you please call him and speak to him, he will speak to you. I know he loves you, you love him and yet you are both being so stubborn. Please call him now, I will take Michael downstairs OK?' I look at her, I can see she is worried and honestly I am too. 'Okay I will.'

Michael and her walk out of the room. I sit on the bed, look at my phone, I take a deep breath and dial his number. Please don't answer I am thinking, but he picks it up on the second ring.

'Bryce it's me are you there?' I ask. Just silence.

I start to speak. 'Honey I just want to say I am sorry for what I said to Simone, I want to say sorry for lying to you in Canada, but there was a reason why I said it, I don't know if you are there or if you are listening but I want to tell you this. I did it because I didn't want you to lose Amy, your livelihood, career, family and everything you have worked for, I lied because I was protecting you, I lied when I said I didn't love you. I was only protecting you, I thought you were back with Simone and for the sake of Amy and your happiness I did it all. But baby, please look after yourself, Amy and your family need you, I need you to be Okay. Baby, are you there? Honey? Bryce?' Nothing but silence, I start to cry. 'I know you will never forgive me but I just want to say, I... I want to say I will love you to the end of time. I will always love you and I will always cherish the time we spent together.'

I then hang up and put my phone on silence. I go looking for Mel and Michael and spot them in the restaurant.

'Mel,' I say, 'the phone answered but he didn't say anything I don't even know if he was there or if someone else was. I tried. Come on mate,' I say, 'we have a plane to catch.'

'A plane?' he asks. 'I thought we were going by train and I thought we were going tomorrow.'

'No mate all changed, I changed it Michael we get there quicker, plus I have a surprise for you.'

I look at Mel, give her a hug and say, 'Mel take care Okay and please keep in contact.'

Michael and I get up and go to our room, we get our bags and go back downstairs. We say goodbye to the staff, hand our keys in and then go outside to get a cab. I can see Mel is on the phone but has her back to us so we walk out without being seen. The driver takes us to the train station and we hop on the train.

'Mum, I thought we were going by plane.'

'I just said that just in case Mel told Bryce baby, plus it only a 5hr trip and we get to see more of the US.'

We go to our seats and sit down to enjoy the trip. I grab my headset, put my music on. I text Roger to say we are on the train and on the way to his town. I give him our hotel details and say will see him tomorrow. Michael is on his tablet playing his games and we are both enjoying the silence. I am about to dose off when my phone rings.

I answer. 'Hello Sandy speaking.'

'Hey Sandy, its Wilma, hi how are you?' I ask. 'Good, I just want to say thank you for calling Bryce, he is in a better mood, he said you called and then he called me and asked me what I thought, I hope you don't mind but I told him everything I guessed and what you confirmed. He said he has sorted out Simone and got his lawyers onto it all. This will help him get Amy full time and she will never be able to try and destroy him again.'

I take a deep breath. 'Oh that is good news Wilma. Please watch him for me, I am glad it is all sorted out and I am glad he did hear me, I was worried, so if I have done something to help him, then that is good.'

'Where are you?' she asks.

We are on the way to see our cousin and then we have had to change our flights to home, so we are leaving early. Why?' I ask.

'Just wondering,' she says. 'Sandy I just wanted to say thank you. We all know how much you love him, to walk away and leave him just to protect him, that is honourable.'

'No it isn't, it was stupid. I should have just told Simone to go fuck herself and tell him what she said, but I was so scared what she was saying was true. Anyway we have to go we are nearly at our destination. Take care Wilma.'

I hang up. We still have a few hours left, so I confirm our hotel reservation again and confirm our cab to pick us up and confirm our flights in a few days. Luckily, no one knows where Roger lives as we never got to discuss this part of our holiday. I will be left alone.

I doze off and when I wake up I hear that we are arriving at Delaware.

'Come on Michael this is us.'

We wait till the train stops get off and go to the cab. He is a lovely man, he drives us to the hotel where we check in and go to our room, have a quick snack, shower and go to bed. Tomorrow is another day and tomorrow we see our relos.

I wake up to ringing in my ear. I am so confused where I am, the room is dark, I turn over and see Michael is still asleep, what time is it I think, I look at the clock on the side table it is 6 am, who is calling me this early. I look at my phone and it is Bryce. Phew, Okay here goes.

'Hello,' I say quietly.

'Sandy, It's me are you there?

'Yeah, hang on for a sec,' I whisper, 'Michael is still sleeping.'

I open the door and walk onto the balcony. 'Hey what is up?' I ask.

'I just wanted to talk to you, I wanted to tell you I don't hate you, I forgive you and I am in the process of getting Amy full time and it is all down to you, before you say anything, I just wanted to tell you my lawyers and I confronted her and she first denied everything, then we went through her phone messages to you and saw what she said, she couldn't deny it. So she has been charged with threatening me and you. She has been advised to drop all charges against us, she has been warned to drop the court cases and to sign parental rights to me. Sandy we did it, you did it.'

'Bryce, I don't think it is right she loses Amy full time, she is still her mum, she still has a right to see her daughter. You need to fix that, you need to go to share custody, it is best for Amy, but you get them to put it in a court order that she can't threaten you or take you to court again.'

'Okay honey I will,' he then says, 'where are you? I will come to you, we need to talk about things, to sort out what we want.'

'Bryce I am with my cousin, how about I call you tonight or tomorrow, you need to sort out everything over there and then we can talk Okay?

'Baby I need to see you,' he says.

'I gotta go honey, Michael is awake, speak soon.' I hang up.

I am happy that he has it sorted out, I am glad that we are talking and I am glad he doesn't hate me. I hate me for all the pain I caused. But at least he can get it all sorted and be happy, that is all I have ever wanted for him to be happy. I turn my phone on silent, but before I do I block Bryce so he can't call, no matter what he says, I know the pain I caused him and I can't be involved anymore, the more I speak to him, the more I want to see him and I know in my heart that if I see him, I know I won't be able to leave again and that I have to do. My life is in Australia, my home is there, my family are there, my job is there, Michael's friends are there, his school. I can't just up and leave it all for a man. A man that no matter what he is saying and I so want to believe him I just can't. I look at my phone, should I block him, I am not a child surely we can still be friends, so I unblock him, then I block him again, I put my phone down, I am awake now so I go in the shower and get ready, by the time I come out I have decided, I will unblock him, it isn't his fault of what happened, it was my fault, I should have the decency to just be an adult and speak to him, I just won't call him, he can call me. Done. That's it no more changes.

By the time Michael wakes up we have to go and see Roger. I am so excited, thanks to Facebook we found out we had cousins in America and if it wasn't for that I wouldn't of come to the states and I wouldn't of met Bryce and fallen in love, OMG, I fell in love, now I know what this pain is, it is a broken heart, I have finally found my forever man and I can't be with him. Oh my goodness life is so unfair, just when I found the man I want to spend the rest of my life with, the man I want to see first thing every morning and the last man at night, it can't happen. I just sit and stare out the balcony.

'Mum, MUM,' I hear.

I turn Michael is looking at me. 'Are we going or what?

'Oh damn yes of course we are baby, sorry just thinking, I know strange and very odd but I do that sometimes', and laugh.

We arrive at Rogers. Oh gosh, the place is huge, the house is surrounded by tall and beautiful trees, flowers and lush green everywhere, we hop out the car go to the back get all the presents out and go to the door. Just as we are about to knock, the door fly's open. 'CUZ I hear', and I am in a big bear hug.

'Hey Rog.' I hug back. No one in my family has ever been so friendly, as kids, we never got hugs and kisses from our parents and that's why I am so loving to my boy. We were never told we were loved but only knocked about being fat and ugly and dumb. No one will ever love you because you're so fat I was told all the time, not just from my grandmother but my dad, I know he loved me and my sister but he was always saying I would never find love if I had a fat ass. But here now my cousin is hugging me.

'Hey Rog, I can't breathe LOL.'

He pulls away. 'Come in and meet the family, we are all so happy to have you both here, shame Louise couldn't come,' he says.

'I agree but she had to stay with Mum and was happy to watch my place,' I say. I add, 'once I get back she is unaware but she is flying over as soon as we get home, my treat, I have changed flights and as we are going home early I was able to use the points and the money for her to fly over. So she will be here in a week. I just haven't told her.' He looks at me amused and laughs. 'Boy Oh boy, you are so going to be in trouble', and we both laugh.

Michael and I go inside meet his wife, Shannon and the kids, they show us around their home and then we sit down and talk.

'So Sandy,' Roger says, 'tell me about this man of yours, I have seen the news, is it true you are dating Bryce Johnston?' I stare and go red and then I start to cry. 'Oh man,' he says, I didn't want to upset you, what is wrong? Shit Shannon,' he says, 'grab some tissues, Sandy are you Okay?' He looks at me with so much concern, I start to shake and cry but look at his concern and start to laugh, man I look like a basket case. Michael puts his headset on, watches his tablet and completely ignores me. I look at Rog and Shan and tell them the whole story, by the time I have finished I have drunk three glasses of wine on an empty stomach and feel quite drunk, my limit is a half of glass!

'WOW that has been an interesting two weeks,' they say, 'and what is happening now?'

'I have no idea,' I say. 'We are here for a few days, he doesn't know where we are, but says he wants to call and talk to me, I just don't know what to do. I have made so many mistakes in the past two weeks, but I know deep in my heart that I love him and always will. I will never not love him and will always watch out for him but at the moment I know I have to walk away and forget about him. I have removed all of my links to him on Facebook, twitter, Instagram and You Tube, I won't be able to see what is happening in his life and maybe, just maybe I can get over him,' I say.

They look at each other then look at me. 'Sandy let me say this, once you fall in love, and it is real love you can't just turn off that love. Trust me,' Cousin Roger says, 'I have been married a few times and when you find that true forever love, it lingers in you always.' I just stare.

'I, I just have to believe that one day I can. It can't happen Roger, he is famous, he is an A-list actor, he lives in LA, I live in Melbourne Australia, everyone knows who he is, no one really cares who I am. He is gorgeous in and out, I am a fat smurf, he couldn't love me, could he?'

He looks at me, then says, 'I saw a picture of you both at the premier, yes Cousin, he does love you, and you love him. It's the same way I look at my Shan.'

'Bugger, I think I am in trouble then.' We all laugh.

We spend the day together, I hand out all the presents, we cook, eat, drink and then what seems like forever my phone rings, I look at the time and realise we have been here all day and it is 8 pm, I focus as I am a bit drunk and see it is Bryce.

'Oh it's him,' I say. I answer the phone. 'Hello this is Sandy, whom am I speaking to?' and giggle.

'Sandy are you Okay? it's Bryce.'

Oh Bryce my darling, yep I am cool up, no honey problem.' I giggle. 'Just a little tipsy ha ha…'

'Okay,' he says, 'I think you are a bit too tipsy. Where are you? I will come and get you,' he says. I laugh.

'You can't me get, we are here and you are there,' I say.

'Honey where is here?'

'It is where we are,' I say.

'Sandy and where is there?' he asks.

'I am with my cousin in America', and laugh.

'Honey, answer me are you Okay? he says.

'Yep all good, me good, Michael is good, Rog and his Shan are good we are having a ball.'

I can hear he is getting a bit worried but I am so drunk I hang up. The phone rings again.

'Hello Sandy here.'

'Sandy, it's me where are you?

'I keep telling you gorgeous I am here and you are there. LOL.'

'Can I speak to your cousin?', and I hand the phone over to Roger.

'Hey man, how you going, Roger says.

'Hey Roger, Bryce here, is Sandy Okay? Well let's just say we have had lots of talks today, she is absolutely in love with you but feels that you can't be with her because of what she said and has happened, don't take this the wrong way dude but she is so drunk I have never seen anyone get drunk on three wines.

153

'Yeah,' says Bryce, 'she doesn't drink much, but she is generally good.

How much has she drunk exactly? he asks.

'Hang on. Shannon how much has Sandy drunk?'

'We have had two bottles but she has only eaten a couple of bits of biscuits plus she has been upset remember.' Bryce hears all the conversation.

'Hey Roger can I ask where you guys live? I want to come and see her.'

'We are in Delaware New Hampshire.'

'Oh,' he says. 'I can't get there probably till tomorrow. Can you watch out for her? I really need to see her and sort out everything.'

'Look man, I know you love her and she loves you,' Roger says, 'but she has been through so much and as her cousin I have to protect her, you need to sort out your shit with your ex and when it is all sorted then come see her, I haven't known Sandy for many years but what I know is she is a kind and beautiful person, she would never intentionally go out and hurt anyone or want to feel she has hurt the ones she loves, you need to give her time to be able to mention you without crying, every time your name comes up she was crying, she is hurt man.'

'Bryce just listens and then says, 'I appreciate what you are saying but I love her you are right with that and I am not going to lose her.'

'Well Bryce, I think you have to let her go and clear her mind, as they say if you love someone you have to let them go, if they come back they were meant to be if they don't it never was.'

154

'I just don't know,' says Bryce, 'I don't want to lose her. I love her, I know it has only been a couple of weeks but it feels like I have known her forever.'

;I get it,' says Roger, 'but let her sleep on it Okay.'

He gives his number to Bryce and says, 'Call me tomorrow, I will talk to her in the morning.'

He then gives the phone back to me. 'Hey honey how is it hanging,' I say.

'Sandy I have to go, but I want you to remember this I love you baby girl and I will always love you and we will get past this Okay,' he says.

Okay dokey, charlie brown love ya back', and hang up.

I feel so happy, I have no idea who I was talking to and go and find Roger and Shan.

'Okay guys we better go back to the hotel and get some sleep. Hey Roger, who was I talking to on the phone or was I dreaming.'

He looks at me, laughs. 'Man oh man, I will tell you later because you are drunk. Come on sugar let's get you back to your hotel and drives us back.'

Once at the hotel, I walk in the room and crash on the bed and fall asleep within seconds, I have no idea what has happened but when I wake up in the morning I have a horrible headache and feel so sick. I look at my mobile and it is dead. I get up and sway and fall back on the bed, Oh my god, I feel so crappy. I crawl to the table plug my phone in the charger and then fall asleep again. I am woken a couple of hours by Michael.

'Come on Mum, wake up, we have to go to see Roger again and this time Mum please don't have a drink.'

I look at him. 'I got drunk last night didn't I baby?

He looks at me and says, 'Yep and boy you were so funny when you were talking to Bryce, I felt so sorry for him but man it was funny.'

I get up look in the mirror and am horrified I look like a monster, make up everywhere, panda eyes and a red nose like Rudolph.

'Give me 30mins baby and we can go.'

By the time I have had a shower, got cleaned up and taken millions of headache tablets I feel like myself. I turn my phone on and there are heaps of messages. Most from Roger asking how I am feeling this morning, one from Bryce asking to call him. I call Rog and tell him all good on this end but plans have changed and we are trying to change our flights back home for ASAP.

He says, 'Just come over and we can talk.'

I agree and Michael and I go down stairs to get a cab back to Rogers'., I decide to stop at the shops to get an apology basket and flowers and anything else that will let them know I am so sorry for last night

We arrive at Rogers and he says, 'Well, someone looks a bit better today?'

'Thanks Cuz, I can't remember much about last night I don't normally drink and if I do two is my limit, I got drunk last night didn't I?' I ask.

'Yep, you certainly did and I hate to tell you this but Bryce called last night and let's say you spoke to him and he was worried about you, so I ended up talking to him,' he said.

'Oh no, I gasp. What happened after I spoke to him and you spoke to him?' I asked. 'Is he Okay?'

'Yes he is. I spoke to him for 20mins or so, I told him how you were, how you were feeling and that I knew you both love each other, I also said that he has to give you space to sort out your head and feelings and then I said that I feel you are both meant to be with each other, but he has sort out his things before he can move on with you.'

I am just staring at him and I move and give him a hug. 'Oh Roger thank you so much, I am so sorry about how I was last night, I have had all these feelings going through my head and all I want to do is go back to LA and be with him but in my mind I keep questioning it all, my feelings, his feelings, what it would mean for me to move here, could I get a job, would I live with him or have to get my own place, how would Michael feel about being here or would it mean I have to leave Michael in Australia to be here with Bryce. I can't do that, I can't leave my baby, that would be my only deal breaker,' I say.

'Sandy the one thing I can tell you is to follow your heart. I can tell you what I think as I know you and have spoken to him but above all it is your life and you have to do what is best for both of you, Bryce and the kids. Don't let his ex-cause any problems, if you both love each other you can both overcome everything. That is what a real relationship is about,' he says.

'Yes I know, in good and bad times,' I say. 'Good times are easy but if you can stick with each other through the bad times it makes your relationship,' I say.

'So change of discussion, what do you want to do today, are you happy to go on a tour of our area, how long are you both staying here?' Roger asks.

I take a deep breath, exhale and then say, 'Tour yes, not sure how long, it depends on if Bryce knows where we are and I will have to make up my mind really quickly too. The thing is, we are booked into the hotel for two more days and I am waiting for confirmation of the flights, I know we were originally going to stay for two weeks here but the longer we stay here the longer we annoy you, the longer we may be found out and the longer it means I will want to go back and see him. So the answer to your question is we will probably be leaving in three days, so that makes it Friday. Is that Okay if we hang for a couple of more days?' 'Absolutely,' he says. 'Okay let's get ready to go on tour of my home town.'

Roger, Michael, Shan and myself climb into their car and off we go. I can't believe how beautiful it is here.

'We saw online through Google earth what a beautiful serene place it is here,' I say, 'but being here wow it is stunning. I could live here so easily and it would be perfect at Christmas with all the snow.'

'It can be nice particularly on Christmas Eve and Christmas day but it takes a lot of work, I have to shovel the snow every morning but yes it is nice too,' he says.

'One day cuz, I want to come back and have a white Christmas and maybe New Year's eve in NY. That is my ultimate dream but I think it maybe a long time coming after this trip.'

'Well Sandy you don't know what the future will hold,' 'Yeah true. Very true. I may win tattslotto and can travel the world.'

We go through town, we see all the sights, we stop for lunch at this restaurant in the hills and as we are taken to our table I see the view.

'OMG what a view, Bryce would love it here, it reminds me of his place in Reno. Hey guys, let's take a picture for memories', and we all jump in and take a selfie.

I am trying to smile but all I think about is Bryce and wish he was here and just then my phone rings.

'Excuse me I have to take this call. Hey Jenny how is it going?'

'Hey Sandy just letting you know I was able to get you and Michael on an earlier flight but it is leaving tomorrow otherwise you will have to wait for another week,' she says.

'Tomorrow,' I quiz, 'what time is the flight?'

'You have to be at the airport by 6 pm for a 9 pm flight. It goes to NY then onto Sydney and then Melbourne, I was able to get you guys on it as there was a cancellation. Do you want to take it or not?' I look at everyone and then Michael and say, 'can I have 5mins to speak to Michael?' 'Sandy it is now or not, there is another couple wanting it, if you don't want it.'

Shit tomorrow, I think. 'Oh Okay yes book us on it. Is there a difference that I can put towards Louise's flight and accommodation?'

'Absolutely, I have worked it out and it will give her a better flight.'

'Good Jenny perfect. Send me the details and I will work it out. Thank you again. Jenny one more thing?'

'Yes,' she says.

'Have you heard from Bryce again since he came to Canada?'

'I have spoken to him but not seen him, he has been up and down but the good thing is he is sorting out everything, I know I shouldn't say this to you but he has asked me where you are staying and I didn't tell him so he spoke to your cousin yesterday,' she says.

'I know that Rog told me I got a little drunk and when he called Rog took the phone and spoke to him, but from my understanding he doesn't know exactly where we are and by the time he finds out we will be gone.' Jenny remains silent and then I say, 'Anyhow I better go we are having lunch thanks Jenny speak soon', and I hang up.

'Hey sorry about that, Michael we are flying out tomorrow night, we have to be at the airport at 6 pm they had a cancellation and it was either tomorrow or when we were meant to leave so I took tomorrow's flight, I hope that is Okay Rog, I know it was meant to be longer but with everything that has happened and I think it is best.'

He looks at me and says, "That is a real shame but I get it, do you think you will come back again?'

'I hope so cuz, I hope so.' We sit in silence and eat our meal. It is a lovely day, very warm and sunny but it is sad as it will be our last time with Roger and Shan. After all the years of wanting to meet I have selfishly made our trip shorter.

'I just want to say sorry about leaving earlier I hope you can understand, I know it has been a long time coming to get here but I just have to go earlier, I hope you don't mind,' I say.

Roger and Shannon look at me and say together, 'You do what is best for you, Okay. We can still Skype and talk and maybe we will see each other again, maybe you can come back soon and have that white Christmas with us all,' says Shannon.

'I would like that, I really would.'

We finish our meal and are driving back when I get a text, *Hey Sandy can you call me Ashley*. Ashley? That is Bryce's sister, well one of them. I call her straight away. 'Hey Ash, it's Sandy what's up?' I ask.

Are you guys coming back to LA soon? I need a favour,' she says.

'No, we aren't we are flying out sooner than expected why, is everything Okay?'

'I just am throwing a surprise party for mum and was hoping you guys could come as we all love you and mum does too.'

'I am sorry Ash, but we are leaving tomorrow and I can't afford to change the flights again.'

'Again?' she asks.

'Yes again, there was a cancellation and we had to take the flight otherwise we would have to stay for our original flight date.'

Are you sure you can't stay longer? I know it would be nice and Bryce would love to see you too,' she says.

'Ash please don't, I just can't plus between you and me, Bryce and I are no longer together.'

She gasps. 'What? He never said anything when I saw him yesterday.'

'I left on Sunday and flew to Canada, he flew up there and we had a talk, we have only just started talking again but we are not a couple anymore, not that I don't want to be with him but I know what is best for him regardless of what he thinks is best. Ash I love him and I always will but it has to be this way. That is all I can say. I have spoken to your mum and she knows everything but please can you accept my decision.'

'Of course I can,' she says. 'Sorry I just want it to be perfect for Mum.'

'I get that Ash, I really do but it has to be this way. But I hope you don't mind if I send something to her and call her on the day is that OK?' I ask.

'Yeah, Okay.'

'Anyway Ash I have to go, speak soon Okay.' She hangs up

Gosh this day is getting so hard, call after call, I feel so drained. I just want to run away, it can't get any harder can it. We finish our sweets and coffees, we all get up and start to drive back. It is very quiet in the car, I am enjoying the view of everything I see, I really could live here.

'Roger this is so gorgeous, I am so jealous. Again I am so sorry about this all.'

'All good, I understand.'

We get dropped off to the hotel as it is late, make plans for breakfast and say goodnight. As we walk in, the receptionist says that there are messages for me, I take them and then go upstairs to our room. I am totally flabbergasted as the messages are from Jenny and it says, *call me ASAP*. I get upstairs and call her.

'Hey, what is up?' I ask.

'Bryce has found out where you are and he says he wants to come and see you.'

'Seriously,' I say, 'how, what, when, why?'

'There was a photo taken today at the restaurant and someone put it online saying check out Bryce's girlfriend having lunch with family. He called me and confirmed it, he wants to fly out and see you, he said he has something urgent to tell you and ask you.'

'Oh shit, does he know where we are staying?' I ask.

'No, but he isn't flying out till tomorrow afternoon, by the time he fly's in you should be flying out. Do you want me to tell him what time you fly out so he doesn't waste his time?'

'Nah it's all good, I will call him and tell him, thanks Jenny, do me a favour I am sure he will cancel the flight. I will text you.'

I go back onto the balcony while Michael is in the shower and I call him. He answers on the second ring.

'Hey how are you?' I ask.

'Sandy I am good, I just wanted to tell you I am flying in tomorrow to see you we need to talk and I have to ask you something that is very important.'

'Bryce you can't fly in tomorrow, we are flying back home shortly, so you need to cancel the flight and save your money Okay.'

'You're going home early?' he asks.

'Yes, we have to I have to get back to work, there is an emergency and Michael has to get back for his competition with soccer and swim trials so I just wanted to call and tell you. This isn't a lie really, he really does have the comps, and I do need to get back to work but not for a week but he doesn't need to know that.'

'Oh,' he says, 'that is a shame honey. I really need to see you, when are you flying out, I will meet you at the airport and we can spend some time together before you fly out.'

'Honey we can't, you have Amy tomorrow and then you have work the next day.'

'Shit I do too.'

'Bugger, can I call you in the morning and talk to you then? he asks.

'Of course you can but if I don't answer just text me, I will have the phone on airplane mode when we fly. Bryce I just want to say this just in case we don't speak before I fly out. I want to thank you for everything, I want to tell you that the time we spent together was the best time of my life, except for having Michael. I always wanted to know what the real person was like and I have and I love, I love you so much and will always love you. I will always watch out for you and hope the best for you and Amy. I love your mum and your family and I think you are the most beautiful, perfect, wonderful, sexy, funny and adorable person I have ever met and I wish things could have been different. I hope you will one day forgive me and I hope you will understand.' He is about to say something and I interrupt. 'Oh look Honey I have to go, Michael needs me, speak soon', and I hang up before he can say anything. There done. I have said everything I need to say. I have told him how I feel and that I love him, it is done and dusted. I go back into the room, tell reception I am not in and if anyone asks we have checked out. We pack our bags and make sure everything is in them and go to bed, when we get up in the morning we will have breakfast with Rog and the family and then check in at the airport and then fly home.

I am not looking forward to it but the good thing is it will be over soon, I will be home and this will be just a memory. I can hear my phone vibrating so I know it is him but I can't answer it, I look at my phone and sure enough it was him, I turn my phone off and finally go to sleep.

If you think I slept well no, all I did was turn around and think, I seriously didn't think I could think anymore, my brain would surely hurt, so I would turn over, close my eyes and sleep would not come. I look through my photos and videos on my phone with us together in LA, at the lake, in his house, the kids playing, us in the backyard and on our walks. I see for the first time how much I loved him. Loved him. Do I still love him? Absolutely. I will love him till the day I die. I know when I get back home, he will forget about me, give it a couple of days and then he will get with a skinny blonde or a model or both. That is his prerogative, nothing to do with me. I will be the fan again, watching from afar, watching his Instagram feed, twitter, Facebook, anywhere I can see him and he can't see me watching. I get up, walk to the balcony, go outside and look at the sky. God I know I don't talk much and when I do I tend to ask for something, but I do need to ask for 2 more things and I promise I will always try to continue being a kind and forgiving person. Please, PLEASE help me get over Bryce, I can't take this wanting, this pain of missing him, please let me get on with my life and Please, help him get everything he wants, he is such a beautiful person, not just looks, but he is beautiful inside too. Please look after him, please make sure he stays as perfect as he is and finds love, he deserves so much, he deserves to be looked after for once in his life, he deserves to find true love, someone who will be there for him and Amy, someone who won't judge him, won't use him and will love him unconditionally. That is all I want. I want him to be happy forever. Please protect him, Amy and his family. I start to feel tears fall down my face but I know that god will help me with this request. I know that Bryce will get his ever after. I don't need anything but my son. I sit on the chair and watch the sunrise. I grab my phone and go to delete all my pictures and videos of us, but before I do I stop and move it to a folder. I can't just wipe him from my life, he is part of my past and what a wonderful past it has been. I will never forget it.

I have been sitting there for so long, I don't hear Michael getting up and coming to the door.

Morning Mum, did you sleep at all?' he asks.

'A little bub, but it is all good. Let's get ready and go see Rog and the family and we are going home today. Are you happy?' I ask.

'I am Mum but I am not,' he says.

Why? I was hoping we could go and see Bryce and his family one more time, he promised to take me water skiing and fishing.'

'Oh baby,' I say. 'I am sorry but we can't we fly out tonight but the good thing is you can always call him, I am sure he won't mind Okay.'

He looks at me. 'Is that Okay with you though?'

'Of course baby, just because we aren't together anymore doesn't mean you can't speak to him. I would never get in your way Okay.' He seems to accept that, goes inside and starts to get ready.

We spend the day with Rog and the family and by the time it starts to get dark, the cab is here to take us to the airport.

'Roger I just want to say to all of you, thank you so much for all you guys have done for us, I wish it could have been longer but as usual I stuffed up and plans had to change, but the good thing is we finally got to meet and one day we will come back and if not myself maybe Michael. Louise will be here in a week so that will be good. She can stay as long as she wants as I have paid for everything for her. But just one thing, if anyone calls to ask about us just say no comment, Okay,' I say.

'Of course Cuz, have a safe flight back home. Let us know when you get home. Will speak to you on Skype.'

I hug him, his kids and the family, we get in the cab and we drive to the airport.

'How long till we get to the airport?' I ask the driver.

'About an hour Miss.'

'Thanks.'

We look out the windows but it is dark and I can't see much, just the moon coming up and the darkness. My phone vibrates and I look at it and see it is his mum.

'Hey Wilma, how are you going?' I ask.

'Hey Sandy, where are you guys?' She asks.

'On the way to the airport as we are flying out shortly. Why?' I ask.

'Just wondering,' she says.

Wilma, can I ask you something, honestly and please don't tell anyone what I am asking?'

'Okay Sandy. What is it Sweetheart?' she says.

Firstly, is Bryce Okay? And Amy? Can you please look after him, I want him to be so happy and get his happy ever after,' I say.

She takes a deep breath. 'Honestly, he is so hurt, he says he knows that you love him and he loves you but he doesn't know why you are not talking to him.'

'I did talk to him,' I say. 'I spoke to him yesterday,' I say, 'I told him I love him but I can't stay,' I say.

'Is it because of his ex?'

'Yes it is, I want him to not lose anything or Amy. I have said all this before over and over but then if I keep saying it maybe I will believe it too. Also, I am so confused and shocked as I can't believe I have met him and all of you, the last two and a bit weeks have been a dream come true, well apart from hurting Bryce but between you and me, I have found the love of my life, but I have to go, I have to walk away so he gets everything. Honestly, if his fans sees him with someone like me, they would go against him, it could destroy his career, I would hate myself if that happened to him.'

'Sandy, you have to listen to me, it won't happen they will see how much you both love each other, how happy he is, I know my son and he loves you and doesn't care what anyone thinks, all I know is you are being stubborn, I understand what you are saying but I still think you should tell him.'

'Oh Wilma, I just can't now, I am so sorry. I hope you don't hate me, I hope we can stay in contact as I value your opinion and understand what you are saying, but I have to do this, I have to do it this way. I hope you can understand?'

'Sandy OK,' she says.

Oh Wilma we have to go we have to go check in. I will speak to you when we get home. Please say goodbye to everyone for me and tell Bryce, tell him, ok here goes, tell him I will love him to the moon and back and beyond the universe and I hope he finds his true love and is forever happy.' I say goodbye and hang up.

So here we are, we are at the airport, we have checked in and we are waiting to board, Michael is watching his tablet, I am listening to my music on my phone and as I look around I see all these couples together, kissing, holding hands and leaning into each other. Oh how it would be good if I didn't have to go home, if life was like a movie, that Bryce and I would be together forever, that we would love each other forever that I could stay here and be with him. I would've moved here to be with him, I would have given up my life in Australia to stay with him. But it wasn't to be. If only life was like the movies, if only.

'Ladies and Gentlemen welcome to gate 12, flight 718 is now boarding for Melbourne Australia. Please make your way to the gate, thank you for flying with Qantas.'

'Come on Mate, let's go,' I say.

Well the time is here, we slowing make our way to the gate, board onto the plane and have 21 hours of flying, the good thing is I should get some sleep I haven't slept properly for days.

We settle into our seats, thank goodness it isn't at the back but near the middle of the plane. I put my bag under the seat and lean into my seat, every time I close my eyes I see his blue eyes, his beautiful smile, I hear his laughter, gosh I have it bad. Give it time, give it time. I look at the movies and what is on, yep one of his movies, even the plane hates me. I laugh, put my headset on, plug my charger in and go to sleep.

'Mum wake up, its breakfast time, food is here.'

I open my eyes, food is in front of me. I feel so sick,

'Oh baby I can't eat, I feel so sick.'

I ask the stewardess to take the food away and ask for a Pepsi max, water and a cup of tea. I just can't stomach food. That is the whole flight, I just can't stomach food, I feel so sick, if I didn't know better I would say I was pregnant but women in their 50s and menopausal don't fall pregnant, it is just love sickness. The flight goes on and on, and what seems like years, we finally arrive back in Melbourne. Home, we are home. I feel a sudden relief but also sadness as I won't ever see Bryce again in the front of me, I will never look into his gorgeous blue eyes, see him smile, the way his eyes light up and he gets these adorable creases in the corner of his eyes, the way he laughs, so perfect, feel his hand in mine, feel him next to me in bed or on the couch, lean into him or just be in

169

the same country as him. I miss him more and more the further away I get from him. I keep saying to myself it is for the best, I had to go or he would have lost everything important to him. This is the best thing for him and then I hear in my head, but is it really? Oh shut up will you I think. God now I am talking to myself and arguing and bet I will lose the fight.

As we come out of customs we see Louise, I walk to her say hi and start to break down. Of course being my older sister she says,' 'Grow the fuck up and get over yourself, enough is enough, you decided to come home early, you decided to act on your feelings and you decided to listen to his ex, so stop crying and grow the fuck up! Just what everyone needs is common sense.'

'Okay,' I say. I turn my phone on and yep there are messages there. 'Crikey,' I say. I look at my phone, show it to Louise and she rolls her eyes.

'You need to speak to them, you need to call him or block him.'

'I can't, I just can't, plus he is probably just saying that it is all sorted and he wants to say thanks for pissing off.' 'Well, then call him.'

I stare at her. 'Yeah, I will eventually.' Knowing I won't, not for a while, plus I have to go back to work in a week, so that gives me time to listen to the messages and forget about him. But I know deep in my heart I will never forget him or stop loving him but maybe one day I will be able to talk to him. This will be my motto from now on. One Day. One Day!

We pull into my driveway and I don't recognise it.

'What the fuck is going on here?' I ask.

'Oh that,' Louise says. 'Bryce paid for the house to be upgraded and fixed, it looks good doesn't it?' She asks.

'How? When? Why didn't you tell me? This isn't my home anymore it is his,' I say.

'Sandy he just got it fixed a bit, I told him about it and he organised it to be painted and fixed inside a bit, it was just finished yesterday.'

'What am I going to do?'

'Just go in and look at it, it isn't that much but trust me it looks fantastic.'

I open the door, it has been painted, there is no mould smell or locked up smell, the couch has been replaced with this gorgeous slim line but stunning couch, the lounge and kitchen is now open planned and the kitchen is stunning, my bedroom has doubled in size and there is a en suite, Michael's room has been doubled as well, the bathroom is massive, we go into the backyard and there is a swimming pool with the spa and the backyard is immaculate.

'It is nothing,' I yell, 'far out, he has spent heaps on this place, I have to call him and tell him I will sell and give him back his money, I can't accept this Louise.'

'Mum, look at my room it is enormous, OMG, this is fantastic, Mum the pool, OMG I love it,' he says.

Great now every time I look at this place I will think of him.

'Mate, yeah it is good.'

Michael goes into the pool after stripping his clothes off and jumps in his jocks. I laugh, sit down and say, 'I have to speak to him don't I?'

'Yep,' Louise says, 'but be strong.'

I look at my phone and realise it is too late over there, so I text him.

Hey honey, just want to say thank you for what you have done to my place, I wish you hadn't of as I now have to work out how much it was and how I can pay you back. Honey, I will pay you back sooner than later, I will sell the place and send you the money. Please don't think I am ungrateful as I am not, I appreciate it but I would never want to use you, I love, I love it and I wish you the best future ever, always and forever your friend Sandy xxx. Sent. Done it is done. I put my phone down and we sit there for a while and relax.

'So, how was the trip apart from the romance bit?' Louise asks.

'Oh it was fantastic, we had so much fun. I have so many souvenirs, so many pictures. I got to drive the fire truck with Bryce, we all went on the lake and I actually went on water skis, I fell off but I had a ball. Louise it was wonderful, I would move over there tomorrow if I could be with him but I know I can't.'

'Oh and you are flying out in three days too.' She looks at me WTF.

'Yeah, the money I saved I have booked a flight for you, you are going to Graceland, NASA and to see Rog. I have put money into your account too for spending money and I have booked a trip to the falls too. So go home and get packed.'

She just stares at me. 'Why?'

'You deserve it,' I say, 'I saved so much staying with him, even leaving money for him and paying for things and shortening my trip I saved enough to send you. So say thank you and enjoy.'

'Thanks and wow.'

I have done something good, I may not be a nice person but I have done something good for my sister. Now to sort out my life and I will be a happy little camper.

Louise goes and we unpack our bags, I still can't believe this is my home, it is so much bigger.

'Mum look at my room I can run around and I have so much space, it is amazing.'

'Yeah mate, it looks good.'

'Mum, you're not even looking,' he says.

'Yes, I am Mate, it looks good,' I say.

'Then, why are you still in your room staring at the wall?' he asks.

Busted. 'Sorry Mate, I just have a lot on my mind, what do you want to do tonight and tomorrow? Do you want to just relax at home tonight and tomorrow how about we go some shopping? We need to get some food and maybe a dog or another cat?'

'Can we Mum, can we get a dog?'

Oh shit. Big mouth. 'Of course honey, let's do it but it has to get on with Sparkie (he is my cat, he is my 12yo cat who has been with me through everything and is sleeping comfortably on my bed) and Pastel (our 2yo cat) and Nugget our rabbit.'

I sit next to him, pat him and then he curls onto my lap, isn't it funny how pets know when you need comfort or love. It seems I have been sitting there for ages as the next minute it is dark in my room, Michael is on the PS4 chatting to his friends and I am just sitting in the same spot I was when we got home.

'Michael, do you want something to eat baby?'

'Nah Mum all good I ate before, ya brought something over.'

Oh good Mate. Great Mum I am. I forgot to feed my son, Oh bugger I have to feed Sparkie, Pastel and Nugget. My brain is like a sieve, but it will take time. That is going to be my motto. It will take time. Love takes time. My heart will heal and I will be surviving this. It is heartache and I can literally feel my heart break in two but que sera, it will get better one day. I feed them, lie on my bed for a minute and fall asleep. I wake up and the house is silent, I look at the clock and it shows 4 am, I go looking for Michael and he is fast asleep in his bed. I walk to the kitchen to get a drink of water and grab my mobile that is in my bag on the table, am I game to look at it and hear the messages? I know I have to do it, I know it is like a band aid, rip it off and don't dally. I turn it on and there are ten messages, and there are voicemails. I listen to the voicemail first.

'Hey Sandy it's Wilma, just wondering if you are still in the US, I have a favour well another favour to ask if you can, call me.'

'Hey Sandy Mel here, Mum has been trying to call you, can you call me back it's urgent?'

'Hey Sandy Honey it's me.' I hang up. Ok I can hear the ones that are not him. God he sounds gorgeous. I call it again and this time I listen. 'Hey Sandy honey it's me, we need to talk, are you still with your cousin? Can you call me please, Mum and I and the family are worried about you, we haven't heard from you.' 'Hey honey it's me again, I am getting worried please call.' 'Sandy it's me, why aren't you answering, are you still in the US?'

'Hey Sandy its Jenny, Bryce has called me a few times asking if you are still in the US he is panicking as he hasn't heard from you, I am assuming you made it on the plane, is it Okay to tell him you went home.' 'Sandy Jenny again, not sure if you did get home you said you would let me know.' 'Honey it's me, I can hear him crying softly, sweetheart please talk to me, I know you said what you said on the phone, I saw the message on the phone so I assume you have got home, but why didn't you call to tell me, why didn't you call to say goodbye, I miss you baby, call me. I know you're in Australia but please honey call me. I need to talk to you. I will let Mum and everyone know you went home. Are you Okay?'

Done, the messages have been heard and will be put away so I don't hear them again. I look at my phone, it is 5am. We are 18 hrs ahead which makes it 10 am in LA. I call his mum.

'Hello Wilma here.'

'Hey Wilma, it's Sandy.'

'Where are you? Did you really go home and not say goodbye to everyone?' She asks.

'Yes I did. But remember I did tell you I had a flight home when we last talked as I had to get home earlier for work.'

'Oh yeah you did,' she says, but I thought when you said you were going home that you had changed your mind and was coming back home to Bryce's.'

'No Wilma, I meant my home, I go back to work on Wednesday so I had to fly in earlier. What's up?' I ask. 'You said it was urgent.'

'It is all sorted, I needed to check on something for you but I just guessed. When are you coming back to the US? I was hoping you would be here for my birthday but obviously you won't be here in a few days again.'

'No sorry Wilma I don't think I will, my budget has taken a hit, but thank you for the offer. I have sent a present for you to Bryce's so just ask him to give it to you when it arrives.'

'Oh you didn't have to do that,' she says.

'I know but it was something I saw and knew you would like it. So when you speak to him please ask him to give it to you on your birthday, Okay,' I say.

'Sandy can I ask you something? And I want the absolute truth,' she asks.

'I will always tell the truth Wilma except the one time that I lied to Bryce as I thought I was doing the right thing.'

'Do you really love my son, wholeheartedly?'

'Yes I do, with my whole being, I will love him to the end of my life and then beyond, between you and me, I would love him even if I never met him but meeting him, spending time with him, Amy and all of you I knew it wouldn't last, I knew I would have had to leave and come home and I knew it was going to be hard but not this hard. I look everywhere I see him, I look in the sky I see his eyes, I hear a song, I see his smile, I see him everywhere and I don't know what to do, he isn't mine, he doesn't love me or want to be with me, it was all in my head. I believed the fairy tale, I believed the lies, I was hooked line and sinker.'

'What do you mean he doesn't love you?' she asks.

'I told you what was said between myself and Simone, I see how much she loves him still, she is fighting for her man and her daughter, I could never come between a family. Plus it wasn't just Simone. There were comments online about what a pity he was with me at the premier, that he could do better with a whale. Then his friends said he could never love me, as I am not anywhere near his league, that he just feels

176

sorry for me, that he was in a bad space and that once I leave which should be sooner than later he will go out with Kate.'

'Kate? who is Kate?' She asks.

'His co-star from the movie, and they are working together on the next one apparently and she would call him all the time, so I guessed it was her he wanted to be with.' 'Oh Sandy, I think you have your wires crossed. Kate is engaged to Matt, Bryce and her are friends and he was helping her with the surprise for Matt's birthday.'

'Oh,' I say. 'Bugger but his friends said he could never love me.'

'Why would they say that if it wasn't true.'

'Well that is something you have to ask them.'

'But I will tell you this just once, I have never seen my son so happy, not even when he was with Simone, he was always smiling, laughing, he always was cheerful and that is because of you. Only you, you made him happy, truly happy.' Oh. What else can I say?'

'Oh well it is too late now, he will be fine Wilma. He will find someone who is better suited for him and his lifestyle, he will only remember me as a crazy fan that got too close.' I think again.

'You have it wrong Sandy, but you need to speak to him eventually.'

'I will but not now if Okay, Michael is awake, I will speak soon. Take care bye.' I hang up.

Shit could it be true, could what she is saying be true. I just don't know who to believe, I could call Christy but would she tell me the truth or what she thinks I want to hear, she has always been honest to me. I just don't know anymore, I am totally lost....

'Mum, I am hungry what is for breakfast.'

'Coming mate.'

I feed him, we get dressed and we go out. It is good to be home, but I miss Bryce so much, we were only away for three weeks but the time I spent with him seemed like a lifetime. It was like we had known each other for ages, it was like coming home. I really could see myself coming home day after day to him, having him there with me all the time. Jeepers woman I think stop, just stop.

We do our shopping, walk around the shops and just look at everything that we haven't seen for ages. It's funny, while we were away I hardly went up the shops, I was happy to just be with Bryce and Amy, we spent so much time together and I know eventually it will be all good memories, it is now. Suddenly, I look up and see people pointing towards Michael and myself, I look behind me and think it is the person behind me and I keep walking towards Kmart. 'Hey Sandy.'

I turn around and I see a few people coming towards me, 'Can you please sign this for us?'

I just stare what are they talking about, they thrust a magazine in my face, on the cover there is Bryce and myself at the premier, I turn the pages and there are pictures of us together in LA at the beach, the shops.

I just stare and say, 'Ummm why?'

'Aren't you his girlfriend?' one of them asks.

'God no. But whoever is his girl would be one lucky duck. But thank you for the compliment, he would never be with a norm like me, I think you have me mistaken.'

I start to walk away.

'We know it is you just sign the fucking mag.'

I turn and am about to tell them what they can do and decide to keep my mouth shut and walk on. We go to Kmart and buy what is needed, by the time we come out there are more people out of the shop, security are holding them back from entering Kmart and as Michael and I walk out they surround us and help us leave. God this is crap, I am not with him why won't they just leave us alone I think. We go to our car, drive off and think how lucky we are, it is just a few skanks who think they know all about me, it will die down and get back to normal soon.

We go past Sandy and Ray to say hi, tell them about our trip and then decide to go home and relax. I call work when I get home to see if they need me back earlier, I am told to relax and to see them in two weeks, unless I want to come back, I say, 'I will see you tomorrow.'

'No, come back on Monday then not a day earlier, work isn't going anywhere.' And then I am left alone at home with Michael. What am I going to do for the rest of the week, if I am doing nothing I am thinking and it is a dangerous thing to do, think. I call the stadium to see if there are any shifts and they say there are some on Friday and the weekend so I only have two days of thinking. Great.

'Hey Michael do you want to go to the movies or out for dinner?'

'Nah Mum I am happy to stay home.'

'OK honey, I am going to go for a walk, do you want to come or should I drop you off to Omi's?'

'Can I go to Omi's?

'Okay baby.'

So, that is what I do. Michael goes to Mum's, I go for a walk, I put my headphones on, and just walk, one minute I am near home, the next thing is I am at the beach, wow, I have walked 10kms, Oh well, I will keep walking for a bit then turn around, at least it is a nice day and I haven't been hassled. I am enjoying my walk when my phone rings, without looking at it I answer.

'Hello Sandy speaking.'

'Hey baby it's me, how are you?' Shit it's Bryce.

'Sorry I can't hear you.' Yeah good one, he will believe that one! 'Hello, hello are you there I can't hear you, if you can hear me it is windy and I can't hear you I will call you back, hello, hello…' I disconnect. You bad girl, very naughty, another lie. I can't keep doing that. It isn't fair. I decide then to block his number. There now he won't call me he will think my number has been changed. Finally, peace and quiet.

By the time I get home, I have been gone for 3hrs. Michael and Louise are at my place and I walk in.

'Hey guys. What's up?'

'How long do you think you were going to be?' she asks. 'As long as I want to. By the way you are not my mother so just don't tell me what to do Okay.'

'Enough is enough, now go pack your bag, you are leaving tomorrow.'

'I am sorry for getting upset Louise I just blocked him, he called and I pretended I couldn't hear him.'

'I think you should unblock him, it isn't fair on him, you need to make peace with him, you can't keep hiding from him.' Shit does she have to seriously make sense. So, I unblock him again. Gosh, I am so childish. I know in my heart I love him. You can't love someone and then act like this. I just have to learn to get on with my life, without him in my life, without seeing him, talking to him, holding him. I really never have felt this way, I really have never been truly in love before, all my other relationships including Michael's dad was a lead up to this, everlasting forever love and I went and screwed it all up. I had to go and fall in love with a dream, a celebrity, someone who is totally out of my league, Oh well such is life.

So this is my life now, Michael and I have a few days left before I have to go to back to work, but do I really want to? But that is the life of a norm, working to pay the bills, to ensure my son has all he wants, well best to my ability.

'Hey Michael, what do you want to do for the next few days?' I ask.

'Not much Mum, I just want to stay home and play my games.'

'Oh ok Honey.'

Now what should I do. Maybe I should write a story about what happened when we went overseas, like a diary. They say that when you write things down it takes all the desires away. Yeah that should be good for me.

So here goes, laptop open. It was meant to be the trip of a lifetime with my son, I had all the plans organised for the US. The trip was going well until a jerk decided to bang right into me, great start of a trip, but what a cutie and also I shouldn't be so nasty and yell at him. No, I can't, all I see is his face. Okay, it was a trip of a lifetime, flying to the US to show Michael what a beautiful world we live in, just don't mention him and it will be Okay. But everything about the US now makes me think of him. I delete it all. I have been sitting here for hours and all I have is the title. The trip of a lifetime! Yep it sure was, it will never be replicated, I have been changed forever.

'Michael I am going for a walk, do you want to come?'
'No Mum, I will stay here.'

'Okay honey.' Won't be long.

This is better, I put on my headset and start listen to my music, I have everything there, Christmas carols, Elvis, Whitney, Southern sons, Mariah, Soundtracks and Bryce's music. I can do this. I keep walking and walking. It is good to be back home but I wish I wasn't, I wish I was back in the US. For goodness sake, this is ridiculous, maybe I just have to wipe everything about him from my world. I go to delete his music, my hand is hovering over the delete button….. I can't, I love his music, it has helped me through so much, it would be like deleting a part of my heart. I will skip past till I can hear it, that is better. I start to listen to Kelly Clarkson's Wrapped in Red, never too early for Christmas carols...LOL and my phone rings.

'Hello this is Sandy.'

'Hey Sandy it's Wilma.' Gulp and deep breath. 'Hey Wilma, how are you all going?'

'Good, just wanted to see how you guys are going.'

'Yep all good here, I go back to work on Monday, so that will be good, it will take my mind off everything. So what has been happening over there, any good news?' I ask. 'Yeah, all great here except Bryce is missing you both.'

'Oh Wilma, we both know he really isn't, but thank you so much for trying. I know that he is happy with Simone and if not her, there are all those girls hanging around, it was on the net yesterday. He looks happy and I am happy for him. You and I know that the feelings I had for him was one sided,

182

that although he said what he said it was just a fun thing for him, but me, It was…It was, god can I say this…It was real for me. I have never felt this way before and I never will again, but now I am home and I have to get on with my life. I will always love him, I will always want the best for him, his happiness is my priority and I know he is happy and always will be. So that is all I need to know.'

'Are you sure about how he feels Sandy?'

'Yes, it wasn't just Simone who told me but it was all his other friends too. I told you this before.'

'Yes you did,' she says, 'but were those friends girls or did Christy tell you?'

'It was all the girls,' I said, 'but it doesn't mean it wasn't the truth. I also saw on the net that he was in Reno with all those girls, so I know he is Okay. I have to just get over him and I will be fine.

Wilma, please don't tell him how I feel. I don't want to be a laughing stock with him, I feel bad as it is, I don't want him to think I am a freak or a loser, so please just keep what we are saying between us Okay?'

'I will try,' she says.

'That is the best I can ask for at least.'

'When are you coming back to the States? she asks.

'I don't think I will, it costs a lot of money and it took ages to save, so I don't think I will ever be able to afford it but in my heart I am over there now. Anyway I better go Wilma I have so much to do. Take care, give my love to everyone. Keep in contact if you want', and I hang up.

God I think, they say if you keep talking to your passed loved ones that they give you an answer, I look up to the clouds and speak out loud, 'Hello dad, helllllooo help, I need your opinion, is he thinking of me and love me?'

'Nope,' I hear, 'you are better to be home.'

Is that my subconscious or is it dad. God I am so confused. I am 53yrs old, totally in love with an celebrity who is A list and I will never see or feel him again and yet he is still in my heart and thoughts. God help me now, I can't do this anymore. Nope, still nothing. What is it, not even my own subconscious is helping, lost cause. So I keep walking, I notice it is getting dark and have no idea where I am, my phone is ringing.

'Mum, where the hell are you?' Michael yells.

'Firstly, don't speak to me like that bub and I have no idea, I have been walking, um hang on.' I look up and realise I am now at the end of Hall road near the freeway, near maccas at the freeway. 'Give me an hour baby and I will be home. I will just turn around and come home.'

I keep walking and walking and realise I am near the shops again, I really need to get home, god I love Melbourne, it is June but it is still nice weather, well it's a bit cold, but always good for a walk. I have to get over him, think of it as a dream, think of it as not really happening, he is in US, I am in Australia. We are 1,000s of kms away and I can guarantee he isn't thinking of me. I go through my contacts to see who I can call, Carla, it rings and goes to voicemail, Shane it rings and goes to voicemail, Mel it rings and goes to voicemail, I even call Mum and it goes to voicemail. God I wish dad was alive still, he would help me, he would tell me it will be Okay. Michael calls and asks if I can bring maccas for dinner, I laugh, by the time I bring it, it will be cold. Tomorrow OK.

I eventually get home, feed him and check with Louise about her flight for the morning, I have to drive her to the airport for her 2 pm flight, so Michael and I can hang in town after. I turn the TV on and guess who is on every channel, Bryce, come on be fair I scream inside, I turn the TV off and try to go to sleep. If it comes, I will be happy.

It takes till 3am to finally fall asleep due to absolute exhaustion. My alarm goes off what seems as 5mins later and realise it isn't the alarm but a call. I look at it is a private number.

'Hello, hey it's me, who is this?'

'It's Christy, Sandy.'

'Hey what's up?

'I need to ask you a question and I want an honest answer?

'And before you ask, no Bryce isn't here, hence the late call or early, call over there.'

'Who told you what?'

'Excuse me?' I ask.

'Who said something to you that made you flip and go?'

'Oh, well firstly Simone did, she said that he doesn't love me and was only using me for publicity and that if I didn't leave he would lose everything including Amy, so I decided to go then, but not after I told her a few home truths and what a bitch she is, then there were messages on my Instagram from Michelle, Arianna, Julie, Cat, Micha, Berlina and Shelly. They all said the same thing and I knew that it was possibly not true but after I had a go at Simone, I knew I had to go. I miss him terribly and know I will get over him but you have to do me a favour Christy, you are his best friend, look out for him. Make sure he is Okay and finds love, he deserves it so much.'

'And what about you? she asks.

'I have given up on love, I had a chance at it, I believed all the lies and fibs and walked away from the only man I could live with till the end of time, he deserves a skinny, blond, vibrant, young female who can give him kids, he deserves to be loved and cherished. I can't do all that, all I could give him was my heart and my love and that isn't enough.'

'How do you know that?' Christy asks.

'I, I, I don't but I have to believe it is for the best. But Christy, I trust you and your opinion, you have been friends with him for years, you know him better than most but unless you have to ask something else, I really need to go as I am getting up in three hrs?

'Do you mind if we keep in contact?' she asks.

'I would be offended if we don't. Night Christy.'

'Night Sandy.'

I hang up and try to go to sleep. I toss and turn, turn and toss and after 30mins, I get up and start cleaning. That is better, if sleep doesn't want to come, then cleaning must.

Michael wakes up at 6 am and comes in the lounge room and just stares, I have moved the furniture around and am just pushing the couch near the window.

'Mum, what the heck have you done?'

'I got bored baby, like it?' I ask.

'No, but I ain't moving it back so it will do.'

I make him breakfast and then do a couple of loads of washing. By the time I look at the clock I realise we have to take Louise to the airport, come on mate, we are leaving in 40mins to take Ya Ya to the airport.

'Mum can I go with her? Back to the US? Yeah, I want to go see Bryce and hang with him,' he says.

I' would love to say yes baby, but he is no longer part of our lives and we wish him nothing but the best life.'

'Do you think he misses us?'

'He will miss you Honey, he would be crazy not to, but me, no way Jose.'

The drive is good, we see Louise off and tell her to have a ball. It is about time she takes time for herself, I ask her to go to Graceland and buy some stuff and get it sent back which she agrees and then waves off and goes to get on the plane.

'Come on Mate, let's go get something to eat, do you want to go to the zoo?'

'Okay Mum.'

That is basically what we do until I go back to work, I try to keep myself distracted till I fall in bed, I only have three more days and back at work, thank god, I realise that although I am thinking about him I am not crying, well I am, but not as much.

So my days are wake, eat, walk, clean, wash, sleep and repeat. Never have I wanted to go to work so much. Finally the day has come, it is Monday morning and I am going to work, I have been home for five days and I will finally be able to keep myself amused.

I walk into work and am bombarded by all the girls.

'Is it true are you dating Bryce Johnston?'

'We saw your pictures at the premier, does this mean him and you are exclusive?'

'I don't want to talk about it Okay, just let me go to my desk and do my work. I will not be discussing it anymore.' Oh someone is shitty says, 'Danica, obviously he dumped you as if he would be with a fat mole like you.'

I look at her and want to hit her.

'Yeah you are right absolutely, now go please.'

Marissa comes up to me and sees that I am crying.

'He didn't did he?'

'No, I left him, Oh Mar I fucked up, I have totally fucked it up and I can never go back, and I love him so much, I want to run to him, I want to go to him, tell him I am so sorry, that I should have never left him but I can't, I lied to him about never loving him. Oh Mar, I am, I am so, I miss him so much.'

'Come on tart, let's go get a cuppa.'

She is a good friend and handy that she is my supervisor. I have support here I know I do. I show her my photos of our trip.

'You guys look so cute together and I can tell you both love each other, so if I had of been over there I would have hog tied you to him until you couldn't leave.'

'Thanks Marissa just what I need a smart ass.'

So back to the grindstone, I don't have time to think about anything about work, anyone who comes near me and asks about Bryce or my trip, Marissa and Noelle cut them off. This is good. I can concentrate on work. This will be my life for the rest of my time. This is good. I put my headset on my left ear and then leave my right ear for the phone. I start to sing as I am alone in the office as *This is me* is playing. *When the sharpest words wanna cut me down, I am going to send a flood I'm gonna drown them out, I am brave I am bruised, I am who I am meant to be.* And I sing it out load. I make no apologies this is me. I know that I deserve his love. I sing and make changes to suit how I am feeling. For we are glorious us, ep ep, this is me. I'm not scared to be seen I make no apologies this is me and I love him, this is me. I know that I deserve his love there is nothing I ain't worthy of. God this is true but it is too late. This is me. I put this on repeat and sing it out load for all to hear. I will get past this This is me. Sandy Oh, I look up its Marissa.

'It's time to go home.'

'Good, this day is awesome, thanks. See ya tomorrow.' And I continue to sing *This is me*. This is going to be my mantra from now on. I will not be put down anymore, I KNOW WHAT I WANT. I WANT Bryce and it will take a while but I deserve his love and I will get it back. Now just have to work it out.

I get home call his mum and talk to her for hours. 'Wilma, I love your son, I am not going to give up, I am going to fight for him, will you help me?' I beg. 'I promise I will never lie to him or any of you guys again, I will never allow anyone to push me away from my fate, my fate is Bryce and I intend until I stop breathing to have him in my life and when that happens I am never going to let go.' I hold my breath and wait for a reply.

'Well, it's about bloody time, Love,' she says, 'a week, it has taken you a week to make up your mind, I already knew on the weds when you left that you guys were perfect for each other as did Bryce.'

'Oh thank God. Now how do I fix this?' I ask.

'I have to go, he is coming for dinner, hang ten can you hold for a second?'

'Yep go for it.'

'Hey Honey, come in.' I hear Wilma.

'How are you Bryce?'

'OK Mum.'

'Really honey?'

'Have you heard from Sandy? I don't think she wants to ever see me again.'

'Well I think a little birdy might have not told you the truth, I know for a fact that you should fight for her, I can guarantee that young lady loves you to the moon and back honey and if you love her, fight for her, I know she will.'

I can't believe what I am hearing, is she letting him know what I said, that I am on the phone. I want to hear what he says and then Michael yells, 'Mum where are you?' Shit I think I am on load speaker and if not they would have heard him I hang up. Meanwhile Wilma is talking to Bryce and telling her everything.

'You have to fight for her Honey, she loves you, she listened to the BS from not just Simone but all the other girls.'

'Yeah I know I spoke to Christy who got it all from Sandy, I was there when she called her and kept quiet. How can I get her to believe that it was not the truth?'

'Tell her Honey. Fly over go to her and tell her. I can't I am leaving for the set tomorrow, and we will be working for the next three months.'

'Call her, message her, keep in contact or if you don't love her wholeheartedly, leave it alone.'

'Thanks Mum, I know what I have to do.'

'Well it better be getting your girl back!'

'Yes mum it is. But I will have to do it after my movie but I will message her tonight and try to call her. We can build on our relationship quietly until she knows what she and Michael mean to me then when she realises I adore her I am going to ask her to marry me!'

'OMG, really?' she shrieks.

'Mum, I have never felt this way, I am going to get the best ring, I am going to go to her and tell her everything and then never let her go again and if it means I have to move to Australia I will.'

'Oh Bryce I am so happy for you. If I can help in anyway let me know.'

They sit down and have dinner, afterwards, he leaves and says, 'Thanks for dinner Mum, speak to you Saturday', and he leaves.

He is on cloud nine, goes through the conversation with his Mum, then thinks back to a noise he heard 'OI', where did that come from? The TV wasn't on, was it the phone? Call mum he says, 'Hello, Hey Mum, it's me, when we were talking before were u on the phone for a bit?'

'Yes I was but I when I went back they had hung up as I was too long, why?' She asks.

'It's just I heard "OI" and I thought it was Michael. I just thought maybe he was on the phone or Sandy was and maybe she had spoken to you.'

'Honey, I speak to her all the time, as does your sisters and brothers. We all love her, and I have been a shoulder for her the past two weeks she has been away, that is how I know how she feels, she is so upset and regrets for walking away, she said to me that she has been crying since she got home, that only now three weeks later she isn't crying everyday but today at work she finally decided that she loves you and wants you in her life and Michael's but still doesn't think you love her, she thinks you are better off without her and although she thinks that she just said she is going to fight for you, for the both of you until her last breath.'

He smiles, takes a deep breath. 'Mum that is the best news I have heard. Gotta go, going to try and call her, Love you Mum.'

'Love you Son.'

Michael has just gone to bed, I am about to go in the shower when the phone rings, I am standing there frozen do I answer it or go in the shower, I go and answer it. Shit it might wake Michael. I grab the phone and answer it just in time.

'Hello.'

'Hey it's me. It is Bryce. Honey, it's me Bryce.'

I smirk I would know his voice anywhere, he snigger, his laugh.

'Hey you, how are you?'

I go into the lounge and sit down.

'I am good, well not really but I think I will be Okay, can you talk?' he asks.

'Yes Michael is asleep and you are beginning to sound like me, indecisive.' I laugh.

He goes on. 'Oh Okay.' He isn't laughing.

'Honey what is wrong,' I say.

'The thing is,' he says, 'I found someone I loved (I noticed the Loved bit) shit. He goes on. 'I thought she loved me and then she just took off, she said she would never lie to me and I find out that she did, I don't really think it is good that she did that but I understand why she did. I am so hurt, that she wouldn't come to me before leaving and I was very hurt and I don't think I can ever forgive her.' He pauses. I am sitting there crying, I can feel a sob come on and cover the phone, Wilma was wrong he doesn't love me, he will never forgive me. He goes on. 'So what do you think I should do? Do you think I should confront her, ask her why or should I just walk away and forget about her? Well what do you think?'

I am wiping my face, trying to stop the sobbing, luckily I have muted the phone so he can't hear me. He goes on. 'So, Sandy what do you think I should do?'

'As a fan I would like your opinion. Now I am just a fan'. I un-mute the phone and try to sound normal. I know I am not, I know if he cared he would know the difference of my Okay voice and my upset voice but he doesn't so I speak. 'Well, it is up to you and how you feel? This person that you love.'

'Loved,' he says.

'Sorry loved, do you still have feelings for her or not? If you don't then forget about her and get on with your life. But if there is some feelings still I would, well if it was me, I would ask her, find out why she did what she did, maybe she was just trying to protect you, so I go on and tell him why I did it but put it in the third person.' I tell him, 'maybe she was confronted by a few people and bombarded and believed them. Maybe just maybe no matter how much she loves you, she thought she was doing the right thing, maybe she didn't want you to lose Amy and everything you had worked for, maybe she thought you were better off with Simone so Amy could have her mum and dad back and maybe she just couldn't believe the fantasy and thought it was just that a fantasy, how could someone so gorgeous, sexy and wonderful as you are inside and outside could even really love her. That maybe she imagined it and would ruin your life if she stayed, so that's why she left.'

He takes a deep breath. 'Yeah it could be all that or it could just be she didn't love me and just couldn't be bothered.'

Stalemate. I am crying again but trying not to let him know.

He says, 'I have a lot to think about, don't I buddy?' 'Yes,' I squeak, 'I guess you do.'

He is smirking on the other side of the phone. He is trying to get me to admit I love him but I am so distracted and hurt and crying I can't concentrate.

'Hey Bryce, I have to go, I am sitting here half-dressed and freezing as I was about to go into the shower. I just want to say I hope it all works out, You deserve all the love and happiness in the world. I am sorry if I hurt you, I will always regret what I did and I hope one day we can be friends.'

'Of course, we are friends Buddy,' he says.

'That is good,' I say.

I am about to hang up when he asks, 'Sandy why are you crying?'

I stop, I thought he didn't hear it. 'I umm, I'm not I have hay fever.'

'In Winter?' He says, 'I don't think so. I thought you would never lie to me,' he says.

'I, it's not a lie, it's a fib.'

'Tell me please,' he asks.

I breath in and out. Here goes. 'Nothing, I am upset as everything I said to you was about me. I did love you, I do love you and I know I fucked it up, but I still can't believe that you allowed me into your life, that someone like you could even love me, I believed the lies, I believed everything that was said to me and then after I had a go at Simone I thought she would destroy you if I stayed and you would lose everything plus as I was rude to Amy's mum and thought you

194

would be angry at me so I left, I did the thing I thought was the best thing for you. I was trying to protect you.'

I can hear him breathing but he is saying nothing.

'I will go now, take care Bryce.'

'Sandy, I didn't say anything, why are you going?'

'You were quiet, I thought, I don't know what I thought. I have been doing that a lot lately. I'm sorry.'

'It's Okay. The thing is, I know everything, I get why you did what you did and I just wanted to tell you that what was said and messaged to you was not true. The way I feel about you is between you and me, no one else has a right to judge or tell you not to love me. The thing is you hurt me when you left.'

'I am so sorry Honey,' I say.

'I know.' He interrupts. 'I know but I want you to make a promise to me, will you?'

'Anything absolutely unless it is illegal,' I say.

Never lie to me again, never listen to anyone about my feelings for you and never hurt me again.'

'That is three things.' I laugh.

'Not funny,' he says.

'Sorry, I promise I will always speak to you first Okay,' I say.

'Good,' he says. I have to go as I am getting up early for a flight to NY we are filming the series again, OK, if you need me anytime call me.'

'Night Bryce.'

'Night my love,' he says. And then hangs up.

So this was good, I am quite happy and realise I am so tired, thank god it is Saturday tomorrow so I can sleep in, I crawl into bed and the minute my head hits the pillow I am sound asleep. I sleep like a baby, I am woken up by Michael in the morning.

'Mum, wake up, I've got soccer soon.'

'Hey baby, what time is it?' I ask.

'It's 10am.'

I look at him and then I smile.

'Okay baby, give me 20mins and we can leave. I just have to pop in the shower.'

I can't believe I slept for 10 hrs, I have not done that since I was a baby. I must have needed it. I go in the shower, get dressed and we are in the car driving to soccer when my phone rings.

'Hello.'

'Hey gorgeous, how did you sleep? I have just finished on set, driving back well getting a lift back to the hotel and thought I'd call to say hi.

'Hey honey.'

'Hi Bryce,' Michael yells out.

I smirk, this is so good, so familiar, I wish he was here I think.

'Hey mate how are you? He asks.

'Good Bryce, Mum is driving me to soccer and then we are going to the pool aren't we Mum?'

'Of course baby, but we have to go back and get our bathers and towels.'

'That's good,' says Bryce.

'So how did it go on the set?' I ask.

No problems. It was good, just a long day, we worked for 14hrs,' he says.

'Shit that is long, are you allowed to work those hours?'

'Yes, as we are not always working but standing around a lot of the times. I did a scene ten times and was absolutely exhausted after it but had to keep going.'

'I'm sorry Honey, I wish I could do something to help.'
'You could.'

'And what is that young man?'

'You and Michael come back, come stay with me while I film in NY. You can stay on set and watch and when I have a break we can spend time together and then I won't be so lonely in the hotel when I get back.'

'Oh honey, If I had the money I would jump on the first plane but I don't plus I don't have anyone to look after the pets and my home. Plus I have to work to pay the bills.'

'Honey, I told you I would help you, I could pay your house off with one month income.'

'Yes I know but that is using you and I won't use you.'
'Really?'

'Yes really.'

I know what he is thinking I would use him in bed, but Michael Is here so I can't say that.

'So, tell me what else happened today?' I ask.

He goes on and tells me everything that happened, how he hurt himself doing a stunt but is Okay, how his co-star is such a sweet young thing and her partner is a funny dude and then he goes quiet.

'Are you Okay?' I ask.

'Yes I was just thinking I will be alone tonight and I miss you and really want you to be here.'

'Oh Bryce, we can't Okay. But I can talk to you until you go to sleep how is that?' and that is exactly what we do, we are on the phone for 3hrs when I say, 'You better go to sleep honey, I will speak to you when you can, Goodnight my sweetheart.'

'Good night, my love' and we both hang up.

I spend the day with Michael and I am in such a good mood, finally my life is getting back on track, he loves me, I love him but the only thing is I have to save to see him. Oh gosh I wish I had the money to go over now.

My phone is ringing.

'Hello.'

'Hey sis, it's me, I have arrived, I am in NY and going down to see Roger tomorrow.'

'Oh can you do me a favour?' I ask.

'Yes what?'

Can you go past and see Bryce he is at the Waldorf, I can get him to call you I just want to see him and thought maybe you could take a photo and video call.'

'NO, I am not doing that, he can video call you. I will go past but I am not going to video him and I won't hang around.'

'Oh ok, I understand at least you will see him. Can you hug him for me?'

'No don't that is too creepy.'

'Nah don't worry about it, I was talking to him for ages, I just miss him', and then I tell her everything that has been said.

'Well thank fuck for that and now maybe you won't be so sad and shitty,' she says.

Only my sister could say that, I know I will be fine.

'Enjoy your trip, keep in contact and we will see you in three weeks.'

So that is my days now. Michael and I spend time together on the weekends, we go past and see Mum. Monday's to

Fridays we have our routine, drop Michael to school, off to work and pick him up from Mum's, cook dinner, clean, speak to Bryce when he can, repeat. This goes on for the three weeks and then it is time for Louise to come back home. We pick her up from the airport and she looks so relaxed. She tells us what she did, how it was good to be with the family and see Graceland and said she was glad to finally get home. I tell her everything that has happened with Bryce and how we are going and we are in a good place.

I can't believe that I have been away from Bryce for nearly two months, I miss him every day, every time I talk to him it makes me sad as I know I can't be with him so I devise a plan and decide to save money so I can go see him at Christmas, I will save all my money from Marlton and stop spending, I put the gym off, cut money wherever I can just so I can go and see him. I will tell him how much he means to me and if all goes to plan we will be together forever. But that is what fantasies are about, do they really come true. Well time will only tell.

Again, everyday it is a routine, I get up Michael goes to school, I go to work, I pay bills, weekends we spend together, I go for a walk every night and around 3am Bryce calls me before he goes to bed most nights, he sounds so exhausted, he has been filming for two months and it is going well but I can tell it is getting to him, he flies on the weekends back to LA to see Amy but I know being away from her is killing him. We talk about everything and nothing at the same time. We have grown closer again and it makes it so hard not to see him but I know it is the way it has to be until I can get over there. I find I am getting so tired but don't want to tell him as if he found out he would stop calling and I would miss him if we didn't speak. Winter is nearly finished over here and he is enjoying summer but is finding it harder and harder, the movie is running overtime but if all goes to plan he said it should finish by August and he can go back home and spend heaps of time with Amy. I am happy for him I just want him to be happy. I want to do something for him but can't think of anything.

I am speaking to his mum every couple of weeks and his sisters and brothers are keeping in contact with me as well. It is funny the longer I am away from him the closer I am getting to him and his family, his mum is wonderful and I feel like I am close to his whole family. Everything has been sorted out with his ex. He listened to me and didn't stop her from seeing Amy but she is on a tight leash, she has been legally gagged to not knock him and changeover has been amicable. She is finally moving on with her new partner and Bryce is so relieved as she is happy she has been so good with him and allows him to spend extra time with Amy. This makes me happy as he is happy. The year is flying by. And then it is suddenly August and my birthday is fast approaching, I don't let on when it is my birthday, it is just another day, all I really want is to be with him, have him here with me for a few weeks, days, hours, even moments but I know it won't happen as he has been busy with the final touches of the series. If only I think what a great present that would be on my birthday to see him. Oh well maybe he will call. And how can he know when you haven't told him my inner voice says, bloody inner voice of reason. I laugh to myself, god I crack myself up.

I hear my phone ring. I look and don't recognise the number.

'Hello.'

'Hi, is this Sandra?'

'Yes it is. I just want to tell you a couple of things, I am a friend of Bryce, well not exactly a friend I am his girlfriend.'

I pause but act like it is not a big deal. 'Yeah so,' I say. 'Well, I just want to tell you or actually warn you to stay the fuck away from him Okay,' she says.

'Really, well let me tell you this thing Missy, I don't give a flying fuck who the hell you think you are and I will not be threatened by anyone ever again, if you are his girlfriend and I would expect him to have one as we are not dating but just friends then if he wants me to stay the fuck away from him, then he will tell me OK,' I yell. 'Now leave me alone, don't ever call me again and I do not ever want to speak about this again. Do you understand what I am saying or is your blonde brain not keeping up?'

'Well I have never and how do you know I am blonde,' she quizzes.

'Just guessing', and I hang up.

Great another bimbo threatening me, I can do two things, I can call him and tell him but that will only upset him if it is true or I can ignore it and forget it ever happened or the third option is Google about him. The third option happens. Okay Google please tell me it is not true, surely he would have told me that he was dating someone?

Bryce Johnston was seen out and about with a few females in Reno on the weekend, one is rumoured to be his new girlfriend, looks like the Aussie girl he was with in June was just a decoy, thank god he has now found someone who is better suited to him and his lifestyle said the article. I go onto E News online. Bryce Johnston has been seen around town with a few females in late, is his dating one or all of them. Our source has said that the Aussie girl he was seen with in June was just a friend and that he is really dating his co-star from his latest movie *Dream catchers*. 'Could this be the forever ever after he is after?' says Jemina.

'Well all I can say,' says her co-host Travis, 'that I think the only one he is dating is Sandy, his Aussie girl and that this is just publicity made up from his co-stars camp to ramp up her exposure.'

'Well we can agree to disagree,' says Jemina.

Let's watch this space as the normally private Bryce Johnston has yet to say anything. So that is it, he is dating his co-star that would be why I haven't heard from him as much. Should I call his mum and ask or should I just forget about it, I chose the latter, forget about it, I knew this was going to happen, I knew all along that we would never be together and now at least I can think of him and not cry, I can think of him and remember the good times we had, I only want him to be happy and If I was a little or actually as I am not little but a fat female, I am a fat blimp in his life that has given him the strength and guidance to finally give love a chance and for that I will forever be grateful.

So I go on with my life, I don't call him or his family. I just do my routine, work is now slowing down at Marlton stadium so I am now only working my full time job so my mind has a little more time to think so I better find something else to do on the weekends.

Oh well tomorrow my week starts again, so another day another dollar. My phone beeps and it shows there is an email from Kaye at Marlton.

Hi all staff, just advising we have just been advised that we are going to be involved in the production of a movie and are asking for staff to give up their weekends for the next couple of weeks, I know it is winter but are requiring at the most 25 staff. Please contact the office before this Wednesday to advise availability. We will require staff during the day and some night shifts, Kaye.

Well that leaves me out as I work during the day and night time I have Michael but the money would be good. My phone then rings and it is Kaye.

'Hey Kaye how are you?' I ask.

'Good Sandy just wondering if you have read the email about the shifts starting from the 16th august?' She asks. 'Well I just read it but the thing is I am working during the week so I won't be able to help unfortunately and at night I have Michael so I can't do that either.'

'The thing is we need you for the work, we have had specific requests for certain characters and you are ideal for one of the roles required.'

'I am sorry Kaye but I can't, it is our busy season at work. Plus this duck doesn't go anywhere near a camera or it will bust.'

'Sandy, the thing is we need you.'

'I don't understand Kaye in what way?'

'The role we need you for is as a female that is funny, kind, generous and very knowledgeable of the stadium and is good with people'

'Well that isn't me Kaye you know that I am the biggest dag and I never shut up.'

'Perfect plus that isn't true. The thing is you have been requested by the big bosses to be available for the two weeks, you will be paid double the pay and there will be a car park under the stadium for you.'

'Kaye I just don't know I will have to check with Marissa at work tomorrow Okay.'

'No need I have already spoken to her,' she says. 'Sorry I don't understand, it has been organised by David here at the stadium.'

'David you mean the general manager?'

'Yep.'

'Well then I guess I am available.' I laugh. 'So what is my role?'

'Well it isn't starting till the 16th August and it will finish around the 31st August, the hours will be from 6 am till no more than 10 pm, but we won't know the hours you are needed till closer to the time.'

'Kaye that is only a week away,' I say. 'Do I really have to do it?'

'If you don't there will be disappointed people.'

'Well I guess I am doing it then.' 'Good I will speak to you on Wednesday.'

I call Marissa.

'Okay woman what the hell is going on and why did you approve this?'

'Oh hi. Happy I guess!'

Silence, if she could see my face she would know I am not a happy Jan.

She says, 'Guess not by the silence.'

'Marissa,' I say, 'tell me what is really going on.'

'I don't know, all I know is I got a call from the Marlton boss from America on video conference and they said they needed you for the movie production they have paid your wages here and said it is only for two weeks.'

'Couldn't you of said no?'

'I tried Sandy but they were very persuasive. So all I can say is have fun.'

'Gee thanks Marissa, thanks.'

Great I have to work on a movie production, probably looking after the drinks that is all I can think of or maybe watching doors or gates, that will be easy but it is cold. Oh well I guess I do this or resign from the stadium but I really need the money as I want to go to the states again at Christmas or even next year and see Roger and the family again but this time just the east coast and stay the way away from the West coast, that way I won't be tempted to see Bryce.

I email Kaye. *Hey Kaye Sandy here, I am on board, let me know when to start and which of the uniforms to wear and I am at your demand.*

She calls straight away. 'Hey Sandy it's Kaye.'

'Are you sleeping at work? I ask.

'No but I have the emails open and I had to put you in before tomorrow as it is closing.'

'You mean if I emailed tomorrow I would have missed out?' I ask.

'Nope you were requested to work during the two weeks.' she says.

'Oh, do you know by who?'

'No but it came from above and we had to make sure you were working. So I need you at the stadium Monday at 6 am, I will email you all the details and car park entry and pass, you will be supplied a uniform when you get here as they have clothes for all the roles. You will have hair and makeup done too,' she says.

'Seriously hair and make up for just watching doors?' 'No you are not watching doors, you will be on screen as security.'

I laugh and snort at the same time. 'I don't think anyone will believe I am security have they not seen me and how short and fat I am.'

'Sandy they know you, all I was told was to get you here. I am assuming it is security but it's changing daily. Just do me a favour this is confidential, you must sign the agreement I am sending you, you cannot speak to anyone about this, Okay.'

'Of course Kaye, just a question how many staff are actually working it.'

'We are only having ten staff and most are on the gates where the filming is happening you are the only one inside.'

'Oh, Okay. I will sign it and re email it tonight, thanks Kaye.'

'See you on Monday Sandy', and hangs up. Now this is a doozy why me? It wouldn't be Bryce coming over here filming surely? Last time he was going to NY. I wonder who it is? And this keeps me awake all night, I have three days before I have to be there so that gives me three days to stalk the internet and try and find out who is filming here.

After three days I am none the wiser, it's not Nicholas Cage, It's not Chris Hemsworth, It's not an Avengers movies, Gosh who is it? All I have found out is Bryce is dating his co-star from his new movie, she is 15yrs younger than him and is an ex model and of course is still able to have children as she is absolutely gorgeous, I am happy for him and wish him nothing but happiness. I keep looking at the picture online of them together laughing on set, he looks so happy in most, his smile is vibrant and he looks relaxed, there is a picture of them hugging each other and I remember the way he hugged me and can almost feel his arms around me, it wasn't the same as it is in the picture but it is close, so that means he is in love with her or at least likes her a lot. I start to cry as I now know it is over, he will never look at me the way he is looking at her. Lucky girl. I wish it was me but know it could never be. I then look closer at one of the pictures, she is looking away from him and is staring at the camera. He doesn't look happy, I can see his frown and his beautiful blue eyes are not shining, I then look at a picture of them both and although he is smiling it isn't reaching his eyes, it is just a put on smile. Does this mean that maybe he isn't dating her. Oh gosh now I am confused. No I am just making something up that isn't there because I want him still. I decide enough is enough, I turn the laptop off and decide never to Google him again, it only brings me heartache. I have the weekend left and then two weeks of doing nothing. I hope.

So Monday has come, I am about to arrive at the stadium, I can see heaps of vans and security, I drive to gate 2 show my pass and am told to drive through and park. I park, get out the car and walk to the boardroom where I have been told to meet Kaye and David. It is 5.30 am I am a bit early but I rather be early than late. I get buzzed in and go the reception and Kaye is there.

'Morning Sandy.'

'Morning Kaye.'

'Sorry for being early but I had a good run, so where do you want me?'

'Just go into the boardroom and meet me there can you, grab a coffee and then I will take you to where you have to go.'

'Okay. Do you want one too?'

'Yeah that will be good Ta.'

I go into the boardroom make a cup of tea for me and a coffee for Kaye. I am in the kitchen and hear the door open I turn around and I see Bryce walk in. Holy Shit he is here. Breathe Sandy, Breathe. Kaye is following him in as is David, pretend you don't know him I think.

'Hi David Coffee?'

'Excuse me sir.'

I look at Bryce. Kaye says, 'Sandy you recognise him don't you he was in all the major movies last year, it is Bryce Johnston.'

'Oh yeah, hi Mr Johnston, Coffee?' I ask.

'That would be great thanks, you know how I like it.' Kaye and David look at me and then him and back to me. 'Um yes I guess as a fan I would know.'

Hopefully that will satisfy them. So, I finish the coffee for David and Bryce and we all sit down at the table, Bryce is next to me and Kaye and David are opposite. I just want to touch him, I can't believe he is actually sitting next to me. God if I only moved my seat a little bit our knees would touch but then I remember he has a girlfriend and I move away.

OK Sandy,' says David, 'you have been asked here today as you were requested to work with the crew in the movie, they are here at the stadium and around Melbourne for the next two weeks, you will be paid handsomely and will have parking available everyday where they are filming.' I can feel Bryce is looking at me and I continue to look at David and Kaye.

'So what exactly am I doing?'

'Bryce answers, 'You will be my personal assistant.'

I turn to him abruptly. 'Excuse me!' I gasp. 'But you have a PA.'

'Yes that is true but I need one that knows Melbourne a lot better and being that you are from here I wanted you.'

I am staring at his beautiful stunning clear blue eyes and he is smiling at me not just with his with mouth that is so tantalising I want to leap over my chair and kiss him senseless. This is the Bryce I remember from the US.

'I am sure you could have anyone you wanted but why me?'

'Because I wanted to see you and you were not taking my calls and when you left in June it broke my heart.'

I am staring. I turn and see Kaye and David staring. Kaye clears her throat and says, 'Sandy we know you guys know each other, Bryce filled us in that is why you were requested.'

'Oh you little shit,' I say, then realise I just swore to my bosses. 'Oh I am so sorry I didn't mean to swear.'

They are both laughing. 'It is all good, we expected a lot more. Now we are going to leave you two to sort out what is happening and on this they leave.'

So, I am sitting next to Bryce at a table that normally fits 20 people and I am starting to shake, I try to calm down and look at him.

'Okay, you got me here talk, tell me what you want to say and then I can go Okay,' I say.

'You can't I, need you for the time I am here,' he says. 'Seriously?'

'Yes Seriously,' he says.

'What about your girlfriend?'

'What girlfriend?' He asks.

Your co-star it was all online, all the pictures of you guys together, cuddling, laughing, I saw it with my own eyes.' I have tears in my eyes and I am trying not to cry so I look away. He grabs my hands turns me towards him, lifts my face up and stares into my eyes.

'Why are you crying? And why are you believing the internet? What did I tell you about that when we were together three months ago hey,' he says. 'Not to believe half the shit that is on there.'

'But you looked happy, you were laughing, hugging her,' I say.

'So, but what you didn't see was we were filming and the moment it stopped I stepped away.'

'Yeah easy to say that now I can't see it.'

'Now Ms Sandy you sound jealous,' he says.

'No not jealous, just don't want to cause any problems.' We are both looking at each other, he looks sad and I look away, tears are forming and I can feel them starting to fall. 'I think this is a mistake Bryce I can't do this, I just can't be here with you, it is just…' And then my voice breaks and the tears are falling. He gets up pulls me into his arms and holds on to me, I am sobbing and leaning into his shoulder and wetting his shirt, gosh he smells so nice. I have missed him so much, I feel myself melting into his arms and leaning into his body, I can feel his heart against my cheek. He is running his hand over my hair and back and allowing me to cry. He then pulls me onto his lap, makes me look at him and says, 'Now baby tell me what is wrong?'

I melt. 'Oh my god. I… I….Oh Bryce, why are you so wonderful, I… I…'

'Yes baby.'

'Here goes, I hate being away from you, I hate not seeing you or being with you but I know we can't be, you are an A list actor, everyone knows who you are, everyone wants to date you girls and guys, they expect you to be with a stunning person not someone like me. I am nothing, I am fat, short, broke, single mother who is trying to do the best, I am trying to lose weight but I have wrinkles, grey hair and no one gives a shit about me, no one knows who I am. Not even my friends really care and all Michael cares about is money and toys.'

He looks at me. 'No that is not right. Sandy I love you, I want you, I don't want to lose you again, the reason why we are filming here is I refused to do the film unless we could come here so I could see you, I wanted to win you again.'

I am looking at him. I know he is an actor but he seems sincere.

'Oh… Yep.' That is all I can say. I am looking at the man I love, the man I would do anything for and he is telling me everything I have wanted to hear but I just can't believe this or can I. I take a deep breath, I am still sitting on his lap.

'I better get off.

'Why?' He asks.

'I don't know', and we both laugh.

'Bryce is this true? Is this really true,' I whisper.

'Yes baby. You are the only I want. I want you and Michael with me forever. I want you to be Amy's step mum and me Michael's dad. You see Sandy I want you and Michael always with me. I don't care what anyone thinks plus as a fan you would want me to be happy yes?'

'Of course,' I say. And so would all the other fans and you make me happy. I want to believe I really do but I never get what I want and it is not real is it?'

'Yes baby it is. So what do you say? are you going to be here with me for the next two weeks? And forever?' 'Well, definitely the next two weeks.

'Good come on let's go.

We walk out holding each other's hands and Kaye and David are nowhere. I go looking for them and ask what I need to do. Kaye is in her office.

'Hey Kaye, so what am I doing?

'You Sandy are there for Bryce, enjoy', and winks and smiles at me. 'He is a wonderful person and loves you very much.

'But Kaye, do you think it can work out? No one knows except now my mum, sister, Michael and you and David. No one else knows over here. His family do but what happens when the world finds out, will it work out, will I be judged and laughed at, will he hate me and push me away?' 'Sandy, I have known you for over ten years and I will tell you this, once someone knows you they love you. If anyone sees what we saw in the board room the way you both look at each other they will be happy.'

'Oh I hope so Kaye, I hope so.'

I go back to Bryce who is talking to a tall guy with David, I go up and he grabs my hand and introduces me. 'Stewart this is Sandy, Sandy this is Stewart the director.' 'The Sandy,' he says.

'Yes The Sandy.'

I look at both of them and I am lost.

'Um guys I am here, what is this The Sandy about? I am only one person nothing special.'

Stewart looks at me. 'Well young lady, you are very important to Bryce and the reason why we have come here to do some scenes with the movie.'

I look at him and Bryce. 'I am sorry I don't understand, what do you mean I am the reason why you are here.'

He looks at Bryce and says, 'We better tell her.'

'Okay.'

He then goes on. 'The thing is, we were looking for a location to finish the movie and Bryce suggested we do it here as Melbourne can be any city plus he wanted to see you as he missed you, and when I say missed I mean MISSED.'

I look at Bryce and he has gone bright red, I have never seen him go this red.

'Oh really you missed me huh!'

He looks at me absolutely and I am not ashamed to say it.

'Oh you are so adorable and gorgeous I missed you too. Hey, I got a phone call three days ago warning me to stay away from you as she was your girlfriend, I told her to fuck off and if you wanted me to stay away from you, you would tell me, so who was that then? And how did she get my number if not from you?'

He looks at me. 'Why are you trying to start an argument?'

'I am not, I am just trying to show you that we are going to constantly get people telling me what is happening in your life and how we are going to have all these obstacles in our way.'

'Well, I can tell you this one thing and I will only say it the once,' he says. 'The only female that I consider to be my girlfriend is a stubborn Aussie girl who happens to be standing in front of me now.'

'I am not stubborn!'

He raises his eyebrows at me.

'Well maybe a little stubborn.' He stares at me.

'OK, OK a lot but at least you know what I am always thinking as I always say it, that is a good thing yes,' I ask.

He grabs me and says, 'I love you Sandy', and gives me a passionate kiss. I melt.

If this is the way it is going to be for the next two weeks then I have died and gone to heaven as heaven in his arms and being around him. I have no idea what I have done but I feel like everything is perfect.

'Hey honey, now that you are here for a couple of weeks where are you staying?'

'Well the crew are staying at Crown and I was hoping that I could stay with you,' he says.

'I can't stay at Crown. Number one I can't afford it plus I have Michael and the pets.'

'No sweetheart, I was hoping to stay with you at your place,' he says.

Oh, yeah that will be Okay. I have space for you plus you can see how good the place looks since you fixed it and we have to discuss how I can pay you back.'

'We won't discuss this Sandy, it was a gift.'

'Oh, a gift. I appreciate it but it was a massive gift.'

'Not to me,' he says, 'it was nothing for the woman I love.'

I look at him. 'You love me?'

'Do you love me?' He asks.

'I asked first...LOL...'

'Yes Sandra I do love you.'

'You called me Sandra and that's nice,' I say and smirk and start to run away, he laughs. 'That's nice, oi come here you cheeky monkey', and grabs me. We are walking towards the centre of the stadium where everyone is waiting.

'So what am I going to do here Bryce, did you get me here to stalk and annoy you or am I actually going to do something?

'Yes you are at my beck and call for whatever I want. 'Oh Okay that will be easy I guess.'

We go into the middle and Stewart is talking.

'Okay guys, thanks for coming we have two weeks here and will be going around Melbourne to finish the movie off, we will be here at the stadium for two days and then I will let you guys know where we are going to from there.'

Bryce goes to the makeup department and tells me to join him. I follow him and think this is a waste of time and money.

'Hey Bryce, do you really need me here? I can't do nothing but be here for you, it is a waste of money.'

'No, you will be an extra too.'

'I don't think so, I am not interested in being on screen. Please let me go back to my day job and I will see you at night or the weekend.'

'Nope you are contracted.'

'Bugger.'

'Hey Sandy, can you come here for a second,' yells Stewart.

'Coming. Hey what's up?'

'Okay I wanted to tell you what you are going to do here.'

'Good.'

'You are here to help with anything Bryce needs, if we need any extra people for scenes will you be Okay with that?'

'Nope.'

'If I went on camera it would break. Do you really need me here for him. It is a waste of money.'

'The studio wants him happy and having you here is what makes him happy.'

'Oh Okay.'

'I will email you where we will be filming so if you want you can drive and meet us there, you will have parking wherever we go.'

'Stewart I don't know what to say, but I think it is too much I am no one.'

'You are too kind he was right, you really have no idea how important you are, do you?' he says.

'I am not, I am just me. I am someone that between you and me who adores Bryce so much, who met him accidentally and fell in love with him the minute he smiled at me and I didn't even recognise him, did he tell you that?' 'Yes, he did and I just thought of a good and happy ending to the movie. Excuse me.' He walks off.

I go back to the makeup department and Bryce is nearly finished, for the little make up he has on it takes ages.

'Hey ladies maybe give him a bright red lipstick to make his eyes pop out.'

He looks at me and chucks a napkin at me, and we all laugh. One of the girls asks if I would like my make up done, 'No all good, but Thank you'.

'Come on Sandy, the rest of the cast are done and I have nothing to do,' says Robyn, 'sit sit', and pulls me onto the seat.

I am just sitting there watching the magic of her work. It only took 15mins and she says to open my eyes and look. 'Oh my god, that isn't me, I look different.'

'We only build on what is there, we can't make you look different.'

I turn to Bryce and he is smiling.

'Now how do you feel?

'I feel like I should be, I have no idea. I feel different.'

'Come on gorgeous, let's go', and we go out of the tent and walk to the set.

I am sitting down on his seat while they are filming, I am watching how he is with his co-star and I can see that he is happy but he is also just working, so maybe the press were wrong, maybe he is just friends with her and I know that they are just co-stars as he told me she has a girlfriend. After they finish doing the scene 10 times, I hear, that's it and both Bryce and the cast sit down.

'Sandy, this is Melinda.'

'Hi Melinda, nice to meet you.'

'I have heard heaps about you the past few months, I must say I have never seen him like this before.'

'Well thank you but if has nothing to do with me,' I say.

'I think it has more to do with you then you think, a girl can tell when someone is in love.' I look at him and he winks at me.

'Yeah I guess you can.'

We sit there talking between scenes and then hear, 'Okay guys, see you tomorrow bright and early, be back here at 8am.'

I look at my watch and it is 9pm. I was wondering why I was feeling tired. I get up and say night to everyone and start to walk to my car.

'Hey Sandy wait up I am coming.'

'Oh sorry honey,' I say to Bryce, 'I thought you may have wanted to just go to the hotel and sleep.'

'Nope I am coming with you.'

We walk to the car and get in, My music comes on and it is Kelly Clarkson's Christmas album.

He looks at me. 'Christmas songs?'

'Yep. I have been listening to them for a month. I love these songs.' I play my favourites while we are driving home.

I still can't believe he is here next to me. I feel like everything is falling into place, could this be my life, could this be actually happening, I look over and he has dozed off, he must be exhausted. I pull into my driveway.

'Honey wake up we are here, come on.' He wakes up, I get his luggage and we go in. He showers and within 1hr we are both lying in bed and fall asleep in each other's arms. I set the alarm for 5am so we have time to get up, get ready and eat breaky.

This is the routine for the next few days. This is perfect, he is with me and we spend heaps of time together. I am glad that Marissa accepted the role for me, otherwise I wouldn't be here now with him.

The press have been trying to find out where he has been staying but no one knows my car and knows where I live, so he has had a relative quiet time while in Australia. On the weekends we spend time with Michael and he meets my mum and my family. We all get on well. Even my nephew thinks he is nice.

'Aunty Sandy, you deserve all the happiness in the world and I can see he makes you happy, just be careful Okay.'
'Okay Sam, thanks for caring.'

Time has flown by so quickly, it feels like I have just seen him walk into the boardroom when it is our last two nights together. It is our last Friday night, we have just got back home from the final scene and he is due to fly out on Monday

218

and I go back to work on Tuesday. We are sitting together on the couch watching TV when I turn to him. 'Bryce, when do you fly out again?'

'I have a flight at 10 am on Monday.'

'Oh Okay. So I will take you to the airport then on Monday morning?'

'Only if you want to,' he says.

'Of course I do. I just wish.'

'What baby? What do you wish?' he asks.

I look at him. 'I just wish this with us didn't have to end, I know it has to but I wish it didn't, I wish this was our normal life, that every morning and night you were with me. But it is just a dream.'

He grabs me and leans me into him. 'It can be if you want.'

'How?'

'Well, you could move to the states and live with me and Amy.'

'I can't, Michael has school here, I have my jobs, my mum, how would I pay for myself if I was over there, how would Michael cope with a different school and life. I couldn't do that to him.' I have tears in my eyes. 'I would do anything to be able to but how could I. You can't move here because your family, Amy and your work is over there.'

He looks at me. 'Well it is a pickle isn't it. I guess we say goodbye on Monday and take this as it is, another two fantastic weeks, full of memories and keep them close to our hearts forever. Is that what you want?' he asks.

'No, I want to be with you always, but how, I can't move and you can't.'

We just lean into each other and go quiet. Me and my bloody mouth but it had to be said.

We have a good weekend with Michael but I am aware the whole time that this is the last time I will see him. Every time I look at him I am counting down to the last time I will see him, the moment he will walk through the gates at the airport. Just breathe, enjoy your time with him and think about it when he goes. I know it is it for me, I will never be the same, I will never get over him now. We have spent in total one month together over the year and it feels so good, so right but also I know that it will end. Life really is unfair.

It is our last night together, he has his bags packed and in my car, Michael and I are taking him to the airport and luckily, the press think we are just friends so they won't think anything of me dropping him off.

'Sandy.'

'Yes Bryce.'

'I need to ask you a question and I want the truth.' he says.

'Of course I always would tell the truth you know that even if I look bad.'

I sit there quietly, I have all these questions going through my head including will you marry me? I then decide that if he does ask me to marry him I will move to America with him, it just means I have to move Michael but if he doesn't want to go I can't force him so he can always stay here with Louise and live at home and I will visit as often as I can or he will fly over until he finishes school, it will be hard but I know that without Bryce my life means nothing. I look at him, 'Yes honey what did you want to ask.'

'I was wondering if you would mind, yes I am thinking, would you mind if we pick up some things on the way to the airport tomorrow I forgot to get some things for mum and the kids.'

My face drops, but then I smile. 'Of course Sweetheart, do you want to go now?

'No all good, I just need to go past the shop at 8 am, I have it all organised to just collect what I need, I just need you to drive me there, is that Okay?' he says.

'Of course Honey, anything. But I think we better go to bed as we are getting up early in the morning.'

We get up, he goes to into the bathroom, I run around and I check everything is locked up, I also grab the present I bought for him and the letter I wrote and put it in his suitcase between his clothes so he gets them when he returns home. I stand there for a few minutes trying not to think that tomorrow he will be gone and try not to cry. You would think that I have no more tears left with him, I seem to always cry when he is going, I am going, or I am with him. If I could lose weight for all the time I have cried over him well I would be skinny.

'Honey, you coming into bed?' and I turn around and he is standing behind me.

'Yep sorry was just locking up.'

We turn and go into the bedroom.

'Bryce, I just want to say this one thing before I don't have the courage again. I love you.'

'I know that,' he says, 'I love you too.'

'No it's not just that. What I wanted to say is I love you, I will always cherish the time we have spent together, my dream was to meet you and get to know the real Bryce and I have and to me he, I mean you are the most wonderful, caring, supportive, loving, funny, adorable, talented, stunning, generous and overall perfect person, some may not agree but to me you are my perfect person. I will always regret that we couldn't make it work and I will always watch out for you, I will always be here for you and when you find love with someone that can be with you I will always wish you well.'

With that the tears are rolling down my face. I look at him and he looks sad.

'Don't you want to be with me?' he asks.

'Yes of course but one of us has to be reasonable and logical, if there was a way to make this work I would jump on the train and never let go, but every scenario I think of doesn't work out.'

He just looks at me and he looks completely heartbroken.

'I am sorry baby I didn't mean to upset you, I just wanted to tell you as it is, I wish there was a different way, I really wish there was.'

We lean into each other for the final time and fall asleep in each other's arms.

All of the sudden it is morning and we have to leave, Michael decides he doesn't want to come to the airport so he goes to Mum's and it is just myself and Bryce in the car. I drop him off to the shops and stay in the car so I don't get in the way. He comes back 20mins later with a package and two parcels.

'All done?' I ask.

'Yep, let's go honey.'

'So, this is the final drive, I take him to the airport where he meets up with the rest of the crew and cast. I help with his bags and go with them to the international gate but can't go into the terminal as I am not flying. I say goodbye to everyone and then it is my turn with Bryce. I am trying to be brave but the tears are welling up.

'Well Honey, be safe, have a good flight, give my love to Amy and your family. I put a present in your bag for Amy it isn't anything illegal, it is a necklace I saw and thought it would be perfect for her. I also have put a gift in your bag for you but it is in your suitcase so you will see it when you get home. Thank you for the last two weeks and the best time of my life with you again.'

He smiles, pulls me close and whispers, 'You are the reason why I want to be a better man, you are my dream and I will try to the end of my breath for us to be together again, don't give up on us Okay my love. I look at him and he has tears in his eyes and I am crying.

'Never ever.'

We kiss and he then has to go. As he walks through the terminal gate he looks at me and winks and blows me a kiss. I am standing there looking at the doors just waiting to see if every time the doors open I can see him but I don't. I must have been standing there for over an hour when I see on the board that his plane has taken off. That is it. It is over. I turn around and walk out of the airport and know that he is gone.

I get in the car and I can smell him, I turn on the stereo and his voice is coming through the speakers. I just sit there and cry and cry and cry. Thank god Michael didn't come he would know what a sook his mum is and I don't want him to see me this weak. This is it. I have never felt this way, I keep saying it, I have never cried over one man in my life as much as I have this one. I have spent 30 days with him in total, surely I have no more tears over this one man. But god dammit I love him so much, I would give my life for him. Pull yourself out of this shit I think, you have 70mins to get over it and then I have to be strong and pretend it is nothing, that him going home is like a friend, no feelings, I have to be strong, I have to show that I am Okay even though I know I am not. Get over yourself useless I think. This is the argument I have all the way home until I pull into the driveway to pick Michael up from Mum's.

'Hey baby I am back, were you good for Omi.'

'Yes Mum,' he says.

'Did Bryce get off Okay?'

'Yes baby all good.'

I give Mum a hug and say thanks for watching Michael.

'Do you guys want to go out to the pub for dinner?' I ask.

'Nah all good.'

'Okay Mate, let's go and I will get you takeaway. Night Mum love you.'

I turn on the radio and *Only love can hurt like this* is playing. It is like the gods know how I feel, don't cry I think. 'Hey Mate, looking forward to going to school tomorrow?'

'Yeah I am, Mum are you at work tomorrow or do you have one more day off?' He asks.

'I go back Tuesday mate, which is tomorrow, isn't it?'

'Yes Mum it is,' he says.

'Why do you ask baby?'

'Do you think I could have the day off so we could go to the zoo?'

'You know what Michael let's do it, we can go see all our relatives there!'

He looks at me, laughs and I say, 'I will call in sick tomorrow…'

'Cool Mum, we can both have a sickie...'

I am such a bad Mum, but let's just have a good day I think.

So plans for tomorrow is the zoo, it should keep my mind off Bryce and whatever our relationship was.

We get up early and spend the day at the zoo. We have been there all day when my phone beeps. It is 2 pm, I look and it is Bryce. I look at the message, *Hey Sandy made it home, got some things to do will speak when I can, all the best B.*

All the best B. For fucks sake he couldn't even write his whole name, what the hell. Is that all I get for everything. Well fuck you Bryce Johnstone, good riddance and to think I wasted all my tears and gave him my heart and all I get is all the best. Go to hell mate I think. There done, better than done. Fuck you!!! Just what I needed to get over this bullshit. To think he said not to give up on us, what a tosser, he was only playing a role. Well good, done and dusted. This anger takes me over and for the next week I do nothing but working, I don't think of him, every time I see his name on my phone, I ignore it, every time there is a text, I don't read it, when he calls me at home, I don't answer it, there, stick it up your banana I think, see how you like it.

'I haven't seen or heard from him for a month, well he has called, messaged and even sent a carrier pigeon, well he didn't but it is like he has tried everything to get in contact with me. He has called Louise, messaged me on Instagram, Telegram, WhatsApp, Messenger, Hangouts, he even has called Carla trying to get in contact with me. All Louise and Carla have said is she will call you or speak to you when she wants. Louise comes over and says, 'He sounds heartbroken and he desperately wants to talk to me.'

'What do I do?' I ask. 'Should I call him?'

'It's up to you but if It was me and you are truly over him, then I would call him and tell him why.' Typical older sister with the right advice, well it's too late. It's 2am over there, I say. So message him and tell him. Yeah good idea he won't get it till he wakes up then I will be asleep.

I text. *Hey Mr Johnston. It's me Sandra. I haven't heard or read any of your messages, I think what we had was just a convenience on your end and I fell for the lie, for the dream, I think we should go back to me being a fan and admiring you from the distance. As you said ALL THE BEST in your last text. So All the best to you and your future. I only want you, Amy and your family to be forever happy. I can't turn off my feelings for you but I will. I hope that you have found love and I hope that you get your forever happy ever after. Thank you for all the good times, for bad times, the tears and the heartache. I have learnt a lot about myself and I now know that love and me do not mix. Regards, Sandra* and I press send.

Done, a minute later the phone rings, Shit it is him. I take a deep breath and answer.

'Hello.'

'Hey, it's me.'

'Who is me?'

'You know who it is, what is that message about?' he asks.

'Did you not read your last message when you got home?' I ask.

'Honey, I had heaps to do I was going to call you back but I got busy with the film and all the shit I had when I got back, what do you mean you go back to being a fan? I don't want you that way, I want you like when we are together.' 'Look

Mate, you are a very good actor, you can fool me a lot of times, but I have seen the press, I can read between the lines, I know how you feel and it isn't the same as how I feel. I have been fooled too many times in my life, treated like shit and I call bullshit.'

'Is that how you really feel?' He asks.

I am crying, but don't let him know I am.

'Look Mate, tell me what I have read is bullshit, tell me that you love me and only want me, tell me that we will be together always and live happy and I will believe you but if you can't say any of that or all of that, then forget it. I am too old to be hurt anymore. I have given my heart for the first time in my life and it cannot take another break, I can feel it breaking every time you leave me or every time I read that you are with someone. My heart is too fragile to take another one.

'I can't promise we won't have arguments,' he says. I can't control what is written in the press but I can assure you I love you wholeheartedly, forever, and I will always love you regardless of how you feel about me,' he says.

'Well, that last comment just proves you have no fucking idea how I feel or what you mean to me. Go to bed Mate. Good bye.' I hang up. The phone rings again and I ignore it, it rings all day and all night. I just keep ignoring it. This goes on for a week and then no more calls. I look in my emails and there are emails from him, again I ignore him. It takes me a while to finally start to feel like my old self. It is nearly Melbourne cup day and I have stopped thinking about him, I have stopped looking at him online, I have my friends all saying he is with a girl here and there, I look at the pictures and see he looks happy but not happy in his eyes, he looks tired. I just want to reach out to him but he doesn't love me. Why waste my time!

'Mum.'

'Yes baby.'

'Can we watch this show at 8.30?' Michael asks.

'Of course.'

We sit down and it is the Jimmy Fallon show.

'Michael, why are we watching this, because there is someone on there I want to watch.'

So, I sit with him.

'Welcome back,' Jimmy says. 'Our first guest is the star of the latest blockbuster series on Netflix, Please welcome my dear friend Bryce Johnstone, Hey welcome.'

'Thanks,' he says.

'So congratulations on the series.'

'Yeah it's been good, it's been a hard few months,' he says.

'I understand it has a green light for 2nd season.'

'Yeah, yeah that's right. So what else has been happening,' asks Jimmy.

'Well the thing is, there has been a lot of press out there about myself and my love life. I want to take this opportunity for the first and only time to clear the air, I know or hope that a certain person is watching this and I want to tell her the only person in my life apart from my daughter and family that I love is her and her son and I will do everything in my power for her to believe me, he is staring right into the camera, If this person is watching and believes me please call me when I get off the show. Love you baby girl.'

'Wow,' says Jimmy. 'Who is this person?' he asks. 'Someone that has been in my life for a while,' Bryce says, 'a lot of people have tried to keep us apart and I won't let them or her keep us apart. Michael I know you are watching get her to call me or come and see me.'

'We will be back after this break,' says Jimmy.

I am sitting there in absolute shock, he is normally very private about his private life, he always said he would never let anyone know anything about his private life as it is his private life. Yet he has just said that on the TV.

'Michael I want to ask you, do you believe him?'

'Yes Mum, I do.

I get my mobile and call his mum.

'Hey Wilma, it's Sandy, how are you?' I ask. 'Good but I guess you are calling as you saw the show?' She asks.

'Yes, I need to ask you an honest question Wilma and I know you won't lie and you will do the best for him.' 'Yes go ahead,' she says.

'Do you think Bryce loves me and means what he just said.'

'YES. Yes and Yes.'

'Are you sure?

'Absolutely yes Sandy.'

'Even after I have ignored him and what I said?'

'Sandy, he showed me the messages and he told me what you said, I told him you were trying to protect yourself and him, I told him that the only time someone would walk away like you did was because you loved him unconditionally and you were trying to protect him and his life.'

'Yes,' I say. But after the way I treated him, I just don't know. Can he forgive me?'

'Sandy, he went on the show purposely to get the message to you,'

'Oh. So, that means he loves me truly?'

'Yes he does.'

'Well then I have to organise a flight and come over there and try to fix this all. Do you think I could come over at Christmas and surprise him, I get two weeks off I might be able to push it to three but do you think I could repair it, let him know I love him?'

'I think if you want to fix it and love him you will.' 'Okay let's call it, save his heart. Give me four weeks and I will be there. Can I stay at your place if it goes shit faced and he tells me to piss off?'

'Of course but I can't see that happening.'

'Thanks Wilma. I want you to know I have never stopped loving him, I only want him to be happy and I know that we will have challenges but I will never hurt him again, please don't tell him I called I want it to be a surprise Okay,' I say.

'Yes of course, but I would call him otherwise he won't think you care,' she says.

'Hmm, good idea. Okay I will call now.'

And so I do. It goes to voicemail.

'Hey, it's Bryce, leave me a message.

'Umm Hi Bryce, it's Sandy, I saw the show, I just want to say I am very sorry for how I have treated you, I only want you to be happy and I thought you didn't love me, that is was just a game, I couldn't fathom that someone like you could actually love someone like me, but you know what, you and Michael and Amy are my life, I love you, I will always love you and if it takes my whole life or the rest of my life to prove it to you, to make it up to you, I will. I really didn't want to leave a message but I wanted to tell you this all straight away. Speak soon' and I hang up.

Okay I have over four weeks to organise flights to LA. I go online and look at the prices. The cost is out of my price range, to fly out on Christmas Eve our time it is going to cost me $3500 return, so for Michael and myself I am looking at $7000, that doesn't count taxes, transfers, accommodation in case I need, spending money or anything. I try to find cheaper flights but they are not near Christmas, they are in January after school holidays, I have to get there over for Christmas I want to surprise him, but I can't afford it. Maybe I will do a DVD instead. I just don't have the money to get over there, I can't afford it. No matter how I try to budget I just can't find the money, all I have in my account is $1000. Shit. This is when I wish I still had my credit card but I got rid of them a when I came back. Oh well, I guess that plan has no air in it. I better call his mum and tell her. But I wonder if I could get the money for just myself. So I look at every angle I can over the next week. But nothing comes to plan, it is all awash. I have to call his mum and tell her.

I decide to do a DVD with a message for him and an attempt at singing to him. So I go and try to work it out my favourite two songs to sing are Wrapped in Red and Underneath the tree. Both very hard songs to sing particularly when you can't sing like me but I am happy to make a fool of myself for the man I love. Carla helps me do the DVD and once I finish it I call his mum to tell her my plans.

'Hey Wilma, hope all is going well?'

'Yeah Okay,' she says. He got your message and is feeling a bit better but he has so much on at the moment that he said he can't get to you.

'Well I have a problem too,' I say. I don't have the money to fly Michael and myself over and If I just fly over I still can't

231

afford it as it is so close to Christmas the prices are inflated, so I can't come over, but what I have done is made a DVD with my two favourite songs and a message for him, I am going to send it to you via email, can you play it when you see him on Christmas day please, you can watch it if you want but please don't let him see it till Christmas and if he forgives me and loves me as much as I love him, please get him to call me Okay.'

'Okay,' she says. 'Are you sure you can't afford it?' and I tell her everything, how much money I have in my account, how much the flights are and that isn't even my visa, taxes, transfers, hotel etc.

'I am so sorry I have to do this one week before Christmas but I just can't afford it.'

'It will work out Sandy don't worry about it Okay,' she says.

'Thanks Wilma, speak soon.' I hang up and send the DVD via email to her. Done.

So leading up to Christmas, everyone is happy, I am putting on a brave smile, wishing everyone a Merry Christmas and occasionally when not thinking a Merry Easter which gives everyone a laugh. I am going through the daily motions of work, home, walk, sleep and repeat. I just keep thinking if only, if only I could find the money I could fly over and tell him that I love him, that I always will forever. I read in the media he is apparently dating his co-star from his latest series, well it is the same series but it has been signed on for at least two more seasons and that makes me happy that he is professionally back on track. I know he isn't dating his co-star as she has a girlfriend and I know he isn't dating anyone as his mum or sisters would tell me. Would they? I think. But

Knowing the press, they are just assuming that they are dating, I know the secrets now of the media and they don't phase me. But I decide to email Wilma and tell her not to worry about the DVD, I don't want to make a fool of myself and I don't want to ruin his Christmas, I want him to enjoy himself plus I haven't spoken to him for ages so I guess he is happy and I don't want to cause any problems.

Hey Wilma, just wanted to say that I haven't heard from Bryce so I assume he has met someone, so I have to ask you NOT to show him the DVD of me making an absolute fool of myself, I am lucky that I couldn't afford the ticket otherwise I would have been out of pocket for that too. I also want to say that I hope we can remain friends, you are like a second Mum to me, you have been so gracious and kind to myself and Michael and I hope that you are happy to stay in contact. I also want to say that Bryce and all the kids are so lucky to have such a loving and caring Mum who never knocks her kids, who is always present with them and the grand kids and I would be so lucky to have someone on my side for Michael. I wish you and the entire family a very Merry Christmas, a safe and Happy New year. I hope that all your wishes and dreams come true and that you always find the love and happiness you all deserve. Finally, thank you from the bottom of my heart for putting up with me while I was over there and for all the drama that I created, for understanding why I did say I never loved Bryce and for hurting him the way I did. I only ever wanted to protect him and Amy. I also want you to know that even though I am a fan of his, I will also ALWAYS LOVE HIM FOREVER, I will always hope and pray that he has found his true love whoever he ends up with and that he

*is always loved and protected as he deserves. Take care with
all my love Sandy.* I press send.

Okay now, back to getting ready for Christmas. I have the
presents all bought, I just have to put the tree up. I just can't
be bothered. I know Michael wants it but my heart is so
broken I just don't have the heart to put one up.

'Mum,' yells Michael.

'Yeah baby.'

'Can we get a real tree this year?' he asks, you did promise
one last year,' he goes on.

'Well baby, they are quite expensive and we do have the
fake one.'

'I know but as we are not going to the states can we
PLEASE get a real one please Mum,' he begs.

'Okay Michael lets go before I change my mind.'

We jump in the car and drive to the Somerville Christmas
tree farm. All around us, I see happy families, Mums and Dads
with the kids, couples all walking around looking lovingly at
each other and then it just Michael and myself.

'Come on Mate, let's go find the best tree that will fit in
our home.'

I haven't been to a tree farm since I was a little girl, the
smell of the pine trees are so gorgeous, it really does feel like
Christmas. We have been walking up and down each row of
trees for at least 2hrs when I hear.

'Mum quick, this is the one, Mum come now.'

'Where are you Mate?'

'In the next row, Mum quick it's the one,' yells Michael.

He is so loud I swear everyone else has heard him and has
just stopped. I walk around and find him and I have to admit

the tree is absolutely stunning, the right amount of leaves, the right height, the smell of the tree is so fresh.

'Mate that is the one, that is it. Stay here I will get one of the guys.'

I walk back to the front and grab one of the guys to cut the tree down for us. I am going to make this the best Christmas ever for Michael. I start to think to myself. It has been such a roller coaster year for both of us. But for Michael he got so close to Bryce in such a short time, then when he came over for the two weeks Michael thought Bryce was going to stay and we were both heartbroken but as a Mum you have to put your hopes and wishes aside and your heartbreaks and put your children first, at times I haven't as I was so lost and just wanted to run away and at times I just wanted to die. I was over my life. I still think I don't deserve to be alive, that everyone would be better without me, Michael would have his home paid for by my life insurance, no other male would miss me and my family wouldn't miss me as I am absolutely useless and stupid but I just don't have the strength to end my life. I pray every night that I won't wake up but not even god helps me, so I am here everyday heart broken and feeling what is the point and keep pushing myself every day.

'Excuse me, the price of the tree is $85.00, do you need a stand as well,' asks the kid.

'Yes please.'

'That is another $80.'

'Oh Okay.'

I pay him, he wraps the tree and puts it on my roof racks and helps tie it down. We hop in the car and off we go home. High ho high ho it's off to home we go, I hum.

'Mum,'

'Yes mate.'

'Can we decorate the tree straight away?' asks Michael.

'I guess so, but we have to set it up first, why don't you call Ya ya and get her to meet us at home, she knows how to set up real trees.'

When we get home Louise is there, she helps us get the tree down and set it in the stand. It fits perfectly with just enough space for the angel on the top. We put on Christmas carols and spend the next two hours decorating the tree. I have to admit to myself this has been a really good day, I just wish that Bryce and Amy were here with us. I stop and think *STOP IT stupid he has a girlfriend and they are probably putting it up themselves together* I feel tears coming to my eyes, be back in a minute just have to go to the ladies room. I sit on there and try to pull myself together. After 10mins I think I have my feelings in check and come back into the lounge, the tree is finished and looks perfect, Michael has put on our favourite Christmas song and we both start to sing badly Underneath the tree. This then gets me to think that I sung this on the DVD to Bryce and it starts me again. Oh shit.

'Mum are you Okay?'

'Yeah mate I just love this song. I really have to pull myself out of this. I can't keep crying. Surely you can only cry for a certain amount of tears over one guy, I keep thinking over and over, surely after a while your body says enough is enough, get over yourself. I know Louise will tell me to GROW THE FUCK UP AND GET OVER HIM. So I will have to.

So, we are nearly ready for Christmas yay fucking yay I am thinking. Christmas movies are back on, I love them but hate that they all end up with happy endings, well as they say life never imitates the movies, ain't that the truth!

Only one more week till Christmas and then one more week till the end of the year. I thought 2020 was bad with Covid but to me personally 2021 has been hard emotionally. We got to have our dream holiday, I got to meet my dream guy in Bryce, fell in love and never fell out of love. They do say it is better to of loved and lost then to never of loved. I guess that Is true but they never said how much loving someone and losing them hurt. I now know that I had never been in love, not even with my ex-husband the prick or ex boyfriends but with Bryce, I fell in love with him as a fan loves the celebrity but even better I got to know the real person, the person that sits on the couch with the dogs and falls asleep after a long day. I got to fall in love with the man that I have always dreamed of, the caring, funny, adorable dag that he is, the one that wears his trackies and slippers, the one that has chocolate on his face, the one that runs around the yard with the kids, the one that I got to lean against and the one that I would fall asleep next to and in the morning he was still there with his beard growth and his beautiful blue majestic eyes and his morning breath. I never thought I could love morning breath but with Bryce it was all perfect. Oh well, I guess it was just good memories.

Work has been busy no rest. Marissa comes up to me, 'Hey Sandy, got a question.'

'Hang ten Marissa just finishing off this email.' I press send. 'Yeah what's up?'

'Well as tomorrow is our last day for a couple of weeks, I was wondering if I can grab a lift to our Christmas break up, I want to drink and need a lift home,' she asks.

'I'm sorry Marissa, I'm not going. I just don't feel like socialising out of work, I just want to go home and try to get through Christmas.'

She looks at me. 'Are you not over him yet?'

I stare at her, try to hold back the tears and can't.

'I don't think I ever will Marissa. I just wish I could run away and never think of him again, but there are too many articles about him and how happy he is, he was seen with Camilla.'

'Who is Camilla?' she asks.

'I am guessing his new squeeze,' I say. She is just his type, skinny, blonde, tall, a model or actress, lives over there and is only 30yrs old, so they can have kids together and Amy can have siblings. Plus there are too many pictures on my phone of him.

'Well give me your phone and I will delete them.'

'NO, I yell. 'Sorry No I can't they are memories, Mar, I really thought he was the one, I really thought I had found my soulmate, stupid huh.'

She looks at me, comes over and gives me a hug.

'It will get easier Sandy. Have you spoken to him.'

'No, he is with someone else, plus I don't have his number anymore, I deleted it and forgot it.'

'Really, you forgot it?'

'No I haven't,' I said, 'but I am trying to forget it', and we both laugh. 'So maybe there will be a time I will be able to forget him,' I say.

'Good girl. Okay, we'll have a good night and a take tomorrow off as we are all not coming into work. Merry Christmas Sandy.'

'Merry Christmas Marissa and Happy New Year.'

I grab my bag, sign off and go home.

Three more days till Christmas. I get home and there is a letter at my door from the post office. I get back into my car and go to the post office to collect the letter. I sign for it and put it in my bag. I go pick up Michael and think I will read it later.

We have been home for a few hours when my mobile rings, I look at the number and see it is Wilma. I take a deep breath and try to sound happy.

'Merry Christmas Wilma, how are you?' I say. 'Hey Sandy, I just got notification that you got the letter from me have you opened it yet?' she asks.

'No I haven't, I just put it in my bag, why?'

'Well, I think you better sit down and go get it,' she says.

'Do I sit down or do I go get it and then sit down?' I ask. 'Sandy, go get it and sit down.'

'Okay no need to get grumpy,' I say.

I grab the letter and go sit down on the lounge.

'Okay, I have it so what do you want me to do.'

'Okay the thing is,' Wilma says, 'the letter has everything explained in it. We have bought you and Michael a return ticket to come and see us for Christmas.'

I am staring at the envelope and the phone.

'Sandy, I have to tell you the whole family put the money together to get both of you over here so you could see Bryce for Christmas.'

'Wilma, he has a girlfriend he is dating Camilla his co-star,' I say.

'No he isn't,' she says. 'The only person he loves is you silly.'

'Me? No he doesn't,' I say.

'YES HE DOES,' she says.

If he loved me why hasn't he called,' I ask.

'He has tried but said he can't get through to you that you are not answering him, so he has been sending you emails. I haven't received any emails from him,' I say.

'Well, he wouldn't say he has sent them if he hasn't.' Then I remember when I came home, I blocked his email so nothing would come through not thinking that he would really send me anything, I deleted his number, home and mobile so I couldn't hear from him.

'Oh, I blocked his details and forgot to unblock them and then he had a different number so I didn't change anything back.'

'Well, that would explain it wouldn't it.'

'Wilma, I can't fly over to the US. I have to do visa's, transfers, accommodation etc.'

'All in the letter, everything has been sorted. Dave is going to pick you guys up from the airport, you will stay with me but I can guarantee Bryce will want you to stay with him and the visas are all paid for. You fly out Christmas eve at 10 pm as I know you celebrate your Christmas on Christmas eve, you will arrive here Christmas Eve around 10 pm and then come over here and I will have him here for lunch on Christmas day, it will be a surprise.'

'Wilma I can't accept this, it is too much plus what happens if he doesn't want us there.'

'A mother knows what her son wants and I know he loves you. So it is all settled Okay. But that is in two days' time.'

'I don't have time to organise anything.'

'Yes, you do I have spoken to your sister Louise, she is going to stay at your place and watch the animals. I have organised a car to pick you up and when you get over here it will be all organised too. All you have to do is grab both of your passports and pack your bags and young lady I will not take the answer no,' she says. If you say no I will be offended.'

'Oh Wilma, I don't know what to say,' I respond. 'Well, the normal thing to say is Thank you very much and I can't wait to spend Christmas with you all.'

'THANK you very much Wilma, I can't wait to spend Christmas with you all but I just hope it isn't the wrong thing.'

She laughs and says, 'It will all work out.'

I hang up and read all the details in the letter.

'Michael, we are going to America on Christmas Eve baby, let's pack our bags.'

'What?' he yells.

'Wilma and all her family have paid for us to go see Bryce and Amy,' I say.

'Woo hoo. I can't wait,' he says.

I think to myself I hope this is not a mistake.

Christmas Eve we have our lunch and afterwards Michael and I get picked up by a car and are taken to the airport. Our flight is on time, it is not a direct flight just via Sydney but that is all good, just means that the flight will take 19hrs but that is Okay, plus we are 18hours ahead of LA so we should basically fly in around the same time we fly out, I think.

We go through the motions, get on the plane settle in for our flight to Sydney but then get advised that due to a mechanical issue the plane has been delayed, that we won't be flying to Sydney but it will be a direct flight to LA, however, we have to wait for the issue to be fixed, that instead of a 10 pm time to depart it will be a 2 am departure time.

Great 4hrs delay. I text Wilma and advised we have been delayed and will not leave till 2 am so that will mean we will be later in LA and that we will organise our own way to her place. I get a call straight away.

'Hey, It's me, all good with whatever time you come in one of the kids will pick you both up Okay, just let me know what time you leave and will arrive.'

'At 1am we hear,

'Ladies and gentleman thank you for your patience, we do apologise for the delay, we have been advised that the part that is needed to repair the plane is coming from Sydney and will arrive approx. 6 am, we can put you up into a hotel for the night or if you prefer you are welcome to stay here at the gate, we are hoping that we will have you in the air shortly after that time. Everyone is peeved but Michael is fast asleep and I text Wilma, *More delays, maybe we should just forget about it, we won't be in LA now till Christmas morning and I will ruin everyone's Christmas day.* I receive a reply: *All good. We will see you then. Don't stress.*

The part arrives and at 9 am we are boarding the plane, we both had a shower at the airport and feel refreshed and are finally on the plane. I really can't believe what they have done for Michael and myself. I am feeling so scared but elated. I know in my heart when I see Bryce that we will be like friends, just friends that he is in love with Camilla and his mother doesn't really know him as well as she thinks but I am looking at our pictures together and wish and pray that I am wrong, that maybe she is right. I am so confused. The flight goes without any issues and we arrive in LA at exactly 9 am.

'Ladies and Gentleman, welcome to LA we apologise for the delay in Melbourne and are happy to offer all of you another flight to US or any destination to the same value for use at a later date. On behalf of Qantas we thank you for flying with us today and for being so understanding. Merry Christmas from myself and all my crew and we hope you have a wonderful holiday.'

'Michael, wake up baby we are here.'

He wakes up and we are both feeling a bit nervous, I have had my phone off since we left. I turn it on once we get off the plane and are heading to customs. Everything seems to be going well. By the time we get out of customs and get our bags it is 10 am. We walk through the doors to go into the terminal and we both look around and see if we can see anyone we know. I am about to give up and walk towards the cabs when I hear 'Sandy', I turn around and it is David. He is waving and running toward us. He gets to us and gives me a massive hug and a hug to Michael.

'Sorry for the lateness we got stuck at an accident, I texted you.'

'Oh sorry I haven't read any texts sorry.'

'It's all good,' he says.

'Now let's get you both home,' he says.

'David, can I ask you a favour?' I ask.

'Of course. Do you think we could go and get changed and showered, we have been in the same clothes since 7 am yesterday and I really would like to look my best for Christmas.'

'Of course, you can come past my place it is on the way to Mum's plus I have to pick up the girls.'

'Thank you, I am sorry I hope I haven't caused any issues.'

'Not at all, it will work out well. Bryce and Amy are due at Mum's just before 12pm so it will work out.'

He calls Wilma. 'Hey mum I have them, yes all good, yes no problem, I am going to drop them past my place as they want to freshen up and change. Yes I know perfect, hang on I will put her on. It's Mum.'

'Hey Wilma, 'I just want to say thank you again but I just hope it doesn't go wrong,' I say.

'It won't,' she says. 'I know my son and I know how he feels,' she says. Now with the DVD, when he gets here, I am going to play it, that will give you time to get here then I think you should then come in. I will guarantee he will be so happy and if he isn't I will apologise and give you $1000US.'

I laugh. 'No need, but maybe you let me change my flight and let me go home early.'

'I don't think that will happen. Gotta go he is here early. See you in a while. Just call me or get Dave to when you are close.'

We arrive at David's go in and get changed, I organise all the Christmas pressies and we are back in the car in 20mins. It is now 11.30 am.

'I am sorry David I hope we haven't made you run late, can I give you some money for petrol?' I ask.

'No, all organised. I will call Mum,' he says.

'Hey mum we are 30mins away. Okay will do.' He hangs up. 'Okay so the plan is mum is going to put the DVD on in 15mins, then when we get there, we will call her and go in the back, then you can surprise them.'

'But David what happens if he has someone with him, what happens if he doesn't want me there?'

'Sandy it is just him and Amy. Trust me I have spoken to him, he loves you.'

I look at him. 'I hope so, I really hope so.'

'Do you love him?' He asks.

'NO, I don't,' I say, 'I adore him, I love him so much it hurts, I have never felt this way about anyone and all I know that if he rejects me which I am expecting my heart will never be in one piece again.'

He looks at me and says, 'Well I know that that won't happen. Okay we are 5mins away let's call Mum.'

'Hey mum it's me, 5mins away, Okay. Sandy, mum wants to speak to you.'

'Okay.'

'He is watching it, he has tears in his eyes. I can't wait for him to see you, hang on stay on the phone.'

I can hear my voice. 'Hi Bryce, I just want to say that I am sorry for everything I said and as it is Christmas I wanted to tell you this, if you can't tell the truth at Christmas then you can't say it... I am absolutely positively irrevocably in love with you, not the celebrity but the real Bryce Johnston, the one that sits on the couch with the dogs, the one that looks adorable in his trackies and a day old beard, the one that laughs with his friends and family and the one man that has made me believe in love at first sight, I feel in love with you before I even knew who you were, the day in the car at the airport when you smiled at me my heart melted and it has never been complete since. I have made a couple of songs for you and it will make me look like a fool but if you can't embarrass yourself for the man you love then who can you. Merry Christmas baby and I will see you when I can.'

I blow him a kiss and Wrapped in Red and Underneath the tree plays. He watches it and I am unsure if he really loves me or if the press are right about him and his co-star but I don't care as this Christmas I am going to risk it all, I am going to stand in front of him and that if he wants I am never leaving him again.

I chose him and don't care about the press or anyone all I want is him and our future.

By this time I have arrived, Michael and I are in the front yard, I can't see him but I can hear Wilma says he is crying, that he is grabbing his phone, luckily I have unblocked him but hope he doesn't try to call me. Dave leads us through the front door.

'Dave, we were going through the back weren't we?' I ask.

'No, it is easier this way, he won't see us.'

So, Michael and I are now walking through the front door and I can see him watching the DVD, I really do sound OK, well only if you are deaf.....LOL... I walk down the steps and I see his family they are all there smiling but trying to stay straight faced. Bryce has his back to the front door and he is watching the DVD. The song finishes and I come on again and say, 'Merry Christmas baby, I miss you.' The DVD goes dark. Wilma is next to him and turns it off. He looks at her.

'Mum, I have to call her, I have to tell her how I feel, I have to fly and see her and I will not stop till she listens to me.'

'Honey, I know she will listen but why don't we have something to eat first and then you can try to call her,' she says.

He grabs his phone and dials my number, I fumble with my phone as it is my bag and I am standing right behind him trying to silence it, I throw it to Dave who throws it to his wife Michelle who is in the kitchen, thankfully it has been silenced. It goes to voicemail. 'Hey thanks for calling Sandy, please leave a message I will get back to you soon.' I am now hiding around the corner hoping he doesn't get up. 'Hey, honey it's me Bryce, I just saw the DVD you sent, we need to talk, I will try again later, I hope you had a good Christmas. Sandy, I love you don't believe the press, we need to talk baby', and he hangs up.

I have tears now rolling down my face. He puts the DVD back on to the part where I am saying Merry Christmas baby. He turns to his mum and I can see he has tears in his eyes too. I look at his mum and decide to walk behind him. He is looking at his phone trying to find flights so he is concentrating. I put my hands over his eyes, lean into his back and say, 'Merry Christmas baby.'

He touches my hands turns around and smiles, he grabs me pulls me onto his lap and gives me a massive kiss right in front of his mum and family. I am laughing but crying at the same time as he is. All his sisters and brother and mum are standing around watching.

'How?' he asks. 'When?'

His mum says, 'We all chipped in and paid for Sandy and Michael to come over and see you.'

I look at him. 'I only found out about it two days ago and the flight was shocking we were delayed for 12hrs so we are lucky to have got here today, but I will pay back your family as it was too much, but your mum said you loved me and I love you.'

His mum looks at us. 'It is about time both of you realise that I know best, I know when two people are meant to be together and regardless of what crap has been thrown to them that they realise that they are meant to be together.'

I am still lying on his lap and look at him.

'Now, can I get off your lap?' I ask.

'No way, you ain't going anywhere,' he says.

'But I will break your back.'

'Don't be silly,' he says. You weigh nothing.

I laugh. 'You must be drunk and need glasses, but you are mine.' We laugh. Eventually he lets me off his lap but is still holding onto my hand. I try to get around to thank all his family for the tickets and for getting us here. Michael comes in and says hi and gives Bryce a hug. I am hugging his mum and chatting to her.

'Okay lunch time,' she says.

We all go into the backyard to eat. We are all sitting down enjoying the meal and talking, I finally am feeling happy, I have my happy ending, the man that I love loves me back. I have three weeks before I have to go back and I know that no matter what anyone says that I will never let anyone come between Bryce and myself. I may not be the model that he is normally with, I may not be the pretty skinny blonde, but I know in my heart that he loves me for me as I love him for him, the real him and I know this is real.

We have been there talking, eating for hours, I look at my watch and realise that Michael and I have been up for over 48 hours and I am starting to waiver and get tired. It is now 4 pm and I look at Bryce. 'Honey can I ask you a favour? do you mind if I go, I am so tired, we have been up since our time

Christmas eve at 6 am, it is 11 am Boxing day and I am buggered.'

He looks at me. 'Of course baby.'

He says to his family he is going to take us home, we hug everyone and go get Michael who happens to be asleep in the spare room. So Bryce, Amy, Michael and I jump in the car and we go to his place. I have started to drift off and am leaning against him, I can feel his arm around me and he kisses my head. I feel safe, happy and content, regardless of what happens from here I don't care, I can die now and be happy.

I am woken up and feel like I am floating, I must be dead, I look up and I am in Bryce's arms, he is carrying me into the house.

'Oh baby put me down, you will break your back,' I say. 'You won't break my back honey, I can lift 250kgs and you do not weigh anything like that, plus you are absolutely wrecked so I can get you in the house quicker.'

I lean into his shoulder I am so tired I can't argue, he takes me into his bedroom, puts me onto the bed and says, 'Do you want to shower or go to sleep?'

'Can I shower?'

'Of course, but I will come back once the bags are in and check on you.' He walks me to the double shower and says, 'Be back in a few minutes.

He runs downstairs grabs all our bags and comes back upstairs, I have washed and have started to dose under the water, when I am woken.

'Come on baby, let's get you in bed.'

He helps dry me and I put on my nightie and go to his bed, he hops in the shower and comes and joins me.

'Hey Bryce, where are the kids?'

'They are both in bed, Michael is in his room, he has had a shower and is sleeping, Amy has too.'

He explained to me that we are going to have a big day tomorrow as everyone is coming over for boxing day lunch, I am leaning into his chest and fall asleep. I wake up what seems as hours later and feel so refreshed, I look up and he is sound asleep still. Gosh he looks beautiful and so rested. I get up and go to the bathroom, I shower and get dressed. I look in the bedroom and he is still asleep. I go downstairs and start to cook breakfast for everyone. I make pancakes, eggs, toast, freshly squeeze orange juice, put a pot of coffee on, make some hot chocolate for the kids, start to make fresh bread for lunch and make myself a cup of tea. I am just stretching from the oven when I feel his arms around me.

'Morning baby', and he nuzzles my neck, I turn around and give him a lingering kiss and then hug.

'Morning Honey. Sleep well?' I ask.

'Yes did you?

'Definitely, the best I have since I was last with you,' I say.

He comes and helps me with the cooking and then goes and gets the kids. We are all sitting together eating and smiling. This is heaven.

'Hey Bryce, what time are your family coming over?'
'Not till 2 pm,' he says, 'it is going to be a late lunch, early dinner,' he says.

'Well, I better get cooking.'

'No need, I have it all covered it is being catered.'

'Why?' I ask.

'So, you can relax,' he says.

'Oh, that is nice, but I can't let you do that,' I say.

'It's all done honey.'

'Okay, but how about if I make some sweets?'

'Okay,' he says, 'we can.'

'So we do, we make a chocolate cake, chocolate mousse, Upside down apple cake, Double chocolate muffins for the kids (just to keep them all bumping along all day...LOL...including the big kids!) and finally I make a rainbow cake. After all the sweets are done, we all sit down near the pool and just enjoy the peace and quiet.'

'Hey Baby,' asks Bryce.

'Yes honey. I have to run up the shops and get a couple of things do you want anything?' he asks.

'All good honey, I may go get cleaned up before your family come and then I want to decorate a bit but thanks for asking.'

I give him a hug and kiss and he goes out the door.

'Hey kids,' I yell, 'can you both come and help me I want to do a surprise for Bryce.'

They both come.

'Yep, what's up?

'I have a surprise for him and need some help to set it up, Amy does daddy have any balloon pumpers or an air pump?'

'Yes, he does it's in the garage.'

'Okay, I will go find it, do you guys want to decorate the room with the streamers and runners? I will blow the balloons.'

I go into the garage with my phone and call Christy.

'Hey Christy, 'Have you got the puppy?'

'Yep on the way now.'

'Cool, I hope he likes him, I know he has girls but this little boy was so cute.'

'Sandy, he will love him as you got him plus he loves dogs,' says Christy.

'Thanks for getting him, he has gone up the shop so when you come we will put him in the office and when everyone is here I will give him the puppy.'

'Okay, I am 5mins away, see you soon', and hangs up.

I grab the air pump, go back into the house and the kids are throwing the streamers all around, the house looks fantastic.

'Hey kids, come on let's do the balloons.'

'Sandy,'

'Yes Amy.'

'I did a sign with Michael for you and Daddy, can I put it up too.'

I begin to wonder what they have done, but reply, 'Of course Sweetheart, do you want me to help?'

'No, we can do it.' and they both go outside in the garden.

'Stay close kids,' I yell.

In the meantime, Christy has come with the puppy. I have decided that as he black as night with speckles I want to call him Starry. I hope Bryce likes the name but the good thing is we can change it. I go upstairs to get quickly washed and changed before Bryce comes back and everyone arrives.

Just as I am about to come back downstairs, Amy and Michael stop me.

'Sandy can you come with us? Daddy said that he doesn't want you to go into the kitchen as the caterers are there and he said to take you downstairs and out to the garden to wait for everyone,' says Amy.

'Okay, let's go. But first do you both want to get changed, they look at me and both run into their rooms.' 'Sandy,' yells Amy.

'Yes,' baby.'

'Can you come here and help?' and I go in straight away. I always wanted a daughter but fate never gave me another child but maybe while I am here I can be a good influence on Amy and regardless how long I am with her I will always treat her like my own.

'What can I do for you sweetheart?'

'Would you mind doing my hair?'

'Of course.'

I sit down on the bed, brush her hair and put it up into a piggy tail as asked, I put a pink ribbon in her hair. Once done, Michael joins us and we all go downstairs and go out back and look for Bryce. As we walk out the patio door, I see him, my handsome man, looking gorgeous in jeans and a shirt. God this man is the most gorgeous person I have seen and that is just his back end. Wow how lucky am I to have such a wonderful man in my life. He looks gorgeous but what is even better is he has such a wonderful heart, so caring, so kind, so funny, he is the perfect package for me. 'Hey honey.' He turns and looks.

'Wow,' he says. 'Baby you look gorgeous.'

I turn bright red. 'I...I...don't, but thanks gorgeous,' I say.

'No, Sandy the dress is perfect, the colours just match you so well.'

I walk to him and hug him, give him a kiss and say, 'Well, thanks honey. But really it is nothing, it is something I bought years ago but I am glad you like it, but the thing is', and I lift the dress up to show. 'I have no shoes on. Pure comfort on my feet.' He grabs me and laughs.

We are all sitting outside, the table is set up, the room is decorated and we are just sitting together enjoying the sunshine when the doorbell goes. We get up and greet his family. I am so happy, I have never had such a large and loving family, it feels so good to have lots of rugrats running around, family on the table and the house full of laughter.

We are all sitting together, partners next to each other, the food and alcohol is flowing and everyone is having fun. I stand up and say, 'Hey, I have a surprise for Bryce and if Okay with everyone now that we have eaten do you mind if I go get it?'

Everyone looks at me, Bryce looks at me and says, 'What have you done honey?'

'Nothing,' I say. 'Just something that I saw and had to get it for you.'

Amy and myself go into the office. Michael stays with Bryce and says, 'You have to close your eyes Bryce', and stands in front of him so he can't see.

Amy sees the puppy and is instantly in love with him. 'Come on Amy, let's give him to daddy.'

I am carrying the puppy and Amy is next to me patting him. I walk outside and everyone goes collectively, 'Awwww so cute!'

This gets Bryce wanting to look but Michael is blocking him. I walk over to Bryce and am standing behind him. 'Okay Honey, open your eyes and turn around.'

As he turns he looks at me and smiles then looks down to my hands and sees the puppy.

'Oh baby, it is so cute.'

He grabs the puppy and hugs him. Both of the other dogs come round to see the new puppy and sniff him.

'The puppy is a little boy, I saw him online this morning and Christy went and got him, I hope you don't mind but I thought it would be something that you have that will remind you of us all together.'

He stands up gives me a hug with the puppy and says, 'He is beautiful, thank you.'

All the kids come up and start wanting to play and hold the puppy, I let Amy and Michael stay in charge of him and then we all sit down and chat and watch. All three dogs are playing together and the kids are running around with them. I feel so content and happy. This feels like home, this feels right, I just hope that I can get transferred over here and then maybe just maybe Bryce and I can be together for real in the same city. But until I hear back from my boss I will keep quiet about it.

'Does anyone want sweets and coffee?' I ask. I get a lot of yes, hell yes and do you want some help? I go into the kitchen to get all the sweets outside on the table, all his sisters and Mum come in and help. The guys are outside chatting and we girls are in the kitchen doing the coffees. 'Wilma can I run something past you without it going to anyone??' I ask.

'Yes, of course.'

'Well, I have spoken to my boss about being transferred over here to the states but before I confirm it, do you think Bryce will be Okay with me moving over here?'

I look at her and stare. She smiles and says, 'I think that if you were able to move over here and be here full time I know that he would be ecstatic, but I think he would be upset with you working.'

'Wilma, I can't not work, I won't rely on him for money, plus I might have to live elsewhere, I know I can stay here for a bit but I won't be able to live here full time,' I say.

'Why not?' she asks.

'Well, I would get in the way and he may not want me to.'

'Hog wash, Sandy he loves you.'

'And I love him, no I adore him, but it just may not be right. But anyway let's get the coffee, tea etc. outside. Please don't tell him, I have to confirm with my boss Okay?'

She looks at me. 'Okay but don't worry about it.'

We walk outside. Everyone just looks at us as we walk out, I give out all the cups hoping I got them right and look for Bryce.

'Where is Bryce?' I ask.

Dave says to me, 'He has gone to the garden to check on something.'

'Oh Okay.'

'You all drink your drinks and eat cakes I will go get him before his coffee gets cold.'

As I leave everyone is looking at me and staring.

'Okay, be back in a second.'

I walk around the table and walk to the garden.

'Bryce Honey, are you there?'

His garden is massive and I walk towards the side where the pathway is.

'Honey, are you there? Your coffee is getting cold.' 'Over here Sandy near the pool.'

I turn the corner and just stare, he has the pool decorated with fairy lights everywhere, the trees, the plants, bushes, even the fence line.

'Oh honey this is gorgeous, Amy will love it, give me a second and I will go get her.'

I turn to see him and he has gone. 'Bryce?'

I look on my other side no Bryce. I turn around and he is kneeling on one knee. 'Sandra Kathleen Jones, the love of my life, I never thought I would ever get married again, you and Michael have brought me back to life, you have given me love, comfort and joy in my life. You have made me believe in love at first sight and soul mates. The first time I met you I loved you and didn't know how I was ever going to be without you and then you left suddenly and I was devastated but knew that you were and always would be the one for me.

Many have tried to keep us apart and failed. You make me the happiest man in the world, if I have to I will live in Australia I will make it work or you can live here with Amy and myself or we can commute but I never want to be apart from you from this day forward. Will you marry me?'

I have tears rolling down my face. 'Can I now answer? I ask. He nods. 'Yes Bryce, l will marry you and we will work it out as I never want to be away from you again.'

We embrace and kiss. 'Do you want the ring?

'I don't need a ring I have you,' I say.

'Yes, but we have to seal the deal with a ring otherwise no one will know you are mine,' he says.

He puts the ring on my finger, it is stunning, it has a diamond heart in the middle and on each side there are mini diamond hearts on a gold band.

'Oh baby, it's beautiful but too big.'

'No, it is perfect,' he says. 'The heart in the middle is for our hearts together and will never be separate like us, the two mini hearts are for Michael and Amy. Our family is complete,' he says. I start to cry again and kiss him.

'Oh honey, how did you do this? When did you get this done?'

'I have had the ring from when we were in Reno, then everything went to shit and you left me, I have had it in my hands the whole time, no matter how long it was going to take I was going to get you back and propose. Sandy you are it for me, you are the woman I want to spend the rest of my life with and no one was going to stop that'.

We kiss and then we hear applause and look up and everyone is staring. We hear cheering, it's about time we hear. 'Oh, thank god finally.'

We turn and he says, 'She said Yes!'

I look and say, 'Was there any doubt?'

Wilma then comes over gives me a hug and said, 'I told you it would work out', and says, 'welcome to the family.'

I stare and then we get all the congratulations and hugs. Amy then pulls down the sign that is on the wall and it reads, 'Welcome to the family Sandy and Michael. I am glad to have you as my step mum and brother!'

I turn to Bryce who is smiling, I go to Amy and give her a massive hug and say, 'Amy, you are a cheeky little monkey but I love you baby girl and I would be honoured to call you my step daughter.'

We go back to the table. Bryce and I are holding hands and I feel like I am walking on air.

Dave says, 'Bugger coffee, who is up for champagne?' And it flows and flows. What a night. Here I was wondering if he would like his new puppy and all along he had this planned.

'So, tell me.' I ask, 'who knew what this young man had planned or was it a surprise?'

Every single hand went up with I knew even Michael's hand.

'Oh come on, everyone knew and no one told me, so not fair,' I say.

Bryce looks at me, 'Hey future wifey.' I smile and he says, 'I like that, I made everyone promise not to say anything so for that you have to blame me.'

'Nah all good honey, it was worth it.'

I am leaning against him and he lifts me onto his knee and wraps his arms around me. How lucky am I, sitting on my fiancé's knee, I can't believe it I am engaged to Bryce. The real man behind the celebrity. The man that sits here with his family and has fun, the man that sits with me on the couch, the man who plays with the kids on the ground and is the biggest dag in the world. He has fun in the snow with his mates, has fun with the kids but also happy to play like a big kid himself. I am looking around the table and staring, everyone is here, the only people who are not, is my family, my mum and sister and my best friend Carla. I will have to call them and tell them. Bryce looks at me and kisses me.

'Are you Okay baby?'

'Of course, never better, I love you Bryce and I am so glad you bumped into me on that first day.'

He kisses my hand, nuzzles my neck and I lean into him. 'Do you want to know when I fell in love with this woman,' he says. 'The moment she yelled at me "what the fuck is your problem", when I bumped into her.'

I am going bright red. 'Yeah but that was just shock,' I say.

'Yes, it was but then you apologised to me for swearing and offered me a lift and I fell deeper in love with you.'

'Oh really,' I say.

'Yes really.'

'Well, I fell in love with you the moment you sat in the car and smiled at me so I guess it was only a matter of time we got together', and I laughed. 'But would you mind if I call Louise and Mum and Carla?'

'Of course go for it.'

'Excuse me, I will be back in a minute.'

I walk into the lounge and call Louise.

'Hey sis, how is everything over there??

'So, did you say yes yet?' She asks.

'You know? Of course, Bryce called and asked for Mum's permission and of course she said yes, he then told me and asked if I wanted to fly over but I had to stay here to watch Mum.'

'Congratulations Sandy, I know I told you that you would never meet him and I said that you needed to grow the fuck up and forget about him once all the shit hit the fan, but I am glad that you didn't listen to me that you got the man of your dreams, I am so proud of you baby sister and I have to admit it will be hard not having you around every day. I will miss you but I know that you are happy and above all that is what is important.'

I am crying. 'Louise I don't know about not seeing me, I am sure I will still be over there, unless I get transferred over here I will be coming back to live.'

'You're not moving over to the US?'

'Louise I will not move over here unless I have a job and get my own green card I am not going to use Bryce in any way.' Oh I just thought. 'Well yes I guess everyone would but just because I am engaged to this amazing man doesn't mean I am going to throw out my values. Anyway I better go give my love to Mum, speak soon', and I hang up.

Next call Carla. 'Hey Carla, it's me.'

'Hey Sandy, how is America?

'Good, I have news but you can't tell anyone Okay?' 'Okay what is up?' She asks.

'Well, Bryce asked me to marry him and I said yes.' 'About fucking time,' she says. 'I knew it, I knew you guys would end up together it was only a matter of time,' she says.

'Well, you could have told me then I wouldn't have been so heartbroken.'

We both start to laugh in the way that us two do, it takes a good 5mins for us to stop.

I say, 'I better go back to him and the family', and hang up.

I really can't believe how this year has gone; our dream holiday brought romance, pain, adventure, heartache, love, everlasting forever love and brought me a larger family, a wonderful step daughter. This year has been so full of life that I never knew which way I was going but knew in my heart that I had finally found love, true honest, everlasting, forever, can't live without love and then I lost it to be found again.

He is the most amazing man and I adore him so much. I walk back outside and just look at everyone, they are all smiling, the night is clear as night with stars blotting the sky like diamonds and at the table is my fiancé. Wow, how lucky am I. I walk to him, sit next to him and give him a kiss and then lean into him. I sit there staring at everyone and I think this is it. This is what people have been talking about when they say that when you find the one, the one that is meant for you in every possible way, then life falls into place.

I have no idea how this is going to work, I know I will be the one that will have to move as his career, family and his beloved daughter is here in the America, but I am not scared or worried. I know it will happen. I will get transferred over here with work and everything will work out. I will have everything I have ever dreamed of, wanted. I have my love and a huge family. Michael and I will never be alone again, he will have a father figure and I feel so content, so in tune with everything around me. His mum comes and sits next to me.

'Sandy, I just want to say that the moment I met you I knew in my heart that you and Bryce would be together. You are so perfect for him, I could not ask for a better person to love my son and my granddaughter more than you do.'

'Thanks Wilma, I do love him so much, I want to pinch myself every moment I am with him and all of you, to think that if he had not of knocked into me on my first day I may never have met him, how my life would have been so different,' I say.

'Sandy, the world works in mysterious ways, you would have met him one way or another as it was meant to be.'

She hugs me and then goes sit back down. We are all around the table talking and drinking, I look at my left hand and think I can't believe I have a ring on my finger, how many times did I dream about being in love, really in love and never thought it would happen that it was just a dream. It could never happen to a person like me and then I smile and I realise that dreams can come true for us norms. You can be at the airport or a shop and bump into your future. That love does exist and I finally have my happy ever after.

Love is possible and dreams come true, you just have to believe and be open to it, you just have to put all your bad experiences aside, you have to put all negativities aside and learn from them otherwise you may just miss out on that one person that will complete your life. No one can complete you but they can make it so much better and make your life just as it needs to be.

Our future is just about to start. I have my fiancé, to the world he is an A list actor, a celebrity, almost like an alien but to me, he is my man, the love of my life, he is my perfection. He is my future, I don't know what will happen, I don't know if his fans and celebrity friends will accept me but all I know is he is it for me. My lover, my best friend, he is the first person I want to see in the morning and the last person I want to see at night. He is the only man I want to kiss for the rest of my life. He is the man that helps my heart keep beating and for the rest of my life I will do anything to ensure his safety and that of Amy and his family and that his reputation never ever takes another beating.

When you fall in love with the real person and not the celebrity you get the most precious gift that can be given to you. Love, true honest love and I wish that everyone one day finds what I have found.

Remember we are all human, we all dress the same way, you can't expect to get anything for free, you have to earn trust and trust has to be earned. It doesn't matter if they have more money than you, or more fame, it doesn't matter if they have less and are like me a norm. Love will find you if you are ready for it. If you love someone and unselfishly then you have found your heaven.

My wish is everyone gets what I have. Love...Honest...Happy contented love and their Happy ever after.

THE END

9 781398 466364